P9-CDO-362

THE
Riverside Library

A Tale of Two Cities

By

CHARLES DICKENS

BOSTON AND NEW YORK
HOUGHTON MIFFLIN COMPANY
The Riverside Press Cambridge
1931

CONTENTS

CONTENTS

BOOK THE THIRD: THE TRACK OF A STORM

A TALE OF TWO CITIES

IN THREE BOOKS

BOOK THE FIRST—RECALLED TO LIFE

CHAPTER I

THE PERIOD

It was the best of times, it was the worst of times, it was the age of wisdom, it was the age of foolishness, it was the epoch of belief, it was the epoch of incredulity, it was the season of Light, it was the season of Darkness, it was the spring of hope, it was the winter of despair, we had everything before us, we had nothing before us, we were all going direct to Heaven, we were all going direct the other way — in short, the period was so far like the present period, that some of its noisiest authorities insisted on its being received, for good or for evil, in the superlative degree of comparison only.

There were a king with a large jaw and a queen with a plain face, on the throne of England; there were a king with a large jaw and a queen with a fair face, on the throne of France. In both countries it was clearer than crystal to the lords of the State preserves of loaves and fishes, that things in general were settled for ever.

It was the year of Our Lord one thousand seven hundred and seventy-five. Spiritual revelations were conceded to England at that favoured period, as at this. Mrs. Southcott had recently attained her five-and-twentieth blessed birthday, of whom a prophetic private in the Life Guards had heralded the sublime appearance by announcing that arrangements were made for the swallowing up of London and Westminster. Even the Cock Lane ghost had been laid only a round dozen of years, after rapping out its messages, as the spirits of this very year last past (supernaturally deficient in originality) rapped out theirs. Mere messages in the earthly order of events had lately come to the English Crown and People, from a congress of British subjects in America: which, strange to relate, have proved more important to the human race than any communications yet received through any of the chickens of the Cock Lane brood.

France, less favoured on the whole as to matters spiritual than her sister of the shield and trident, rolled with exceeding smoothness down hill, making paper money and spending it. Under the guidance of her Christian pastors, she entertained herself, besides, with such humane achievements as sentencing a youth to have his hands cut off, his tongue torn out with pincers, and his body burned alive, because he had not kneeled down in the rain to do honour to a dirty procession of monks which passed within his view, at a distance of some fifty or sixty yards. It is likely enough that, rooted in the woods of France and Norway, there were growing trees, when that sufferer was put to death, already marked by the Woodman, Fate, to come down and be sawn into boards, to make a certain movable framework with a sack and a knife in it, terrible in history. It is likely enough that in the rough outhouses of some tillers of the heavy lands adjacent to Paris, there were sheltered from the weather that very day, rude carts, bespattered with rustic mire, snuffed about by pigs, and roosted in by poultry, which the Farmer, Death, had already set apart to be his tumbrils of the Revolution. But that Woodman and that Farmer, though they work unceasingly, work silently, and no one heard them as they went about with muffled tread: the rather, forasmuch as to entertain any suspicion that they were awake was to be atheistical and traitorous.

In England, there was scarcely an amount of order and protection to justify much national boasting. Daring burglaries by armed men, and highway robberies, took place in the capital itself every night; families were publicly cautioned not to go out of town without removing their furniture to upholsterers' warehouses for security; the highwayman in the dark was a City tradesman in the light, and, being recognised and challenged by his fellow-tradesman whom he stopped in his character of "the Captain," gallantly shot him through the head and rode away; the mail was waylaid by seven robbers, and the guard shot three dead, and then got shot dead himself by the other four, "in consequence of the failure of his ammunition:" after which the mail was robbed in peace; that magnificent potentate, the Lord Mayor of London, was made to stand and deliver on Turnham Green, by one highwayman, who despoiled the illustrious creature in sight of all his retinue; prisoners in London jails fought battles with their turnkeys, and the majesty of the law fired blunderbusses in among them, loaded with rounds of shot and ball; thieves snipped off diamond crosses from the necks of noble lords at Court drawing-rooms; musketeers went into St. Giles's, to search for contraband goods, and the mob fired on the musketeers, and the musketeers fired on the mob, and nobody thought any of these occurrences much out of the common way. In the midst of them, the hangman, ever busy and ever worse than useless, was in constant requisition; now, stringing up long rows of miscellaneous criminals; now, hanging a housebreaker on Saturday who had been taken on Tuesday; now, burning people in the hand at Newgate by the dozen, and now burning pamphlets at the door of Westminster Hall; to-day, taking the life of an atrocious murderer, and to-morrow of a wretched pilferer who had robbed a farmer's boy of sixpence.

All these things, and a thousand like them, came to pass in and close upon the dear old year one thousand seven hundred and seventy-five. Environed by them, while the Woodman and the Farmer worked unheeded, those two of the large jaws, and those other two of the plain and the fair faces, trod with stir enough, and carried their divine rights with a high hand. Thus did the year one thousand seven hundred and seventy-five conduct their Greatnesses, and myriads of small creatures — the creatures of this chronicle among the rest — along the roads that lay before them.

CHAPTER II

THE MAIL

IT was the Dover road that lay, on a Friday night late in November, before the first of the persons with whom this history has business. The Dover road lay, as to him, beyond the Dover mail, as it lumbered up Shooter's Hill. He walked up-hill in the mire by the side of the mail, as the rest of the passengers did; not because they had the least relish for walking exercise, under the circumstances, but because the hill, and the harness, and the mud, and the mail, were all so heavy, that the horses had three times already come to a stop, besides once drawing the coach across the road, with the mutinous intent of taking it back to Blackheath. Reins and whip and coachman and guard, however, in combination, had read that article of war which forbade a purpose otherwise strongly in favour of the argument, that some brute animals are endued with Reason; and the team had capitulated and returned to their duty.

With drooping heads and tremulous tails, they mashed their way through the thick mud, floundering and stumbling between whiles as if they were falling to pieces at the larger joints. As often as the driver rested them and brought them to a stand, with a wary "Wo-ho! so-ho then!" the near leader violently shook his head and everything upon it — like an unusually emphatic horse, denying that the coach could be got up the hill. Whenever the leader made this rattle, the passenger started, as a nervous passenger might, and was disturbed in mind.

There was a steaming mist in all the hollows, and it had roamed in its forlornness up the hill, like an evil spirit, seeking rest and finding none. A clammy and intensely cold mist, it made its slow way through the air in ripples that visibly followed and overspread one another, as the waves of an unwholesome sea might do. It was dense enough to shut out everything from the light of the coach-lamps but these its own workings, and a few yards of road; and the reek of the labouring horses steamed into it, as if they had made it all.

Two other passengers, besides the one, were plodding up the hill by the side of the mail. All three were wrapped to the cheek-bones and over the ears, and wore jack-boots. Not one of the three could have said, from anything he saw, what either of the other two was like; and each was hidden under almost as many wrappers from the eyes of the mind, as from the eyes of the body, of his two companions. In those days, travellers were very shy of being confidential on a short notice, for anybody on the road might be a robber or in league with robbers. As to the latter, when every posting-house and alehouse could produce somebody in "the Captain's" pay, ranging from the landlord to the lowest stable nondescript, it was the likeliest thing upon the cards. So the guard of the Dover mail thought to himself, that Friday night in November one thousand seven hundred and seventy-five, lumbering up Shooter's Hill, as he stood on his own particular perch behind the mail, beating his feet, and keeping an eye and a hand on the arm-chest before him, where a loaded blunderbuss lay at the top of six or eight loaded horse-pistols, deposited on a substratum of cutlass.

The Dover mail was in its usual genial position that the guard suspected the passengers, the passengers suspected one another and the guard, they all suspected everybody else, and the coachman was sure of nothing but the horses; as to which cattle he could with a clear conscience have taken his oath on the two Testaments that they were not fit for the journey.

"Wo-ho!" said the coachman. "So, then! One more pull and you're at the top and be damned to you, for I have had trouble enough to get you to it! — Joe!"

"Halloa!" the guard replied.

"What o'clock do you make it, Joe?"

"Ten minutes, good, past eleven."

"My blood!" ejaculated the vexed coachman, "and not atop of Shooter's yet? Tst! Yah! Get on with you!"

The emphatic horse, cut short by the whip in a most decided negative, made a decided scramble for it, and the three other horses followed suit. Once more, the Dover mail struggled on, with the jack-boots of its passengers squashing along by its side. They had stopped when the coach stopped, and they kept close company with it. If any one of the three had had the hardihood to propose to another to walk on a little ahead into the mist and darkness, he would have put himself in a fair way of getting shot instantly as a highwayman.

The last burst carried the mail to the summit of the hill. The horses stopped to breathe again, and the guard got down to skid the wheel for the descent, and open the coach-door to let the passengers in.

" Tst !   Joe ! " cried the coachman, in a warning voice, looking down from his box.

" What do you say, Tom ? "

They both listened.

" I say a horse at a canter coming up, Joe."

" *I* say a horse at a gallop, Tom," returned the guard, leaving his hold of the door, and mounting nimbly to his place. " Gentlemen !   In the king's name, all of you ! "

With this hurried adjuration, he cocked his blunderbuss, and stood on the offensive.

The passenger booked by this history was on the coach-step, getting in; the two other passengers were close behind him, and about to follow.   He remained on the step, half in the coach and half out of it ; they remained in the road below him.   They all looked from the coachman to the guard, and from the guard to the coachman, and listened.   The coachman looked back, and the guard looked back, and even the emphatic leader pricked up his ears and looked back, without contradicting.

The stillness consequent on the cessation of the rumbling and labouring of the coach, added to the stillness of the night, made it very quiet indeed.   The panting of the horses communicated a tremulous motion to the coach, as if it were in a state of agitation.   The hearts of the passengers beat loud enough perhaps to be heard ; but at any rate, the quiet pause was audibly expressive of people out of breath, and holding the breath, and having the pulses quickened by expectation.

The sound of a horse at a gallop came fast and furiously up the hill

" So-ho ! " the guard sang out, as loud as he could roar. " Yo there !   Stand !   I shall fire ! "

The pace was suddenly checked, and, with much splashing and floundering, a man's voice called from the mist, " Is that the Dover mail ? "

" Never you mind what it is ! " the guard retorted.   " What are you ? "

" *Is* that the Dover mail ? "

" Why do you want to know ? "

" I want a passenger, if it is."

" What passenger ? "

" Mr. Jarvis Lorry."

Our booked passenger showed in a moment that it was his name.   The guard, the coachman, and the two other passengers, eyed him distrustfully.

" Keep where you are," the guard called to the voice in the mist, " because, if I should make a mistake, it could never be set right in your lifetime.   Gentleman of the name of Lorry answer straight."

" What is the matter ? " asked the passenger, then, with mildly quavering speech.   " Who wants me ?   Is it Jerry ? "

(" I don't like Jerry's voice, if it is Jerry," growled the guard to himself.   " He's hoarser than suits me, is Jerry.")

" Yes, Mr. Lorry."

" What is the matter ? "

" A despatch sent after you from over yonder.   T. and Co."

" I know this messenger, guard," said Mr. Lorry, getting down into the road — assisted from behind more swiftly than politely by the other two passengers, who immediately scrambled into the coach, shut the door, and pulled up the window. " He may come close ; there's nothing wrong."

" I hope there ain't, but I can't make so 'Nation sure of that," said the guard, in gruff soliloquy.   " Hallo you ! "

" Well ! And hallo you ! " said Jerry, more hoarsely than before.

" Come on at a footpace; d' ye mind me ?   And if you've got holsters to that saddle o' yourn, don't let me see your hand go nigh 'em.   For I 'm a devil at a quick mistake, and when I make one it takes the form of Lead.   So now let's look at you."

The figures of a horse and rider came slowly through the eddying mist, and came to the side of the mail, where the passenger stood.   The rider stooped, and, casting up his eyes at the guard, handed the passenger a small folded paper.   The rider's horse was blown, and both horse and rider were covered with mud, from the hoofs of the horse to the hat of the man.

"Guard!" said the passenger, in a tone of quiet business confidence.

The watchful guard, with his right hand at the stock of his raised blunderbuss, his left at the barrel, and his eye on the horseman, answered curtly, "Sir."

"There is nothing to apprehend. I belong to Tellson's Bank. You must know Tellson's Bank in London. I am going to Paris on business. A crown to drink. I may read this?"

"If so be as you're quick, sir."

He opened it in the light of the coach-lamp on that side, and read — first to himself and then aloud: "'Wait at Dover for Mam'selle.' It's not long, you see, guard. Jerry, say that my answer was, RECALLED TO LIFE."

Jerry started in his saddle. "That's a Blazing strange answer, too," said he, at his hoarsest.

"Take that message back, and they will know that I received this, as well as if I wrote. Make the best of your way. Good night."

With those words the passenger opened the coach-door and got in; not at all assisted by his fellow-passengers, who had expeditiously secreted their watches and purses in their boots, and were now making a general pretence of being asleep. With no more definite purpose than to escape the hazard of originating any other kind of action.

The coach lumbered on again, with heavier wreaths of mist closing round it as it began the descent. The guard soon replaced his blunderbuss in his arm-chest, and having looked to the rest of its contents, and having looked to the supplementary pistols that he wore in his belt, looked to a smaller chest beneath his seat, in which there were a few smith's tools, a couple of torches, and a tinder-box. For he was furnished with that completeness, that if the coach-lamps had been blown and stormed out, which did occasionally happen, he had only to shut himself up inside, keep the flint and steel sparks well off the straw, and get a light with tolerable safety and ease (if he were lucky) in five minutes.

"Tom!" softly over the coach-roof.

"Hallo, Joe."

"Did you hear the message?"

"I did, Joe."

"What did you make of it, Tom?"

"Nothing at all, Joe."

"That's a coincidence, too," the guard mused, "for I made the same of it myself."

Jerry, left alone in the mist and darkness, dismounted meanwhile, not only to ease his spent horse, but to wipe the mud from his face, and to shake the wet out of his hat-brim, which might be capable of holding about half a gallon. After standing with the bridle over his heavily splashed arm, until the wheels of the mail were no longer within hearing and the night was quite still again, he turned to walk down the hill.

"After that there gallop from Temple Bar, old lady, I won't trust your fore-legs till I get you on the level," said this hoarse messenger, glancing at his mare. "'Recalled to life.' That's a Blazing strange message. Much of that would n't do for you, Jerry! I say, Jerry! You'd be in a Blazing bad way, if recalling to life was to come into fashion, Jerry!"

CHAPTER III

THE NIGHT SHADOWS

A WONDERFUL fact to reflect upon, that every human creature is constituted to be that profound secret and mystery to every other. A solemn consideration, when I enter a great city by night, that every one of those darkly clustered houses incloses its own secret; that every room in every one of them incloses its own secret; that every beating heart in the hundreds of thousands of breasts there is, in some of its imaginings, a secret to the heart nearest it! Something of the awfulness, even of Death itself, is referable to this. No more can I turn the leaves of this dear book that I loved, and vainly hope in time to read it all. No more can I look into the depths of this unfathomable water, wherein, as momentary lights glanced into it, I have had glimpses of buried treasure and other things submerged. It was appointed that the book should shut with a spring, for ever and for ever, when I had read but a page. It was appointed that the water should be locked in an eternal frost, when the light was playing on its surface, and I stood in ignorance on the shore. My friend is dead, my neighbour is dead, my love, the darling of my soul, is dead; it is the inexorable consolation and perpetuation of the secret that was always in that individuality, and which I shall carry in mine to my life's end. In any of the burial-places in this city through which I pass, is there a sleeper more inscrutable than its busy inhabitants are, in their innermost personality, to me, or than I am to them?

As to this, his natural and not to be alienated inheritance, the messenger on horseback had exactly the same possessions as the King, the first Minister of State, or the richest merchant in London. So with the three passengers shut up in the narrow compass of one lumbering old mail-coach; they were mysteries to one another, as complete as if each had been in his own coach and six, or his own coach and sixty, with the breadth of a county between him and the next.

The messenger rode back at an easy trot, stopping pretty often at alehouses by the way to drink, but evincing a tendency to keep his own counsel, and to keep his hat cocked over his eyes. He had eyes that assorted very well with that decoration, being of a surface black, with no depth in the colour or form, and much too near together — as if they were afraid of being found out in something, singly, if they kept too far apart. They had a sinister expression, under an old cocked hat like a three-cornered spittoon, and over a great muffler for the chin and throat, which descended nearly to the wearer's knees. When he stopped for drink, he moved this muffler with his left hand, only while he poured his liquor in with his right; as soon as that was done, he muffled again.

"No, Jerry, no!" said the messenger, harping on one theme as he rode. "It would n't do for you, Jerry. Jerry, you honest tradesman, it would n't suit *your* line of business! Recalled —! Bust me if I don't think he'd been a drinking!"

His message perplexed his mind to that degree that he was fain, several times, to take off his hat to scratch his head. Except on the crown, which was raggedly bald, he had stiff, black hair, standing jaggedly all over it, and growing down-hill almost to his broad, blunt nose. It was so like smith's work, so much more like the top of a strongly spiked wall than a head of hair, that the best of players at leap-frog might have declined him, as the most dangerous man in the world to go over.

While he trotted back with the message he was to deliver to the night watchman in his box at the door of Tellson's Bank, by Temple Bar, who was to deliver it to greater authorities within, the shadows of the night took such shapes to him as arose out of the message, and took such shapes to the mare as arose out of *her* private topics of uneasiness. They seemed to be numerous, for she shied at every shadow on the road.

What time, the mail-coach lumbered, jolted, rattled, and bumped upon its tedious way, with its three fellow-inscrutables inside. To whom, likewise, the shadows of the night revealed themselves, in the forms their dozing eyes and wandering thoughts suggested.

Tellson's Bank had a run upon it in the mail. As the bank passenger — with an arm drawn through the leathern strap, which did what lay in it to keep him from pounding against the next passenger, and driving him into his corner, whenever the coach got a special jolt — nodded in his place with half-shut eyes, the little coach-windows, and the coach-lamp dimly gleaming through them, and the bulky bundle of opposite passenger, became the bank, and did a great stroke of business. The rattle of the harness was the chink of money, and more drafts were honoured in five minutes than even Tellson's, with all its foreign and home connection, ever paid in thrice the time. Then the strong-rooms underground, at Tellson's, with such of their valuable stores and secrets as were known to the passenger (and it was not a little that he knew about them), opened before him, and he went in among them with the great keys and the feebly burning candle, and found them safe, and strong, and sound, and still, just as he had last seen them.

But though the bank was almost always with him, and though the coach (in a confused way, like the presence of pain under an opiate) was always with him, there was another current of impression that never ceased to run, all through the night. He was on his way to dig some one out of a grave.

Now, which of the multitude of faces that showed themselves before him was the true face of the buried person, the shadows of the night did not indicate; but they were all the faces of a man of five-and-forty by years, and they differed principally in the passions they expressed, and in the ghastliness of their worn and wasted state. Pride, contempt, defiance, stubbornness, submission, lamentation, succeeded one another; so did varieties of sunken cheek, cadaverous colour, emaciated hands and fingers. But the face was in the main one face, and every head was prematurely white. A hundred times the dozing passenger inquired of this spectre : —

"Buried how long ? "

The answer was always the same : " Almost eighteen years."

" You had abandoned all hope of being dug out ? "

" Long ago."

" You know that you are recalled to life ? "

" They tell me so."

" I hope you care to live ? "

" I can't say."

" Shall I show her to you ? Will you come and see her ? "

The answers to this question were various and contradictory. Sometimes the broken reply was, " Wait ! It would kill me if I saw her too soon." Sometimes, it was given in a tender rain of tears, and then it was, "Take me to her." Sometimes, it was staring and bewildered, and then it was, "I don't know her. I don't understand."

After such imaginary discourse, the passenger in his fancy would dig, and dig, dig — now with a spade, now with a great key, now with his hands — to dig this wretched creature out. Got out at last, with earth hanging about his face and hair, he would suddenly fall away to dust. The passenger would then start to himself, and lower the window, to get the reality of mist and rain on his cheek.

Yet even when his eyes were opened on the mist and rain, on the moving patch of light from the lamps, and the hedge at the roadside retreating by jerks, the night shadows outside the coach would fall into the train of the night shadows within. The real Banking-house by Temple Bar, the real business of the past day, the real strong-rooms, the real express sent after him, and the real message returned, would all be there. Out of the midst of them, the ghostly face would rise, and he would accost it again.

" Buried how long ? "

"Almost eighteen years."

" I hope you care to live ? "

" I can't say."

Dig — dig — dig — until an impatient movement from one of the two passengers would admonish him to pull up the window, draw his arm securely through the leathern strap, and speculate upon the two slumbering forms, until his mind lost its hold of them, and they again slid away into the bank and the grave.

" Buried how long ? "

"Almost eighteen years."

" You had abandoned all hope of being dug out ? "

" Long ago."

The words were still in his hearing as just spoken — distinctly in his hearing as ever spoken words had been in his life — when the weary passenger started to the consciousness of daylight, and found that the shadows of the night were gone.

He lowered the window, and looked out at the rising sun. There was a ridge of ploughed land, with a plough upon it where it had been left last night when the horses were unyoked ; beyond, a quiet coppice-wood, in which many leaves of burning red and golden yellow still remained upon the trees. Though the earth was cold and wet, the sky was clear, and the sun rose bright, placid, and beautiful.

"Eighteen years!" said the passenger, looking at the sun. "Gracious Creator of Day! To be buried alive for eighteen years!"

CHAPTER IV

THE PREPARATION

WHEN the mail got successfully to Dover, in the course of the forenoon, the head-drawer at the Royal George Hotel opened the coach-door as his custom was. He did it with some flourish of ceremony, for a mail journey from London in winter was an achievement to congratulate an adventurous traveller upon.

By that time, there was only one adventurous traveller left to be congratulated; for the two others had been set down at their respective roadside destinations. The mildewy inside of the coach, with its damp and dirty straw, its disagreeable smell, and its obscurity, was rather like a larger dog-kennel. Mr. Lorry, the passenger, shaking himself out of it in chains of straw, a tangle of shaggy wrapper, flapping hat, and muddy legs, was rather like a larger sort of dog.

"There will be a packet to Calais to-morrow, drawer?"

"Yes, sir, if the weather holds and the wind sets tolerable fair. The tide will serve pretty nicely at about two in the afternoon, sir. Bed, sir?"

"I shall not go to bed till night; but I want a bedroom, and a barber."

"And then breakfast, sir? Yes, sir. That way, sir, if you please. Show Concord! Gentleman's valise and hot water to Concord. Pull off gentleman's boots in Concord. (You will find a fine sea-coal fire, sir.) Fetch barber to Concord. Stir about, there, now, for Concord!"

The Concord bed-chamber being always assigned to a passenger by the mail, and passengers by the mail being always heavily wrapped up from head to foot, the room had the odd interest for the establishment of the Royal George that although but one kind of man was seen to go into it, all kinds and varieties of men came out of it. Consequently another drawer, and two porters, and several maids, and the landlady, were all loitering by accident at various points of the road between the Concord and the coffee-room, when a gentleman of sixty, formally dressed in a brown suit of clothes, pretty well worn, but very well kept, with large square cuffs and large flaps to the pockets, passed along on his way to his breakfast.

The coffee-room had no other occupant, that forenoon, than the gentleman in brown. His breakfast-table was drawn before the fire, and as he sat, with its light shining on him, waiting for the meal, he sat so still, that he might have been sitting for his portrait.

Very orderly and methodical he looked, with a hand on each knee, and a loud watch ticking a sonorous sermon under his flapped waistcoat, as though it pitted its gravity and longevity against the levity and evanescence of the brisk fire. He had a good leg, and was a little vain of it, for his brown stockings fitted sleek and close, and were of a fine texture ; his shoes and buckles, too, though plain, were trim. He wore an odd little sleek crisp flaxen wig, setting very close to his head : which wig, it is to be presumed, was made of hair, but which looked far more as though it were spun from filaments of silk or glass. His linen, though not of a fineness in accordance with his stockings, was as white as the tops of the waves that broke upon the neighbouring beach, or the specks of sail that glinted in the sunlight far at sea. A face habitually suppressed and quieted was still lighted up under the quaint wig by a pair of moist bright eyes that it must have cost their owner, in years gone by, some pains to drill to the composed and reserved expression of Tellson's Bank. He had a healthy colour in his cheeks, and his face, though lined, bore few traces of anxiety. But perhaps the confidential bachelor clerks in Tellson's Bank were principally occupied with the cares of other people ; and perhaps second-hand cares, like second-hand clothes, come easily off and on.

Completing his resemblance to a man who was sitting for his portrait, Mr. Lorry dropped off asleep. The arrival of his breakfast roused him, and he said to the drawer, as he moved his chair to it : —

" I wish accommodation prepared for a young lady who may come here at any time to-day. She may ask for Mr. Jarvis Lorry, or she may only ask for a gentleman from Tellson's Bank. Please to let me know."

" Yes, sir. Tellson's Bank in London, sir ? "

" Yes."

" Yes, sir. We have oftentimes the honour to entertain your gentlemen in their travelling backwards and forwards betwixt London and Paris, sir. A vast deal of travelling, sir, in Tellson and Company's House."

" Yes. We are quite a French house, as well as an English one."

" Yes, sir. Not much in the habit of such travelling yourself, I think, sir ? "

" Not of late years. It is fifteen years since we — since I — came last from France."

" Indeed, sir ? That was before my time here, sir. Before our people's time here, sir. The George was in other hands at that time, sir."

" I believe so."

" But I would hold a pretty wager, sir, that a House like Tellson and Company was flourishing, a matter of fifty, not to speak of fifteen years ago ? "

" You might treble that, and say a hundred and fifty, yet not be far from the truth."

" Indeed, sir ! "

Rounding his mouth and both his eyes, as he stepped backward from the table, the waiter shifted his napkin from his right arm to his left, dropped into a comfortable attitude, and stood surveying the guest while he ate and drank, as from an observatory or watch-tower. According to the immemorial usage of waiters in all ages.

When Mr. Lorry had finished his breakfast, he went out for a stroll on the beach. The little, narrow, crooked town of Dover hid itself away from the beach, and ran its head into the chalk cliffs, like a marine ostrich. The beach was a desert of heaps of sea and stones tumbling wildly about, and the sea did what it liked, and what it liked was destruction. It thundered at the town, and thundered at the cliffs, and brought the coast down madly. The air among the houses was of so strong a piscatory flavour that one might have supposed sick fish went up to be dipped in it, as sick people went down to be dipped in the sea. A little fishing was done in the port, and a quantity of strolling about by night, and looking seaward : particularly at those times when the tide made, and was near flood. Small tradesmen, who did no business whatever, sometimes unaccountably realised large fortunes, and it was remarkable that nobody in the neighbourhood could endure a lamplighter.

As the day declined into the afternoon, and the air, which had been at intervals clear enough to allow the French coast to be seen, became again charged with mist and vapour, Mr. Lorry's thoughts seemed to cloud too. When it was dark, and he sat before the coffee-room fire, awaiting his dinner as he had awaited his breakfast, his mind was busily digging, digging, digging, in the live red coals.

A bottle of good claret after dinner does a digger in the red coals no harm, otherwise than as it has a tendency to throw him out of work. Mr. Lorry had been idle a long time, and had just poured out his last glassful of wine with as complete an appearance of satisfaction as is ever to be found in an elderly gentleman of a fresh complexion who has got to the end of a bottle, when a rattling of wheels came up the narrow street, and rumbled into the inn-yard.

He set down his glass untouched. " This is Mam'selle ! " said he.

In a very few minutes the waiter came in, to announce that Miss Manette had arrived from London, and would be happy to see the gentleman from Tellson's.

" So soon ? "

Miss Manette had taken some refreshment on the road, and required none then, and was extremely anxious to see the gentleman from Tellson's immediately, if it suited his pleasure and convenience.

The gentleman from Tellson's had nothing left for it but to empty his glass with an air of stolid desperation, settle his odd little flaxen wig at the ears, and follow the waiter to Miss Manette's apartment. It was a large, dark room, furnished in a funereal manner with black horsehair, and loaded with heavy dark tables. These had been oiled and oiled, until the two tall candles on the table in the middle of the room were gloomily reflected on every leaf ; as if *they* were buried, in deep graves of black mahogany, and no light to speak of could be expected from them until they were dug out.

The obscurity was so difficult to penetrate that Mr. Lorry, picking his way over the well-worn Turkey carpet, supposed Miss Manette to be, for the moment, in some adjacent room, until, having got past the two tall candles, he saw standing to receive him by the table between them and the fire, a young lady of not more than seventeen, in a riding-cloak, and still holding her straw travelling-hat by its ribbon in her hand. As his eyes rested on a short, slight, pretty figure, a quantity of golden hair, a pair of blue eyes that met his own with an inquiring look, and a forehead with a singular capacity (remembering how young and smooth it was) of lifting and knitting itself into an expression that was not quite one of perplexity, or wonder, or alarm, or merely of a bright fixed attention, though it included all the four expressions — as his eyes rested on these things, a sudden vivid likeness passed before him, of a child whom he had held in his arms on the passage across that very Channel, one cold time, when the hail drifted heavily and the sea ran high. The likeness passed away, say, like a breath along the surface of the gaunt pier-glass behind her, on the frame of which, a hospital procession of negro cupids, several headless and all cripples, were offering black baskets of Dead Sea fruit to black divinities of the feminine gender — and he made his formal bow to Miss Manette.

"Pray take a seat, sir." In a very clear and pleasant young voice : a little foreign in its accent, but a very little indeed.

"I kiss your hand, miss," said Mr. Lorry, with the manners of an earlier date, as he made his formal bow again, and took his seat.

"I received a letter from the Bank, sir, yesterday, informing me that some intelligence — or discovery — "

"The word is not material, miss ; either word will do."

" — respecting the small property of my poor father whom I never saw — so long dead — "

Mr. Lorry moved in his chair, and cast a troubled look towards the hospital procession of negro cupids. As if *they* had any help for anybody in their absurd baskets!

" — rendered it necessary that I should go to Paris, there to communicate with a gentleman of the Bank, so good as to be despatched to Paris for the purpose."

"Myself."

"As I was prepared to hear, sir."

She curtseyed to him (young ladies made curtseys in those days), with a pretty desire to convey to him that she felt how much older and wiser he was than she. He made her another bow.

"I replied to the Bank, sir, that as it was considered neces-sary, by those who know, and who are so kind as to advise me, that I should go to France, and that as I am an orphan and have no friend who could go with me, I should esteem it highly if I might be permitted to place myself during the journey, under that worthy gentleman's protection. The gentleman had left London, but I think a messenger was sent after him to beg the favour of his waiting for me here."

"I was happy," said Mr. Lorry, "to be entrusted with the charge. I shall be more happy to execute it."

"Sir, I thank you indeed. I thank you very gratefully. It was told me by the Bank that the gentleman would explain to me the details of the business, and that I must prepare myself to find them of a surprising nature. I have done my best to prepare myself, and I naturally have a strong and eager interest to know what they are."

"Naturally," said Mr. Lorry. "Yes — I — "

After a pause, he added, again settling the crisp flaxen wig at the ears : —

"It is very difficult to begin."

He did not begin, but in his indecision met her glance. The young forehead lifted itself into that singular expression — but it was pretty and characteristic, besides being singular — and she raised her hand, as if with an involuntary action she caught at, or stayed, some passing shadow.

"Are you quite a stranger to me, sir ? "

"Am I not ? " Mr. Lorry opened his hands, and extended them outward with an argumentative smile.

Between the eyebrows and just over the little feminine nose, the line of which was as delicate and fine as it was possible to be, the expression deepened itself as she took her seat thought-fully in the chair by which she had hitherto remained standing. He watched her as she mused, and the moment she raised her eyes again, went on : —

"In your adopted country, I presume, I cannot do better than address you as a young English lady, Miss Manette ? "

"If you please, sir."

"Miss Manette, I am a man of business. I have a business charge to acquit myself of. In your reception of it, don't heed me any more than if I was a speaking machine — truly, I am not much else. I will, with your leave, relate to you, miss, the story of one of our customers."

"Story!"

He seemed wilfully to mistake the word she had repeated, when he added in a hurry, "Yes, customers; in the banking business we usually call our connection our customers. He was a French gentleman; a scientific gentleman; a man of great acquirements — a doctor."

"Not of Beauvais?"

"Why, yes, of Beauvais. Like Monsieur Manette, your father, the gentleman was of Beauvais. Like Monsieur Manette, your father, the gentleman was of repute in Paris. I had the honour of knowing him there. Our relations were business relations, but confidential. I was at that time in our French House, and had been — oh! twenty years."

"At that time — I may ask, at what time, sir?"

"I speak, miss, of twenty years ago. He married — an English lady — and I was one of the trustees. His affairs, like the affairs of many other French gentlemen and French families, were entirely in Tellson's hands. In a similar way, I am, or I have been, trustee of one kind or other for scores of our customers. These are mere business relations, miss; there is no friendship in them, no particular interest, nothing like sentiment. I have passed from one to another, in the course of my business life, just as I pass from one of our customers to another in the course of my business day; in short, I have no feelings; I am a mere machine. To go on —"

"But this is my father's story, sir; and I begin to think" — the curiously roughened forehead was very intent upon him — "that when I was left an orphan through my mother's surviving my father only two years, it was you who brought me to England. I am almost sure it was you."

Mr. Lorry took the hesitating little hand that confidingly advanced to take his, and he put it with some ceremony to his lips. He then conducted the young lady straightway to her chair again, and, holding the chair-back with his left hand, and using his right by turns to rub his chin, pull his wig at the ears, or point what he said, stood looking down into her face while she sat looking up into his.

"Miss Manette, it *was* I. And you will see how truly I spoke of myself just now, in saying I had no feelings, and that all the relations I hold with my fellow-creatures are mere business relations, when you reflect that I have never seen you since. No; you have been the ward of Tellson's House since, and I have been busy with the other business of Tellson's House since. Feelings! I have no time for them, no chance of them. I pass my whole life, miss, in turning an immense pecuniary Mangle."

After this odd description of his daily routine of employment, Mr. Lorry flattened his flaxen wig upon his head with both hands (which was most unnecessary, for nothing could be flatter than its shining surface was before), and resumed his former attitude.

"So far, miss (as you have remarked), this is the story of your regretted father. Now comes the difference. If your father had not died when he did — Don't be frightened! How you start!"

She did, indeed, start. And she caught his wrist with both her hands.

"Pray," said Mr. Lorry, in a soothing tone, bringing his left hand from the back of the chair to lay it on the supplicatory fingers that clasped him in so violent a tremble, "pray control your agitation — a matter of business. As I was saying — "

Her look so discomposed him that he stopped, wandered, and began anew : —

"As I was saying; if Monsieur Manette had not died; if he had suddenly and silently disappeared; if he had been spirited away; if it had not been difficult to guess to what dreadful place, though no art could trace him; if he had an enemy in some compatriot who could exercise a privilege that I in my own time have known the boldest people afraid to speak of in a whisper, across the water there, for instance, the privilege of filling up blank forms for the consignment of any one to the oblivion of a prison for any length of time; if his wife had implored the king, the queen, the court, the clergy, for any tidings of him, and all quite in vain; — then the history of your father would have been the history of this unfortunate gentleman, the Doctor of Beauvais."

"I entreat you to tell me more, sir."

"I will. I am going to. You can bear it?"

"I can bear anything but the uncertainty you leave me in at this moment."

"You speak collectedly, and you — are collected. That's good!" (Though his manner was less satisfied than his words.) "A matter of business. Regard it as a matter of business — business that must be done. Now, if this Doctor's wife, though a lady of great courage and spirit, had suffered so intensely from this cause before her little child was born — "

"The little child was a daughter, sir."

"A daughter. A — a — matter of business — don't be distressed. Miss, if the poor lady had suffered so intensely before her little child was born, that she came to the determination of sparing the poor child the inheritance of any part of the agony she had known the pains of, by rearing her in the belief that her father was dead — No, don't kneel! In Heaven's name why should you kneel to me!"

"For the truth. O dear, good, compassionate sir, for the truth!"

"A — a matter of business. You confuse me, and how can I transact business if I am confused? Let us be clear-headed. If you could kindly mention now, for instance, what nine times ninepence are, or how many shillings in twenty guineas, it would be so encouraging. I should be so much more at my ease about your state of mind."

Without directly answering to this appeal, she sat so still when he had very gently raised her, and the hands that had not ceased to clasp his wrists were so much more steady than they had been, that she communicated some reassurance to Mr. Jarvis Lorry.

"That's right, that's right. Courage! Business! You have business before you; useful business. Miss Manette, your mother took this course with you. And when she died — I believe broken-hearted — having never slackened her unavailing search for your father, she left you, at two years old, to grow to be blooming, beautiful, and happy, without the dark cloud upon you of living in uncertainty whether your father soon wore his heart out in prison, or wasted there through many lingering years."

As he said the words, he looked down, with an admiring pity, on the flowing golden hair; as if he pictured to himself that it might have been already tinged with grey.

"You know that your parents had no great possession, and that what they had was secured to your mother and to you. There has been no new discovery, of money, or of any other property; but — "

He felt his wrist held closer, and he stopped. The expression in the forehead, which had so particularly attracted his notice, and which was now immovable, had deepened into one of pain and horror.

"But he has been — been found. He is alive. Greatly changed, it is too probable; almost a wreck, it is possible; though we will hope the best. Still, alive. Your father has been taken to the house of an old servant in Paris, and we are going there: I, to identify him, if I can: you, to restore him to life, love, duty, rest, comfort."

A shiver ran through her frame, and from it through his. She said, in a low, distinct, awe-stricken voice, as if she were saying it in a dream: —

"I am going to see his Ghost! It will be his Ghost — not him!"

Mr. Lorry quietly chafed the hands that held his arm. "There, there, there! See now, see now! The best and the worst are known to you now. You are well on your way to the poor wronged gentleman, and, with a fair sea voyage, and a fair land journey, you will be soon at his dear side."

She repeated in the same tone, sunk to a whisper, "I have been free, I have been happy, yet his Ghost has never haunted me!"

"Only one thing more," said Mr. Lorry, laying stress upon it as a wholesome means of enforcing her attention: "he has been found under another name; his own, long forgotten or long concealed. It would be worse than useless now to inquire which; worse than useless to seek to know whether he has been for years overlooked, or always designedly held prisoner. It would be worse than useless now to make any inquiries, because it would be dangerous. Better not to mention the subject anywhere or in any way, and to remove him — for a while at all events — out of France. Even I, safe as an Englishman, and even Tellson's, important as they are to French credit, avoid all naming of the matter. I carry about me not a scrap of writing openly referring to it. This is a secret service altogether. My credentials, entries, and memoranda, are all comprehended in the one line, 'Recalled to Life;' which may mean anything. But what is the matter! She does n't notice a word! Miss Manette!"

Perfectly still and silent, and not even fallen back in her

chair, she sat under his hand, utterly insensible; with her eyes open and fixed upon him, and with that last expression looking as if it were carved or branded into her forehead. So close was her hold upon his arm, that he feared to detach himself lest he should hurt her; therefore he called out loudly for assistance without moving.

A wild-looking woman, whom even in his agitation, Mr. Lorry observed to be all of a red colour, and to have red hair, and to be dressed in some extraordinary tight-fitting fashion, and to have on her head a most wonderful bonnet like a Grenadier wooden measure, and good measure too, or a great Stilton cheese, came running into the room in advance of the inn servants, and soon settled the question of his detachment from the poor young lady, by laying a brawny hand upon his chest, and sending him flying back against the nearest wall.

("I really think this must be a man!" was Mr. Lorry's breathless reflection, simultaneously with his coming against the wall.)

"Why, look at you all!" bawled this figure, addressing the inn servants. "Why don't you go and fetch things, instead of standing there staring at me? I am not so much to look at, am I? Why don't you go and fetch things? I'll let you know, if you don't bring smelling-salts, cold water, and vinegar, quick, I will!"

There was an immediate dispersal for these restoratives, and she softly laid the patient on a sofa, and tended her with great skill and gentleness: calling her "my precious!" and "my bird!" and spreading her golden hair aside over her shoulders with great pride and care.

"And you in brown!" she said, indignantly turning to Mr. Lorry; "couldn't you tell her what you had to tell her, without frightening her to death? Look at her, with her pretty pale face and her cold hands. Do you call *that* being a Banker?"

Mr. Lorry was so exceedingly disconcerted by a question so hard to answer, that he could only look on, at a distance, with much feebler sympathy and humility, while the strong woman, having banished the inn servants under the mysterious penalty of "letting them know" something not mentioned if they stayed there, staring, recovered her charge by a regular series of gradations, and coaxed her to lay her drooping head upon her shoulder.

"I hope she will do well now," said Mr. Lorry.

"No thanks to you in brown, if she does. My darling pretty!"

"I hope," said Mr. Lorry, after another pause of feeble sympathy and humility, "that you accompany Miss Manette to France?"

"A likely thing, too!" replied the strong woman. "If it was ever intended that I should go across salt water, do you suppose Providence would have cast my lot in an island?"

This being another question hard to answer, Mr. Jarvis Lorry withdrew to consider it.

CHAPTER V

THE WINE-SHOP

A LARGE cask of wine had been dropped and broken in the
street. The accident had happened in getting it out of a cart;
the cask had tumbled out with a run, the hoops had burst, and
it lay on the stones just outside the door of the wine-shop,
shattered like a walnut-shell.

All the people within reach had suspended their business,
or their idleness, to run to the spot and drink the wine. The
rough, irregular stones of the street, pointing every way, and
designed, one might have thought, expressly to lame all living
creatures that approached them, had dammed it into little
pools; these were surrounded, each by its own jostling group
or crowd, according to its size. Some men kneeled down,
made scoops of their two hands joined, and sipped, or tried to
help women, who bent over their shoulders, to sip, before the
wine had all run out between their fingers. Others, men and
women, dipped in the puddles with little mugs of mutilated
earthenware, or even with handkerchiefs from women's heads,
which were squeezed dry into infants' mouths; others made
small mud-embankments, to stem the wine as it ran; others,
directed by lookers-on up at high windows, darted here and
there, to cut off little streams of wine that started away in new
directions; others devoted themselves to the sodden and lee-
dyed pieces of the cask, licking, and even champing the moister
wine-rotted fragments with eager relish. There was no drain-
age to carry off the wine, and not only did it all get taken up,
but so much mud got taken up along with it, that there might
have been a scavenger in the street, if anybody acquainted with
it could have believed in such a miraculous presence.

A shrill sound of laughter and of amused voices — voices
of men, women, and children — resounded in the street while
this wine-game lasted. There was little roughness in the
sport, and much playfulness. There was a special companion-

ship in it, an observable inclination on the part of every one
to join some other one, which led, especially among the luckier
or lighter-hearted, to frolicsome embraces, drinking of healths,
shaking of hands, and even joining of hands and dancing, a
dozen together.   When the wine was gone, and the places
where it had been most abundant were raked into a gridiron-
pattern by fingers, these demonstrations ceased, as suddenly as
they had broken out.   The man who had left his saw sticking
in the firewood he was cutting, set it in motion again ; the
woman who had left on a door-step the little pot of hot ashes,
at which she had been trying to soften the pain in her own
starved fingers and toes, or in those of her child, returned to it ;
men with bare arms, matted locks, and cadaverous faces, who
had emerged into the winter light from cellars, moved away
to descend again ; and a gloom gathered on the scene that
appeared more natural to it than sunshine.

The wine was red wine, and had stained the ground of the
narrow street in the suburb of Saint Antoine, in Paris, where it
was spilled.   It had stained many hands, too, and many faces,
and many naked feet, and many wooden shoes.   The hands of
the man who sawed the wood left red marks on the billets ; and
the forehead of the woman who nursed her baby was stained
with the stain of the old rag she wound about her head again.
Those who had been greedy with the staves of the cask had
acquired a tigerish smear about the mouth ; and one tall joker
so besmirched, his head more out of a long squalid bag of a
nightcap than in it, scrawled upon a wall with his finger dipped
in muddy wine lees — BLOOD.

The time was to come, when that wine too would be spilled
on the street stones, and when the stain of it would be red upon
many there.

And now that the cloud settled on Saint Antoine, which a
momentary gleam had driven from his sacred countenance, the
darkness of it was heavy — cold, dirt, sickness, ignorance, and
want, were the lords in waiting on the saintly presence — nobles
of great power all of them ; but, most especially, the last.
Samples of a people who had undergone a terrible grinding and
re-grinding in the mill, and certainly not in the fabulous mill
which ground old people young, shivered at every corner, passed
in and out at every doorway, looked from every window, flut-
tered in every vestige of a garment that the wind shook.   The

mill which had worked them down was the mill that grinds
young people old; the children had ancient faces and grave
voices; and upon them, and upon the grown faces, and ploughed
into every furrow of age and coming up afresh, was the sign,
Hunger. It was prevalent everywhere. Hunger was pushed
out of the tall houses in the wretched clothing that hung upon
poles and lines; Hunger was patched into them with straw and
rag and wood and paper; Hunger was repeated in every fragment of the small modicum of firewood that the man sawed off;
Hunger stared down from the smokeless chimneys, and started up
from the filthy street that had no offal, among its refuse, of anything to eat. Hunger was the inscription on the baker's shelves,
written in every small loaf of his scanty stock of bad bread; at
the sausage-shop, in every dead-dog preparation that was offered
for sale. Hunger rattled its dry bones among the roasting
chestnuts in the turned cylinder; Hunger was shred into atomies
in every farthing porringer of husky chips of potato, fried with
some reluctant drops of oil.

Its abiding-place was in all things fitted to it. A narrow
winding street, full of offence and stench, with other narrow
winding streets diverging, all peopled by rags and nightcaps,
and all smelling of rags and nightcaps, and all visible things
with a brooding look upon them that looked ill. In the hunted
air of the people there was yet some wild-beast thought of the
possibility of turning at bay. Depressed and slinking though
they were, eyes of fire were not wanting among them; nor compressed lips, white with what they suppressed; nor foreheads
knitted into the likeness of the gallows rope they mused about
enduring, or inflicting. The trade signs (and they were almost
as many as the shops) were, all, grim illustrations of Want.
The butcher and the porkman painted up only the leanest
scrags of meat; the baker the coarsest of meagre loaves. The
people, rudely pictured as drinking in the wine-shops, croaked
over their scanty measures of thin wine and beer, and were
gloweringly confidential together. Nothing was represented in a
flourishing condition, save tools and weapons; but the cutler's
knives and axes were sharp and bright, the smith's hammers
were heavy, and the gunmaker's stock was murderous. The
crippling stones of the pavement, with their many little reservoirs
of mud and water, had no footways, but broke off abruptly at
the doors. The kennel, to make amends, ran down the middle

of the street — when it ran at all : which was only after heavy rains, and then it ran, by many eccentric fits, into the houses. Across the streets, at wide intervals, one clumsy lamp was slung by a rope and pulley ; at night, when the lamplighter had let these down, and lighted, and hoisted them again, a feeble grove of dim wicks swung in a sickly manner overhead, as if they were at sea. Indeed they were at sea, and the ship and crew were in peril of tempest.

For the time was to come, when the gaunt scarecrows of that region should have watched the lamplighter, in their idleness and hunger, so long, as to conceive the idea of improving on his method, and hauling up men by those ropes and pulleys, to flare upon the darkness of their condition. But the time was not come yet ; and every wind that blew over France shook the rags of the scarecrows in vain, for the birds, fine of song and feather, took no warning.

The wine-shop was a corner shop, better than most others in its appearance and degree, and the master of the wine-shop had stood outside it, in a yellow waistcoat and green breeches, looking on at the struggle for the lost wine. " It 's not my affair," said he, with a final shrug of the shoulders. " The people from the market did it. Let them bring another."

There, his eyes happening to catch the tall joker writing up his joke, he called to him across the way : —

" Say, then, my Gaspard, what do you do there ? "

The fellow pointed to his joke with immense significance, as is often the way with his tribe. It missed its mark and completely failed, as is often the way with his tribe too.

" What now ? Are you a subject for the mad-hospital ? " said the wine-shop keeper, crossing the road, and obliterating the jest with a handful of mud, picked up for the purpose, and smeared over it. " Why do you write in the public streets ? Is there — tell me, thou — is there no other place to write such words in ? "

In his expostulation he dropped his cleaner hand (perhaps accidentally, perhaps not) upon the joker's heart. The joker rapped with his own, took a nimble spring upward, and came down in a fantastic dancing attitude, with one of his stained shoes jerked off his foot into his hand, and held out. A joker of an extremely, not to say wolfishly, practical character, he looked, under those circumstances.

" Put it on, put it on," said the other. " Call wine, wine ;
and finish there." With that advice, he wiped his soiled
hand upon the joker's dress, such as it was — quite deliberately,
as having dirtied the hand on his account; and then recrossed
the road and entered the wine-shop.

This wine-shop keeper was a bull-necked, martial-looking
man of thirty, and he should have been of a hot temperament,
for, although it was a bitter day, he wore no coat, but carried
one slung over his shoulder. His shirt-sleeves were rolled up,
too, and his brown arms were bare to the elbows. Neither did
he wear anything more on his head than his own crisply curling,
short dark hair. He was a dark man altogether, with good eyes
and a good bold breadth between them. Good-humoured looking on the whole, but implacable-looking, too ; evidently a man
of a strong resolution and a set purpose ; a man not desirable to
be met rushing down a narrow pass with a gulf on either side,
for nothing would turn the man.

Madame Defarge, his wife, sat in the shop behind the counter as he came in. Madame Defarge was a stout woman of
about his own age, with a watchful eye that seldom seemed to
look at anything, a large hand heavily ringed, a steady face,
strong features, and great composure of manner. There was a
character about Madame Defarge, from which one might have
predicated that she did not often make mistakes against herself
in any of the reckonings over which she presided. Madame
Defarge, being sensitive to cold, was wrapped in fur, and had a
quantity of bright shawl twined about her head, though not to
the concealment of her large ear-rings. Her knitting was before
her, but she had laid it down to pick her teeth with a toothpick. Thus engaged, with her right elbow supported by her
left hand, Madame Defarge said nothing when her lord came
in, but coughed just one grain of cough. This, in combination
with the lifting of her darkly defined eyebrows over her toothpick by the breadth of a line, suggested to her husband that he
would do well to look round the shop among the customers for
any new customer who had dropped in while he stepped over
the way.

The wine-shop keeper accordingly rolled his eyes about, until
they rested upon an elderly gentleman and a young lady, who
were seated in a corner. Other company were there : two playing cards, two playing dominoes, three standing by the counter

lengthening out a short supply of wine. As he passed behind the counter, he took notice that the elderly gentleman said in a look to the young lady, "This is our man."

"What the devil do *you* do in that galley there!" said Monsieur Defarge to himself; "I don't know you."

But he feigned not to notice the two strangers, and fell into discourse with the triumvirate of customers who were drinking at the counter.

"How goes it, Jacques?" said one of these three to Monsieur Defarge. "Is all the spilt wine swallowed?"

"Every drop, Jacques," answered Monsieur Defarge.

When this interchange of Christian name was effected, Madame Defarge, picking her teeth with her toothpick, coughed another grain of cough, and raised her eyebrows by the breadth of another line.

"It is not often," said the second of the three, addressing Monsieur Defarge, "that many of these miserable beasts know the taste of wine, or of anything but black bread and death. Is it not so, Jacques?"

"It is so, Jacques," Monsieur Defarge returned.

At this second interchange of the Christian name, Madame Defarge, still using her toothpick with profound composure, coughed another grain of cough, and raised her eyebrows by the breadth of another line.

The last of the three now said his say, as he put down his empty drinking vessel and smacked his lips.

"Ah! So much the worse! A bitter taste it is that such poor cattle always have in their mouths, and hard lives they live, Jacques. Am I right, Jacques?"

"You are right, Jacques," was the response of Monsieur Defarge.

This third interchange of the Christian name was completed at the moment when Madame Defarge put her toothpick by, kept her eyebrows up, and slightly rustled in her seat.

"Hold then! True!" muttered her husband. "Gentlemen — my wife!"

The three customers pulled off their hats to Madame Defarge. with three flourishes. She acknowledged their homage by bending her head, and giving them a quick look. Then she glanced in a casual manner round the wine-shop, took up her knitting with great apparent calmness and repose of spirit, and became absorbed in it.

" Gentlemen," said her husband, who had kept his bright eye observantly upon her, " good day. The chamber, furnished bachelor-fashion, that you wished to see, and were inquiring for when I stepped out, is on the fifth floor. The doorway of the staircase gives on the little courtyard close to the left here," pointing with his hand, " near to the window of my establishment. But, now that I remember, one of you has already been there, and can show the way. Gentlemen, adieu ! "

They paid for their wine, and left the place. The eyes of Monsieur Defarge were studying his wife at her knitting, when the elderly gentleman advanced from his corner, and begged the favour of a word.

" Willingly, sir," said Monsieur Defarge, and quietly stepped with him to the door.

Their conference was very short, but very decided. Almost at the first word, Monsieur Defarge started and became deeply attentive. It had not lasted a minute, when he nodded and went out. The gentleman then beckoned to the young lady, and they, too, went out. Madame Defarge knitted with nimble fingers and steady eyebrows, and saw nothing.

Mr. Jarvis Lorry and Miss Manette, emerging from the wine-shop thus, joined Monsieur Defarge in the doorway to which he had directed his other company just before. It opened from a stinking little black courtyard, and was the general public entrance to a great pile of houses, inhabited by a great number of people. In the gloomy tile-paved entry to the gloomy tile-paved staircase, Monsieur Defarge bent down on one knee to the child of his old master, and put her hand to his lips. It was a gentle action, but not at all gently done ; a very remarkable transformation had come over him in a few seconds. He had no good-humour in his face, nor any openness of aspect left, but had become a secret, angry, dangerous man.

" It is very high ; it is a little difficult. Better to begin slowly." Thus, Monsieur Defarge, in a stern voice, to Mr. Lorry, as they began ascending the stairs.

" Is he alone ? " the latter whispered.

" Alone ! God help him who should be with him ! " said the other, in the same low voice.

" Is he always alone, then ? "

" Yes."

" Of his own desire ? "

"Of his own necessity. As he was when I first saw him after they found me and demanded to know if I would take him, and, at my peril, be discreet — as he was then, so he is now."

"He is greatly changed?"

"Changed!"

The keeper of the wine-shop stopped to strike the wall with his hand, and mutter a tremendous curse. No direct answer could have been half so forcible. Mr. Lorry's spirits grew heavier and heavier, as he and his two companions ascended higher and higher.

Such a staircase, with its accessories, in the older and more crowded parts of Paris, would be bad enough now ; but at that time it was vile indeed to unaccustomed and unhardened senses. Every little habitation within the great foul nest of one high building — that is to say, the room or rooms within every door that opened on the general staircase — left its own heap of refuse on its own landing, besides flinging other refuse from its own windows. The uncontrollable and hopeless mass of decomposition so engendered would have polluted the air, even if poverty and deprivation had not loaded it with their intangible impurities ; the two bad sources combined made it almost insupportable. Through such an atmosphere, by a steep dark shaft of dirt and poison, the way lay. Yielding to his own disturbance of mind, and to his young companion's agitation, which became greater every instant, Mr. Jarvis Lorry twice stopped to rest. Each of these stoppages was made at a doleful grating, by which any languishing good airs that were left uncorrupted seemed to escape, and all spoilt and sickly vapours seemed to crawl in. Through the rusted bars, tastes, rather than glimpses, were caught of the jumbled neighbourhood ; and nothing within range, nearer or lower than the summits of the two great towers of Notre-Dame, had any promise on it of healthy life or wholesome aspirations.

At last, the top of the staircase was gained, and they stopped for the third time. There was yet an upper staircase, of a steeper inclination and of contracted dimensions, to be ascended, before the garret story was reached. The keeper of the wine-shop, always going a little in advance, and always going on the side which Mr. Lorry took, as though he dreaded to be asked any question by the young lady, turned himself about here, and, carefully feeling in the pockets of the coat he carried over his shoulder, took out a key.

"The door is locked then, my friend?" said Mr. Lorry, surprised.

"Ay. Yes," was the grim reply of Monsieur Defarge.

"You think it necessary to keep the unfortunate gentleman so retired?"

"I think it necessary to turn the key." Monsieur Defarge whispered it closer in his ear, and frowned heavily.

"Why?"

"Why! Because he has lived so long, locked up, that he would be frightened — rave — tear himself to pieces — die — come to I know not what harm — if his door was left open."

"Is it possible!" exclaimed Mr. Lorry.

"Is it possible?" repeated Defarge bitterly. "Yes. And a beautiful world we live in, when it *is* possible, and when many other such things are possible, and not only possible, but done — done, see you! — under that sky there, every day. Long live the Devil. Let us go on."

This dialogue had been held in so very low a whisper, that not a word of it had reached the young lady's ears. But by this time she trembled under such strong emotion, and her face expressed such deep anxiety, and, above all, such dread and terror, that Mr. Lorry felt it incumbent on him to speak a word or two of reassurance.

"Courage, dear miss! Courage! Business! The worst will be over in a moment; it is but passing the room door, and the worst is over. Then, all the good you bring to him, all the relief, all the happiness you bring to him, begin. Let our good friend here assist you on that side. That's well, friend Defarge. Come, now. Business, business!"

They went up slowly and softly. The staircase was short, and they were soon at the top. There, as it had an abrupt turn in it, they came all at once in sight of three men, whose heads were bent down close together at the side of a door, and who were intently looking into the room to which the door belonged, through some chinks or holes in the wall. On hearing footsteps close at hand, these three turned, and rose, and showed themselves to be the three of one name who had been drinking in the wine-shop.

"I forgot them in the surprise of your visit," explained

Monsieur Defarge. " Leave us, good boys; we have business here."

The three glided by, and went silently down.

There appearing to be no other door on that floor, and the keeper of the wine-shop going straight to this one when they were left alone, Mr. Lorry asked him in a whisper, with a little anger : —

" Do you make a show of Monsieur Manette ? "

" I show him, in the way you have seen, to a chosen few."

" Is that well ? "

" *I* think it is well."

" Who are the few ?   How do you choose them ? "

" I choose them as real men, of my name, — Jacques is my name, — to whom the sight is likely to do good.   Enough; you are English; that is another thing.   Stay there, if you please, a little moment."

With an admonitory gesture to keep them back, he stooped, and looked in through the crevice in the wall.   Soon raising his head again, he struck twice or thrice upon the door — evidently with no other object than to make a noise there. With the same intention, he drew the key across it, three or four times, before he put it clumsily into the lock, and turned it as heavily as he could.

The door slowly opened inward under his hand, and he looked into the room and said something.   A faint voice answered something.   Little more than a single syllable could have been spoken on either side.

He looked back over his shoulder, and beckoned them to enter.   Mr. Lorry got his arm securely round the daughter's waist, and held her; for he felt that she was sinking.

" A — a — a — business, business ! " he urged, with a moisture that was not of business shining on his cheek.   " Come in, come in ! "

" I am afraid of it," she answered, shuddering.

" Of it ?   What ? "

" I mean of him.   Of my father."

Rendered in a manner desperate, by her state and by the beckoning of their conductor, he drew over his neck the arm that shook upon his shoulder, lifted her a little, and hurried her into the room.   He set her down just within the door, and held her, clinging to him.

Defarge drew out the key, closed the door, locked it on the inside, took out the key again, and held it in his hand. All this he did, methodically, and with as loud and harsh an accompaniment of noise as he could make. Finally, he walked across the room with a measured tread to where the window was. He stopped there, and faced round.

The garret, built to be a depository for firewood and the like, was dim and dark; for the window of dormer shape was in truth a door in the roof, with a little crane over it for the hoisting up of stores from the street — unglazed, and closing up the middle in two pieces, like any other door of French construction. To exclude the cold, one half of this door was fast closed, and the other was opened but a very little way. Such a scanty portion of light was admitted through these means, that it was difficult, on first coming in, to see anything; and long habit alone could have slowly formed in any one the ability to do any work requiring nicety in such obscurity. Yet, work of that kind was being done in the garret; for with his back towards the door, and his face towards the window, where the keeper of the wine-shop stood looking at him, a white-haired man sat on a low bench, stooping forward and very busy, making shoes.

CHAPTER VI

THE SHOEMAKER

"Good day!" said Monsieur Defarge, looking down at the white head that bent low over the shoemaking.

It was raised for a moment, and a very faint voice responded to the salutation, as if it were at a distance : —

"Good day!"

"You are still hard at work, I see?"

After a long silence, the head was lifted for another moment, and the voice replied, "Yes — I am working." This time, a pair of haggard eyes had looked at the questioner, before the face had dropped again.

The faintness of the voice was pitiable and dreadful. It was not the faintness of physical weakness, though confinement and hard fare no doubt had their part in it. Its deplorable peculiarity was, that it was the faintness of solitude and disuse. It was like the last feeble echo of a sound made long and long ago. So entirely had it lost the life and resonance of the human voice, that it affected the senses like a once beautiful colour, faded away into a poor weak stain. So sunken and suppressed it was, that it was like a voice underground. So expressive it was, of a hopeless and lost creature, that a famished traveller, wearied out by lonely wandering in a wilderness, would have remembered home and friends in such a tone before lying down to die.

Some minutes of silent work had passed, and the haggard eyes had looked up again — not with any interest or curiosity, but with a dull mechanical perception, beforehand, that the spot where the only visitor they were aware of had stood was not yet empty.

"I want," said Defarge, who had not removed his gaze from the shoemaker, "to let in a little more light here. You can bear a little more?"

The shoemaker stopped his work; looked, with a vacant air

of listening, at the floor on one side of him; then, similarly, at the floor on the other side of him; then, upward at the speaker.

"What did you say?"

"You can bear a little more light?"

"I must bear it, if you let it in." (Laying the palest shadow of a stress upon the second word.)

The opened half door was opened a little further, and secured at that angle for the time. A broad ray of light fell into the garret, and showed the workman, with an unfinished shoe upon his lap, pausing in his labour. His few common tools and various scraps of leather were at his feet and on his bench. He had a white beard, raggedly cut, but not very long, a hollow face, and exceedingly bright eyes. The hollowness and thinness of his face would have caused them to look large, under his yet dark eyebrows and his confused white hair, though they had been really otherwise; but they were naturally large, and looked unnaturally so. His yellow rags of shirt lay open at the throat, and showed his body to be withered and worn. He, and his old canvas frock, and his loose stockings, and all his poor tatters of clothes, had, in a long seclusion from direct light and air, faded down to such a dull uniformity of parchment-yellow, that it would have been hard to say which was which.

He had put up a hand between his eyes and the light, and the very bones of it seemed transparent. So he sat, with a steadfastly vacant gaze, pausing in his work. He never looked at the figure before him, without first looking down on this side of himself, then on that, as if he had lost the habit of associating place with sound; he never spoke, without first wandering in this manner, and forgetting to speak.

"Are you going to finish that pair of shoes to-day?" asked Defarge, motioning to Mr. Lorry to come forward.

"What did you say?"

"Do you mean to finish that pair of shoes to-day?"

"I can't say that I mean to. I suppose so. I don't know."

But the question reminded him of his work, and he bent over it again.

Mr. Lorry came silently forward, leaving the daughter by the door. When he had stood, for a minute or two, by the side of Defarge, the shoemaker looked up. He showed no surprise at seeing another figure, but the unsteady fingers of one of his hands strayed to his lips as he looked at it (his lips and his nails were of the same pale lead-colour), and then the hand dropped to his work, and he once more bent over the shoe. The look and the action had occupied but an instant.

"You have a visitor, you see," said Monsieur Defarge.

"What did you say?"

"Here is a visitor."

The shoemaker looked up as before, but without removing a hand from his work.

"Come!" said Defarge. "Here is monsieur, who knows a well-made shoe when he sees one. Show him that shoe you are working at. Take it, monsieur."

Mr. Lorry took it in his hand.

"Tell monsieur what kind of shoe it is, and the maker's name."

There was a longer pause than usual, before the shoemaker replied : —

"I forget what it was you asked me. What did you say?"

"I said, could n't you describe the kind of shoe, for monsieur's information?"

"It is a lady's shoe. It is a young lady's walking-shoe. It is in the present mode. I never saw the mode. I have had a pattern in my hand." He glanced at the shoe, with some little passing touch of pride.

"And the maker's name?" said Defarge.

Now that he had no work to hold, he laid the knuckles of the right hand in the hollow of the left, and then the knuckles of the left hand in the hollow of the right, and then passed a hand across his bearded chin, and so on in regular changes, without a moment's intermission. The task of recalling him from the vacancy into which he always sank when he had spoken was like recalling some very weak person from a swoon, or endeavouring, in the hope of some disclosure, to stay the spirit of a fast-dying man.

"Did you ask me for my name?"

"Assuredly I did."

"One Hundred and Five, North Tower."

"Is that all?"

"One Hundred and Five, North Tower."

With a weary sound that was not a sigh, nor a groan, he bent to work again, until the silence was again broken.

"You are not a shoemaker by trade?" said Mr. Lorry, looking steadfastly at him.

His haggard eyes turned to Defarge as if he would hav transferred the question to him; but as no help came from tha quarter, they turned back on the questioner when they had sought the ground.

"I am not a shoemaker by trade? No, I was not a shoemaker by trade. I — I learnt it here. I taught myself. I asked leave to —"

He lapsed away, even for minutes, ringing those measured changes on his hands the whole time. His eyes came slowly back, at last, to the face from which they had wandered; when they rested on it, he started, and resumed, in the manner of a sleeper that moment awake, reverting to a subject of last night.

"I asked leave to teach myself, and I got it with much difficulty after a long while, and I have made shoes ever since."

As he held out his hand for the shoe that had been taken from him, Mr. Lorry said, still looking steadfastly in his face : —

"Monsieur Manette, do you remember nothing of me?"

The shoe dropped to the ground, and he sat looking fixedly at the questioner.

"Monsieur Manette," — Mr. Lorry laid his hand upon Defarge's arm, — "do you remember nothing of this man? Look at him. Look at me. Is there no old banker, no old business, no old servant, no old time, rising in your mind, Monsieur Manette?"

As the captive of many years sat looking fixedly, by turns at Mr. Lorry and at Defarge, some long-obliterated marks of an actively intent intelligence in the middle of the forehead, gradually forced themselves through the black mist that had fallen on him. They were overclouded again, they were fainter, they were gone; but they had been there. And so exactly was the expression repeated on the fair young face of her who had crept along the wall to a point where she could see him, and where she now stood looking at him, with hands which at first had been only raised in frightened compassion, if not even to keep him off and shut out the sight of him, but which were now extending towards him, trembling with eagerness to lay the spectral face upon her warm young breast, and love it back to life and hope — so exactly was the expression repeated (though in stronger characters) on her fair young face, that it looked as though it had passed, like a moving light, from him to her.

Darkness had fallen on him in its place. He looked at the two, less and less attentively, and his eyes in gloomy abstraction sought the ground and looked about him in the old way. Finally, with a deep long sigh, he took the shoe up, and resumed his work.

"Have you recognised him, monsieur?" asked Defarge, in a whisper.

"Yes; for a moment. At first I thought it quite hopeless, but I have unquestionably seen, for a single moment, the face that I once knew well. Hush! Let us draw further back. Hush!"

She had moved from the wall of the garret very near to the bench on which he sat. There was something awful in his unconsciousness of the figure that could have put out its hand and touched him as he stooped over his labour.

Not a word was spoken, not a sound was made. She stood, like a spirit, beside him, and he bent over his work.

It happened, at length, that he had occasion to change the instrument in his hand for his shoemaker's knife. It lay on that side of him which was not the side on which she stood. He had taken it up, and was stooping to work again, when his eyes caught the skirt of her dress. He raised them, and saw her face. The two spectators started forward, but she stayed them with a motion of her hand. She had no fear of his striking at her with the knife, though they had.

He stared at her with a fearful look, and after a while his lips began to form some words, though no sound proceeded from them. By degrees, in the pauses of his quick and laboured breathing, he was heard to say: —

"What is this!"

With the tears streaming down her face, she put her two hands to her lips, and kissed them to him; then clasped them on her breast, as if she laid his ruined head there.

"You are not the jailer's daughter?"

She sighed, "No."

"Who are you?"

Not yet trusting the tones of her voice, she sat down on the bench beside him. He recoiled, but she laid her hand upon his arm. A strange thrill struck him when she did so, and visibly passed over his frame; he laid the knife down softly, as he sat staring at her.

Her golden hair, which she wore in long curls, had been hurriedly pushed aside, and fell down over her neck. Advancing his hand by little and little, he took it up, and looked at it. In the midst of the action he went astray, and, with another deep sigh, fell to work at his shoemaking.

But not for long. Releasing his arm, she laid her hand upon his shoulder. After looking doubtfully at it, two or three times, as if to be sure that it was really there, he laid down his work, put his hand to his neck, and took off a blackened string with a scrap of folded rag attached to it. He opened this, carefully, on his knee, and it contained a very little quantity of hair: not more than one or two long golden hairs, which he had, in some old day, wound off upon his finger.

He took her hair into his hand again, and looked closely at it. "It is the same. How can it be! When was it! How was it!"

As the concentrating expression returned to his forehead, he seemed to become conscious that it was in hers too. He turned her full to the light, and looked at her.

"She had laid her head upon my shoulder, that night when I was summoned out — she had a fear of my going, though I had none — and when I was brought to the North Tower they found these upon my sleeve. 'You will leave me them? They can never help me to escape in the body, though they may in the spirit.' Those were the words I said. I remember them very well."

He formed this speech with his lips many times before he could utter it. But when he did find spoken words for it, they came to him coherently, though slowly.

"How was this? — *Was it you?*"

Once more, the two spectators started, as he turned upon her with a frightful suddenness. But she sat perfectly still in his grasp, and only said, in a low voice, "I entreat you, good gentlemen, do not come near us, do not speak, do not move!"

"Hark!" he exclaimed. "Whose voice was that?"

His hands released her as he uttered this cry, and went up to his white hair, which they tore in a frenzy. It died out, as everything but his shoemaking did die out of him, and he refolded his little packet and tried to secure it in his breast; but he still looked at her, and gloomily shook his head.

" No, no, no ; you are too young, too blooming. It can't be. See what the prisoner is. These are not the hands she knew, this is not the face she knew, this is not a voice she ever heard. No, no. She was — and He was — before the slow years of the North Tower — ages ago. What is your name, my gentle angel ? "

Hailing his softened tone and manner, his daughter fell upon her knees before him, with her appealing hands upon his breast.

" Oh, sir, at another time you shall know my name, and who my mother was, and who my father, and how I never knew their hard, hard history. But I cannot tell you at this time, and I cannot tell you here. All that I may tell you, here and now, is, that I pray to you to touch me and to bless me. Kiss me, kiss me ! Oh, my dear, my dear ! "

His cold white head mingled with her radiant hair, which warmed and lighted it as though it were the light of Freedom shining on him.

" If you hear in my voice — I don't know that it is so, but I hope it is — if you hear in my voice any resemblance to a voice that once was sweet music in your ears, weep for it, weep for it ! If you touch, in touching my hair, anything that recalls a beloved head that lay in your breast when you were young and free, weep for it, weep for it ! If, when I hint to you of a Home there is before us, where I will be true to you with all my duty and with all my faithful service, I bring back the remembrance of a Home long desolate, while your poor heart pined away, weep for it, weep for it ! "

She held him closer round the neck, and rocked him on her breast like a child.

" If when I tell you, dearest dear, that your agony is over, and that I have come here to take you from it, and that we go to England to be at peace and at rest, I cause you to think of your useful life laid waste, and of our native France so wicked to you, weep for it, weep for it ! And if, when I shall tell you of my name, and of my father who is living, and of my mother who is dead, you learn that I have to kneel to my honoured father, and implore his pardon for having never for his sake striven all day and lain awake and wept all night, because the love of my poor mother hid his torture from me, weep for it, weep for it! Weep for her, then, and for me! Good gentlemen, thank God! I feel his sacred tears upon my face, and his sobs strike against my heart. Oh, see! Thank God for us, thank God!"

He had sunk in her arms, with his face dropped on her breast : a sight so touching, yet so terrible in the tremendous wrong and suffering which had gone before it, that the two beholders covered their faces.

When the quiet of the garret had been long undisturbed, and his heaving breast and shaken form had long yielded to the calm that must follow all storms — emblem to humanity, of the rest and silence into which the storm called Life must hush at last — they came forward to raise the father and daughter from the ground. He had gradually drooped to the floor, and lay there in a lethargy, worn out. She had nestled down with him, that his head might lie upon her arm; and her hair drooping over him curtained him from the light.

"If, without disturbing him," she said, raising her hand to Mr. Lorry as he stooped over them, after repeated blowings of his nose, "all could be arranged for our leaving Paris at once, so that, from the very door, he could be taken away — "

"But consider. Is he fit for the journey ?" asked Mr. Lorry.

"More fit for that, I think, than to remain in this city, so dreadful to him."

"It is true," said Defarge, who was kneeling to look on and hear. "More than that; Monsieur Manette is, for all reasons, best out of France. Say, shall I hire a carriage and post-horses ?"

"That's business," said Mr. Lorry, resuming on the shortest notice his methodical manners; "and if business is to be done, I had better do it."

"Then be so kind," urged Miss Manette, "as to leave us here. You see how composed he has become, and you cannot be afraid to leave him with me now. Why should you be? If you will lock the door to secure us from interruption, I do not doubt that you will find him, when you come back, as quiet as you leave him. In any case, I will take care of him until you return, and then we will remove him straight."

Both Mr. Lorry and Defarge were rather disinclined to this

course, and in favour of one of them remaining. But as there were not only carriage and horses to be seen to, but travelling-papers; and as time pressed, for the day was drawing to an end, it came at last to their hastily dividing the business that was necessary to be done, and hurrying away to do it.

Then, as the darkness closed in, the daughter laid her head down on the hard ground close at the father's side, and watched him. The darkness deepened and deepened, and they both lay quiet, until a light gleamed through the chinks in the wall.

Mr. Lorry and Monsieur Defarge had made all ready for the journey, and had brought with them, besides travelling-cloaks and wrappers, bread and meat, wine, and hot coffee. Monsieur Defarge put this provender, and the lamp he carried, on the shoemaker's bench (there was nothing else in the garret but a pallet bed), and he and Mr. Lorry roused the captive, and assisted him to his feet.

No human intelligence could have read the mysteries of his mind, in the scared blank wonder of his face. Whether he knew what had happened, whether he recollected what they had said to him, whether he knew that he was free, were questions which no sagacity could have solved. They tried speaking to him; but he was so confused, and so very slow to answer, that they took fright at his bewilderment, and agreed for the time to tamper with him no more. He had a wild, lost manner of occasionally clasping his head in his hands, that had not been seen in him before; yet, he had some pleasure in the mere sound of his daughter's voice, and invariably turned to it when she spoke.

In the submissive way of one long accustomed to obey under coercion, he ate and drank what they gave him to eat and drink, and put on the cloak and other wrappings that they gave him to wear. He readily responded to his daughter's drawing her arm through his, and took — and kept — her hand in both of his own.

They began to descend; Monsieur Defarge going first with the lamp, Mr. Lorry closing the little procession. They had not traversed many steps of the long main staircase when he stopped, and stared at the roof and round at the walls.

"You remember the place, my father? You remember coming up here?"

"What did you say?"

But before she could repeat the question, he murmured an answer as if she had repeated it.

"Remember? No, I don't remember. It was so very long ago."

That he had no recollection whatever of his having been brought from his prison to that house was apparent to them. They heard him mutter, "One Hundred and Five, North Tower;" and when he looked about him, it evidently was for the strong fortress-walls which had long encompassed him. On their reaching the courtyard, he instinctively altered his tread, as being in expectation of a drawbridge; and when there was no drawbridge, and he saw the carriage waiting in the open street, he dropped his daughter's hand and clasped his head again.

No crowd was about the door; no people were discernible at any of the many windows; not even a chance passer-by was in the street. An unnatural silence and desertion reigned there. Only one soul was to be seen, and that was Madame Defarge — who leaned against the door-post, knitting, and saw nothing.

The prisoner had got into the coach, and his daughter had followed him, when Mr. Lorry's feet were arrested on the step by his asking, miserably, for his shoemaking tools and the unfinished shoes. Madame Defarge immediately called to her husband that she would get them, and went, knitting, out of the lamplight, through the courtyard. She quickly brought them down and handed them in; — and immediately afterwards leaned against the door-post, knitting, and saw nothing.

Defarge got upon the box, and gave the word "To the Barrier!" The postilion cracked his whip, and they clattered away under the feeble over-swinging lamps.

Under the over-swinging lamps — swinging ever brighter in the better streets, and ever dimmer in the worse — and by lighted shops, gay crowds, illuminated coffee-houses, and theatre doors, to one of the city gates. Soldiers with lanterns, at the guard-house there. "Your papers, travellers!" "See here then, Monsieur the Officer," said Defarge, getting down, and taking him gravely apart, "these are the papers of monsieur inside, with the white head. They were consigned to me, with him, at the —." He dropped his voice, there was a flutter among the military lanterns, and one of them being handed into the coach by an arm in uniform, the eyes connected with the

arm looked, not an every day or an every night look, at monsieur with the white head. "It is well. Forward!" from the
uniform. "Adieu!" from Defarge. And so, under a short
grove of feebler and feebler over-swinging lamps, out under the
great grove of stars.

Beneath that arch of unmoved and eternal lights: some, so
remote from this little earth that the learned tell us it is doubt-
ful whether their rays have even yet discovered it, as a point in
space where anything is suffered or done: the shadows of the
night were broad and black. All through the cold and restless
interval, until dawn, they once more whispered in the ears of
Mr. Jarvis Lorry — sitting opposite the buried man who had
been dug out, and wondering what subtle powers were for ever
lost to him, and what were capable of restoration — the old
inquiry : —

"I hope you care to be recalled to life?"

And the old answer: —

"I can't say."

BOOK THE SECOND — THE GOLDEN THREAD

CHAPTER I

FIVE YEARS LATER

TELLSON'S Bank by Temple Bar was an old-fashioned place, even in the year one thousand seven hundred and eighty. It was very small, very dark, very ugly, very incommodious. It was an old-fashioned place, moreover, in the moral attribute that the partners in the House were proud of its smallness, proud of its darkness, proud of its ugliness, proud of its incommodiousness. They were even boastful of its eminence in those particulars, and were fired by an express conviction that, if it were less objectionable, it would be less respectable. This was no passive belief, but an active weapon which they flashed at more convenient places of business. Tellson's (they said) wanted no elbow-room, Tellson's wanted no light, Tellson's wanted no embellishment. Noakes and Co.'s might, or Snooks Brothers' might; but Tellson's, thank Heaven! —

Any one of these partners would have disinherited his son on the question of rebuilding Tellson's. In this respect the House was much on a par with the Country; which did very often disinherit its sons for suggesting improvements in laws and customs that had long been highly objectionable, but were only the more respectable.

Thus it had come to pass, that Tellson's was the triumphant perfection of inconvenience. After bursting open a door of idiotic obstinacy with a weak rattle in its throat, you fell into Tellson's down two steps, and came to your senses in a miserable little shop, with two little counters, where the oldest of men made your cheque shake as if the wind rustled it, while they examined the signature by the dingiest of windows, which were always under a shower-bath of mud from Fleet Street, and which were made the dingier by their own iron bars proper, and the heavy shadow of Temple Bar. If your business necessitated your seeing "the House," you were put into a species of Condemned Hold at the back, where you meditated on a misspent life, until the House came with its hands in its pockets, and you could hardly blink at it in the dismal twilight. Your money came out of, or went into, wormy old wooden drawers, particles of which flew up your nose and down your throat when they were opened and shut. Your bank-notes had a musty odour, as if they were fast decomposing into rags again. Your plate was stowed away among the neighbouring cesspools, and evil communications corrupted its good polish in a day or two. Your deeds got into extemporised strong-rooms made of kitchens and sculleries, and fretted all the fat out of their parchments into the Banking-house air. Your lighter boxes of family papers went up stairs into a Barmecide room, that always had a great dining-table in it and never had a dinner, and where, even in the year one thousand seven hundred and eighty, the first letters written to you by your old love, or by your little children, were but newly released from the horror of being ogled through the windows, by the heads exposed on Temple Bar with an insensate brutality and ferocity worthy of Abyssinia or Ashantee.

But indeed, at that time, putting to death was a recipe much in vogue with all trades and professions, and not least of all with Tellson's. Death is Nature's remedy for all things, and why not Legislation's? Accordingly, the forger was put to Death; the utterer of a bad note was put to Death; the unlawful opener of a letter was put to Death; the purloiner of forty shillings and sixpence was put to Death; the holder of a horse at Tellson's door, who made off with it, was put to Death; the coiner of a bad shilling was put to Death; the sounders of three fourths of the notes in the whole gamut of Crime were put to Death. Not that it did the least good in the way of prevention — it might almost have been worth remarking that the fact was exactly the reverse — but it cleared off (as to this world) the trouble of each particular case, and left nothing else connected with it to be looked after. Thus, Tellson's, in its day like greater places of business, its contemporaries, had taken so many lives, that, if the heads laid low before it had been ranged on Temple Bar instead of being privately disposed of, they would probably have excluded what little light the ground-floor had, in a rather significant manner.

Cramped in all kinds of dim cupboards and hutches at Tellson's, the oldest of men carried on the business gravely. When they took a young man into Tellson's London house, they hid him somewhere till he was old. They kept him in a dark place, like a cheese, until he had the full Tellson flavour and blue-mould upon him. Then only was he permitted to be seen, spectacularly poring over large books, and casting his breeches and gaiters into the general weight of the establishment.

Outside Tellson's — never by any means in it, unless called in — was an odd-job-man, an occasional porter and messenger, who served as the live sign of the House. He was never absent during business hours, unless upon an errand, and then he was represented by his son : a grisly urchin of twelve, who was his express image. People understood that Tellson's, in a stately way, tolerated the odd-job-man. The House had always tolerated some person in that capacity, and time and tide had drifted this person to the post. His surname was Cruncher, and on the youthful occasion of his renouncing by proxy the works of darkness, in the easterly parish church of Houndsditch, he had received the added appellation of Jerry.

The scene was Mr. Cruncher's private lodging in Hanging-sword Alley, Whitefriars ; the time, half-past seven of the clock on a windy March morning, Anno Domini seventeen hundred and eighty. (Mr. Cruncher himself always spoke of the year of our Lord as Anna Dominoes : apparently under the impression that the Christian era dated from the invention of a popular game, by a lady who had bestowed her name upon it.)

Mr. Cruncher's apartments were not in a savoury neighbourhood, and were but two in number, even if a closet with a single pane of glass in it might be counted as one. But they were very decently kept. Early as it was, on the windy March morning, the room in which he lay abed was already scrubbed throughout ; and between the cups and saucers arranged for breakfast, and the lumbering deal table, a very clean white cloth was spread.

Mr. Cruncher reposed under a patchwork counterpane, like a Harlequin at home. At first, he slept heavily, but, by degrees, began to roll and surge in bed, until he rose above the surface, with his spiky hair looking as if it must tear the sheets to ribbens. At which juncture, he exclaimed, in a voice of dire exasperation : —

" Bust me, if she ain't at it agin ! "

A woman of orderly and industrious appearance rose from her knees in a corner, with sufficient haste and trepidation to show that she was the person referred to.

"What!" said Mr. Cruncher, looking out of bed for a boot. "You're at it agin, are you?"

After hailing the morn with this second salutation, he threw a boot at the woman as a third. It was a very muddy boot, and may introduce the odd circumstance connected with Mr. Cruncher's domestic economy, that, whereas he often came home after banking hours with clean boots, he often got up next morning to find the same boots covered with clay.

"What," said Mr. Cruncher, varying his apostrophe after missing his mark — "what are you up to, Aggerawayter?"

"I was only saying my prayers."

"Saying your prayers. You're a nice woman! What do you mean by flopping yourself down and praying agin me?"

"I was not praying against you; I was praying for you."

"You weren't. And if you were, I won't be took the liberty with. Here! your mother's a nice woman, Young Jerry, going a praying agin your father's prosperity. You've got a dutiful mother, you have, my son. You've got a religious mother, you have, my boy — going and flopping herself down, and praying that the bread and butter may be snatched out of the mouth of her only child!"

Master Cruncher (who was in his shirt) took this very ill, and, turning to his mother, strongly deprecated any praying away of his personal board.

"And what do you suppose, you conceited female," said Mr. Cruncher, with unconscious inconsistency, "that the worth of *your* prayers may be? Name the price that you put *your* prayers at!"

"They only come from the heart, Jerry. They are worth no more than that."

"Worth no more than that," repeated Mr. Cruncher. "They ain't worth much, then. Whether or no, I won't be prayed agin, I tell you. I can't afford it. I'm not a going to be made unlucky by *your* sneaking. If you must go flopping yourself down, flop in favour of your husband and child, and not in opposition to 'em. If I had had any but a unnat'ral wife, and this poor boy had had any but a unnat'ral mother, I might have made some money last week, instead of being coun-

terprayed and countermined and religiously circumwented into
the worst of luck. Bu-u-ust me!" said Mr. Cruncher, who
all this time had been putting on his clothes, "if I ain't, what
with piety and one blowed thing and another, been choused this
last week into as bad luck as ever a poor devil of a honest
tradesman met with! Young Jerry, dress yourself, my boy,
and while I clean my boots keep a eye upon your mother now
and then, and if you see any signs of more flopping, give me a
call. For I tell you," here he addressed his wife once more,
"I won't be gone agin, in this manner. I am as rickety as a
hackney-coach, I'm as sleepy as laudanum, my lines is strained
to that degree that I should n't know, if it was n't for the pain
in 'em, which was me and which somebody else, yet I'm none
the better for it in pocket; and it's my suspicion that you've
been at it from morning to night to prevent me from being the
better for it in pocket, and I won't put up with it, Aggerawayter, and what do you say now!"

Growling, in addition, such phrases as, "Ah! yes! You're
religious, too. You would n't put yourself in opposition to the
interests of your husband and child, would you? Not you!"
and throwing off other sarcastic sparks from the whirling grind-
stone of his indignation, Mr. Cruncher betook himself to his
boot-cleaning and his general preparations for business. In the
mean time, his son, whose head was garnished with tenderer
spikes, and whose young eyes stood close by one another, as his
father's did, kept the required watch upon his mother. He
greatly disturbed that poor woman at intervals, by darting out
of his sleeping-closet, where he made his toilet, with a suppressed cry of "You are going to flop, mother. — Halloa,
father!" and after raising this fictitious alarm, darting in again
with an undutiful grin.

Mr. Cruncher's temper was not at all improved when he
came to his breakfast. He resented Mrs. Cruncher's saying
Grace with particular animosity.

"Now, Aggerawayter! What are you up to? At it
agin?"

His wife explained that she had merely "asked a blessing."

"Don't do it!" said Mr. Cruncher, looking about, as if he
rather expected to see the loaf disappear under the efficacy of
his wife's petitions. "I ain't a going to be blest out of house

and home. I won't have my wittles blest off my table. Keep still!"

Exceedingly red-eyed and grim, as if he had been up all night at a party which had taken anything but a convivial turn, Jerry Cruncher worried his breakfast rather than ate it, growling over it like any four-footed inmate of a menagerie. Towards nine o'clock he smoothed his ruffled aspect, and, presenting as respectable and business-like an exterior as he could overlay his natural self with, issued forth to the occupation of the day.

It could scarcely be called a trade, in spite of his favourite description of himself as "a honest tradesman." His stock consisted of a wooden stool, made out of a broken-backed chair cut down, which stool Young Jerry, walking at his father's side, carried every morning to beneath the Banking-house window that was nearest Temple Bar; where, with the addition of the first handful of straw that could be gleaned from any passing vehicle to keep the cold and wet from the odd-job-man's feet, it formed the encampment for the day. On this post of his, Mr. Cruncher was as well known to Fleet Street and the Temple, as the Bar itself — and was almost as ill-looking.

Encamped at a quarter before nine, in good time to touch his three-cornered hat to the oldest of men as they passed in to Tellson's, Jerry took up his station on this windy March morning, with Young Jerry standing by him, when not engaged in making forays through the Bar, to inflict bodily and mental injuries of an acute description on passing boys who were small enough for his amiable purpose. Father and son, extremely like each other, looking silently on at the morning traffic in Fleet Street, with their two heads as near to one another as the two eyes of each were, bore a considerable resemblance to a pair of monkeys. The resemblance was not lessened by the accidental circumstance that the mature Jerry bit and spat out straw, while the twinkling eyes of the youthful Jerry were as restlessly watchful of him as of everything else in Fleet Street.

The head of one of the regular in-door messengers attached to Tellson's establishment was put through the door, and the word was given : —

"Porter wanted!"

"Hooray, father! Here's an early job to begin with!"

Having thus given his parent God-speed, Young Jerry seated

himself on the stool, entered on his reversionary interest in the straw his father had been chewing, and cogitated.

"Al-ways rusty! His fingers is al-ways rusty!" muttered Young Jerry. "Where does my father get all that iron-rust from? He don't get no iron-rust here!"

CHAPTER II

A SIGHT

"You know the Old Bailey well, no doubt?" said one of the oldest of clerks to Jerry the messenger.

"Ye-es, sir," returned Jerry, in something of a dogged manner. "I *do* know the Bailey."

"Just so. And you know Mr. Lorry?"

"I know Mr. Lorry, sir, much better than I know the Bailey. Much better," said Jerry, not unlike a reluctant witness at the establishment in question, "than I, as a honest tradesman, wish to know the Bailey."

"Very well. Find the door where the witnesses go in, and show the doorkeeper this note for Mr. Lorry. He will then let you in."

"Into the court, sir?"

"Into the court."

Mr. Cruncher's eyes seemed to get a little closer to one another, and to interchange the inquiry, "What do you think of this?"

"Am I to wait in the court, sir?" he asked, as the result of that conference.

"I am going to tell you. The doorkeeper will pass the note to Mr. Lorry, and do you make any gesture that will attract Mr. Lorry's attention, and show him where you stand. Then what you have to do is to remain there until he wants you."

"Is that all, sir?"

"That's all. He wishes to have a messenger at hand. This is to tell him you are there."

As the ancient clerk deliberately folded and superscribed the note, Mr. Cruncher, after surveying him in silence until he came to the blotting-paper stage, remarked: —

"I suppose they 'll be trying Forgeries this morning?"

"Treason!"

"That's quartering," said Jerry. "Barbarous!"

"It is the law," remarked the ancient clerk, turning his surprised spectacles upon him. "It is the law."

"It's hard in the law to spile a man, I think. It's hard enough to kill him, but it's wery hard to spile him, sir."

"Not at all," returned the ancient clerk. "Speak well of the law. Take care of your chest and voice, my good friend, and leave the law to take care of itself. I give you that advice."

"It's the damp, sir, what settles on my chest and voice," said Jerry. "I leave you to judge what a damp way of earning a living mine is."

"Well, well," said the old clerk, "we all have our various ways of gaining a livelihood. Some of us have damp ways, and some of us have dry ways. Here is the letter. Go along."

Jerry took the letter, and, remarking to himself with less internal deference than he made an outward show of, "You are a lean old one, too," made his bow, informed his son, in passing, of his destination, and went his way.

They hanged at Tyburn, in those days, so the street outside Newgate had not obtained one infamous notoriety that has since attached to it. But the jail was a vile place, in which most kinds of debauchery and villainy were practised, and where dire diseases were bred, that came into court with the prisoners, and sometimes rushed straight from the dock at my Lord Chief Justice himself, and pulled him off the bench. It had more than once happened, that the judge in the black cap pronounced his own doom as certainly as the prisoner's, and even died before him. For the rest, the Old Bailey was famous as a kind of deadly inn-yard, from which pale travellers set out continually, in carts and coaches, on a violent passage into the other world; traversing some two miles and a half of public street and road, and shaming few good citizens, if any. So powerful is use, and so desirable to be good use in the beginning. It was famous, too, for the pillory, a wise old institution, that inflicted a punishment of which no one could foresee the extent; also, for the whipping-post, another dear old institution, very humanising and softening to behold in action; also, for extensive transactions in blood-money, another fragment of ancestral wisdom, systematically leading to the most frightful mercenary crimes that could be committed under Heaven. Altogether, the Old Bailey, at that date, was a choice illustration of the precept, that "Whatever is, is right;" an aphorism that would be as final as it is lazy, did it not include the troublesome consequence, that nothing that ever was, was wrong.

Making his way through the tainted crowd, dispersed up and down this hideous scene of action, with the skill of a man accustomed to make his way quietly, the messenger found out the door he sought, and handed in his letter through a trap in it. For people then paid to see the play at the Old Bailey, just as they paid to see the play in Bedlam — only the former entertainment was much the dearer. Therefore, all the Old Bailey doors were well guarded — except, indeed, the social doors by which the criminals got there, and those were always left wide open.

After some delay and demur, the door grudgingly turned on its hinges a very little way, and allowed Mr. Jerry Cruncher to squeeze himself into court.

"What's on?" he asked, in a whisper, of the man he found himself next to.

"Nothing yet."

"What's coming on?"

"The Treason case."

"The quartering one, eh?"

"Ah!" returned the man, with a relish; "he'll be drawn on a hurdle to be half hanged, and then he'll be taken down and sliced before his own face, and then his inside will be taken out and burnt while he looks on, and then his head will be chopped off, and he'll be cut into quarters. That's the sentence."

"If he's found Guilty, you mean to say?" Jerry added, by way of proviso.

"Oh! they'll find him Guilty," said the other. "Don't you be afraid of that."

Mr. Cruncher's attention was here diverted to the doorkeeper, whom he saw making his way to Mr. Lorry, with the note in his hand. Mr. Lorry sat at a table, among the gentlemen in wigs, not far from a wigged gentleman, the prisoner's counsel, who had a great bundle of papers before him, and nearly opposite another wigged gentleman with his hands in his pockets, whose whole attention, when Mr. Cruncher looked at him then or afterwards, seemed to be concentrated on the ceil-

ing of the court.   After some gruff coughing and rubbing of his
chin and signing with his hand, Jerry attracted the notice of
Mr. Lorry, who had stood up to look for him, and who quietly
nodded, and sat down again.

" What's *he* got to do with the case ? " asked the man he
had spoken with.

" Blest if I know," said Jerry.

" What have *you* got to do with it, then, if a person may
inquire ? "

" Blest if I know that either," said Jerry.

The entrance of the Judge, and a consequent great stir and
settling-down in the court, stopped the dialogue.   Presently,
the dock became the central point of interest.   Two jailers,
who had been standing there, went out, and the prisoner was
brought in, and put to the bar.

Everybody present, except the one-wigged gentleman who
looked at the ceiling, stared at him.   All the human breath in
the place rolled at him, like a sea, or a wind, or a fire.   Eager
faces strained round pillars and corners, to get a sight of him ;
spectators in back rows stood up, not to miss a hair of him ;
people on the floor of the court laid their hands on the shoulders of the people before them, to help themselves, at anybody's
cost, to a view of him — stood a-tiptoe, got upon ledges, stood
upon next to nothing, to see every inch of him.   Conspicuous
among these latter, like an animated bit of the spiked wall of
Newgate, Jerry stood ; aiming at the prisoner the beery breath
of a whet he had taken as he came along, and discharging it
to mingle with the waves of other beer, and gin, and tea, and
coffee, and what not, that flowed at him, and already broke
upon the great windows behind him in an impure mist and
rain.

The object of all this staring and blaring was a young man
of about five-and-twenty, well-grown and well-looking, with a
sunburnt cheek and a dark eye.   His condition was that of
a young gentleman.   He was plainly dressed in black, or very
dark grey, and his hair, which was long and dark, was gathered
in a ribbon at the back of his neck, more to be out of his way
than for ornament.   As an emotion of the mind will express
itself through any covering of the body, so the paleness which
his situation engendered came through the brown upon his
cheek, showing the soul to be stronger than the sun.   He was

otherwise quite self-possessed, bowed to the Judge, and stood quiet.

The sort of interest with which this man was stared and breathed at was not a sort that elevated humanity. Had he stood in peril of a less horrible sentence, — had there been a chance of any one of its savage details being spared, — by just so much would he have lost in his fascination. The form that was to be doomed to be so shamefully mangled, was the sight ; the immortal creature that was to be so butchered and torn asunder, yielded the sensation. Whatever gloss the various spectators put upon the interest, according to their several arts and powers of self-deceit, the interest was, at the root of it, Ogreish.

Silence in the court ! Charles Darnay had yesterday pleaded Not Guilty to an indictment denouncing him (with infinite jingle and jangle) for that he was a false traitor to our serene, illustrious, excellent, and so forth, prince, our Lord the King, by reason of his having, on divers occasions, and by divers means and ways, assisted Lewis, the French King, in his wars against our said serene, illustrious, excellent, and so forth ; that was to say, by coming and going between the dominions of our said serene, illustrious, excellent, and so forth, and those of the said French Lewis, and wickedly, falsely, traitorously, and otherwise evil-adverbiously, revealing to the said French Lewis what forces our said serene, illustrious, excellent, and so forth, had in preparation to send to Canada and North America. This much, Jerry, with his head becoming more and more spiky as the law terms bristled it, made out with huge satisfaction, and so arrived circuitously at the understanding that the aforesaid, and over and over again aforesaid, Charles Darnay, stood there before him upon his trial ; that the jury were swearing in ; and that Mr. Attorney-General was making ready to speak.

The accused, who was (and who knew he was) being mentally hanged, beheaded, and quartered, by everybody there, neither flinched from the situation, nor assumed any theatrical air in it. He was quiet and attentive ; watched the opening proceedings with a grave interest ; and stood with his hands resting on the slab of wood before him, so composedly, that they had not displaced a leaf of the herbs with which it was strewn. The court was all bestrewn with herbs and sprinkled with vinegar, as a precaution against jail air and jail fever.

Over the prisoner's head there was a mirror, to throw the

light down upon him. Crowds of the wicked and the wretched had been reflected in it, and had passed from its surface and this earth's together. Haunted in a most ghastly manner that abominable place would have been, if the glass could ever have rendered back its reflections, as the ocean is one day to give up its dead. Some passing thought of the infamy and disgrace for which it had been reserved may have struck the prisoner's mind. Be that as it may, a change in his position making him conscious of a bar of light across his face, he looked up; and when he saw the glass his face flushed, and his right hand pushed the herbs away.

It happened that the action turned his face to that side of the court which was on his left. About on a level with his eyes, there sat, in that corner of the Judge's bench, two persons upon whom his look immediately rested; so immediately, and so much to the changing of his aspect, that all the eyes that were turned upon him, turned to them.

The spectators saw in the two figures, a young lady of little more than twenty, and a gentleman who was evidently her father; a man of a very remarkable appearance in respect of the absolute whiteness of his hair, and a certain indescribable intensity of face: not of an active kind, but pondering and self-communing. When this expression was upon him, he looked as if he were old; but, when it was stirred and broken up — as it was now, in a moment, on his speaking to his daughter — he became a handsome man, not past the prime of life.

His daughter had one of her hands drawn through his arm, as she sat by him, and the other pressed upon it. She had drawn close to him, in her dread of the scene, and in her pity for the prisoner. Her forehead had been strikingly expressive of an engrossing terror and compassion that saw nothing but the peril of the accused. This had been so very noticeable, so very powerfully and naturally shown, that starers who had had no pity for him were touched by her; and the whisper went about, "Who are they?"

Jerry the messenger, who had made his own observations in his own manner, and who had been sucking the rust off his fingers in his absorption, stretched his neck to hear who they were. The crowd about him had pressed and passed the inquiry on to the nearest attendant, and from him it had been more slowly pressed and passed back; at last it got to Jerry: —

"Witnesses."

"For which side?"

"Against."

"Against what side?"

"The prisoner's."

The Judge, whose eyes had gone in the general direction, recalled them, leaned back in his seat, and looked steadily at the man whose life was in his hand, as Mr. Attorney-General rose to spin the rope, grind the axe, and hammer the nails into the scaffold.

CHAPTER III

A DISAPPOINTMENT

MR. ATTORNEY-GENERAL had to inform the jury, that the prisoner before them, though young in years, was old in the treasonable practices which claimed the forfeit of his life. That this correspondence with the public enemy was not a correspondence of to-day, or of yesterday, or even of last year, or of the year before. That, it was certain the prisoner had, for longer than that, been in the habit of passing and repassing between France and England, on secret business of which he could give no honest account. That, if it were in the nature of traitorous ways to thrive (which happily it never was), the real wickedness and guilt of his business might have remained undiscovered. That Providence, however, had put it into the heart of a person who was beyond fear and beyond reproach, to ferret out the nature of the prisoner's schemes, and, struck with horror, to disclose them to his Majesty's Chief Secretary of State and most honourable Privy Council. That, this patriot would be produced before them. That, his position and attitude were, on the whole, sublime. That, he had been the prisoner's friend, but, at once in an auspicious and an evil hour detecting his infamy, had resolved to immolate the traitor he could no longer cherish in his bosom, on the sacred altar of his country. That, if statues were decreed in Britain, as in ancient Greece and Rome, to public benefactors, this shining citizen would assuredly have had one. That, as they were not so decreed, he probably would not have one. That, Virtue, as had been observed by the poets (in many passages which he well knew the jury would have, word for word, at the tips of their tongues; whereat the jury's countenances displayed a guilty consciousness that they knew nothing about the passages), was in a manner contagious; more especially the bright virtue known as patriotism, or love of country. That, the lofty example of this immaculate and unimpeachable witness for the

Crown, to refer to whom however unworthily was an honour, had communicated itself to the prisoner's servant, and had engendered in him a holy determination to examine his master's table-drawers and pockets, and secrete his papers. That, he (Mr. Attorney-General) was prepared to hear some disparagement attempted of this admirable servant; but that, in a general way, he preferred him to his (Mr. Attorney-General's) brothers and sisters, and honoured him more than his (Mr. Attorney-General's) father and mother. That, he called with confidence on the jury to come and do likewise. That, the evidence of these two witnesses, coupled with the documents of their discovering that would be produced, would show the prisoner to have been furnished with lists of his Majesty's forces, and of their disposition and preparation, both by sea and land, and would leave no doubt that he had habitually conveyed such information to a hostile power. That, these lists could not be proved to be in the prisoner's handwriting; but that it was all the same; that, indeed, it was rather the better for the prosecution, as showing the prisoner to be artful in his precautions. That, the proof would go back five years, and would show the prisoner already engaged in these pernicious missions, within a few weeks before the date of the very first action fought between the British troops and the Americans. That, for these reasons, the jury, being a loyal jury (as he knew they were), and being a responsible jury (as *they* knew they were), must positively find the prisoner Guilty, and make an end of him, whether they liked it or not. That, they never could lay their heads upon their pillows; that, they never could tolerate the idea of their wives laying their heads upon their pillows; that, they never could endure the notion of their children laying their heads upon their pillows; in short, that there never more could be, for them or theirs, any laying of heads upon pillows at all, unless the prisoner's head was taken off. That head Mr. Attorney-General concluded by demanding of them, in the name of everything he could think of with a round turn in it, and on the faith of his solemn asseveration that he already considered the prisoner as good as dead and gone.

When the Attorney-General ceased, a buzz arose in the court as if a cloud of great blue-flies were swarming about the prisoner, in anticipation of what he was soon to become. When it toned down again, the unimpeachable patriot appeared in the witness-box.

Mr. Solicitor-General then, following his leader's lead, examined the patriot: John Barsad, gentleman, by name. The story of his pure soul was exactly what Mr. Attorney-General had described it to be — perhaps, if it had a fault, a little too exactly. Having released his noble bosom of its burden, he would have modestly withdrawn himself, but that the wigged gentleman with the papers before him, sitting not far from Mr. Lorry, begged to ask him a few questions. The wigged gentleman sitting opposite, still looking at the ceiling of the court.

Had he ever been a spy himself? No, he scorned the base insinuation. What did he live upon? His property. Where was his property? He did n't precisely remember where it was. What was it? No business of anybody's. Had he inherited it? Yes, he had. From whom? Distant relation. Very distant? Rather. Ever been in prison? Certainly not. Never in a debtors' prison? Did n't see what that had to do with it. Never in a debtors' prison? — Come, once again. Never? Yes. How many times? Two or three times. Not five or six? Perhaps. Of what profession? Gentleman. Ever been kicked? Might have been. Frequently? No. Ever kicked down stairs? Decidedly not; once received a kick on the top of a staircase, and fell down stairs of his own accord. Kicked on that occasion for cheating at dice? Something to that effect was said by the intoxicated liar who committed the assault, but it was not true. Swear it was not true? Positively. Ever live by cheating at play? Never. Ever live by play? Not more than other gentlemen do. Ever borrow money of the prisoner? Yes. Ever pay him? No. Was not this intimacy with the prisoner, in reality a very slight one, forced upon the prisoner in coaches, inns, and packets? No. Sure he saw the prisoner with these lists? Certain. Knew no more about the lists? No. Had not procured them himself, for instance? No. Expect to get anything by this evidence? No. Not in regular government pay and employment, to lay traps? Oh, dear no. Or to do anything? Oh, dear no. Swear that? Over and over again. No motives but motives of sheer patriotism? None whatever.

The virtuous servant, Roger Cly, swore his way through the case at a great rate. He had taken service with the prisoner, in good faith and simplicity, four years ago. He had asked the prisoner, aboard the Calais packet, if he wanted a handy fellow, and the prisoner had engaged him. He had not asked the prisoner to take the handy fellow as an act of charity — never thought of such a thing. He began to have suspicions of the prisoner, and to keep an eye upon him, soon afterwards. In arranging his clothes, while travelling, he had seen similar lists to these in the prisoner's pockets, over and over again. He had taken these lists from the drawer of the prisoner's desk. He had not put them there first. He had seen the prisoner show these identical lists to French gentlemen at Calais, and similar lists to French gentlemen, both at Calais and Boulogne. He loved his country, and could n't bear it, and had given information. He had never been suspected of stealing a silver teapot; he had been maligned respecting a mustard-pot, but it turned out to be only a plated one. He had known the last witness seven or eight years; that was merely a coincidence. He did n't call it a particularly curious coincidence; most coincidences were curious. Neither did he call it a curious coincidence that true patriotism was *his* only motive too. He was a true Briton, and hoped there were many like him.

The blue-flies buzzed again, and Mr. Attorney-General called Mr. Jarvis Lorry.

"Mr. Jarvis Lorry, are you a clerk in Tellson's bank?"

"I am."

"On a certain Friday night in November one thousand seven hundred and seventy-five, did business occasion you to travel between London and Dover by the mail?"

"It did."

"Were there any other passengers in the mail?"

"Two."

"Did they alight on the road in the course of the night?"

"They did."

"Mr. Lorry, look upon the prisoner. Was he one of those two passengers?"

"I cannot undertake to say that he was."

"Does he resemble either of these two passengers?"

"Both were so wrapped up, and the night was so dark, and we were all so reserved, that I cannot undertake to say even that."

"Mr. Lorry, look again upon the prisoner. Supposing him

wrapped up as those two passengers were, is there anything in his bulk and stature to render it unlikely that he was one of them ? "

" No."

" You will not swear, Mr. Lorry, that he was not one of them ? "

" No."

" So at least you say he may have been one of them ? "

" Yes.   Except that I remember them both to have been — like myself — timorous of highwaymen, and the prisoner has not a timorous air."

" Did you ever see a counterfeit of timidity, Mr. Lorry ? "

" I certainly have seen that."

" Mr. Lorry, look once more upon the prisoner.   Have you seen him, to your certain knowledge, before ? "

" I have."

" When ? "

" I was returning from France a few days afterwards, and, at Calais, the prisoner came on board the packet-ship in which I returned, and made the voyage with me."

" At what hour did he come on board ? "

" At a little after midnight."

" In the dead of the night.   Was he the only passenger who came on board at that untimely hour ? "

" He happened to be the only one."

" Never mind about 'happening,' Mr. Lorry.   He was the only passenger who came on board in the dead of the night ? "

" He was."

" Were you travelling alone, Mr. Lorry, or with any companion ? "

" With two companions.   A gentleman and lady.   They are here."

" They are here.   Had you any conversation with the prisoner ? "

" Hardly any.   The weather was stormy, and the passage long and rough, and I lay on a sofa, almost from shore to shore."

" Miss Manette ! "

The young lady, to whom all eyes had been turned before, and were now turned again, stood up where she had sat.   Her father rose with her, and kept her hand drawn through his arm.

" Miss Manette, look upon the prisoner."

To be confronted with such pity, and such earnest youth and beauty, was far more trying to the accused than to be confronted with all the crowd. Standing, as it were, apart with her on the edge of his grave, not all the staring curiosity that looked on could, for the moment, nerve him to remain quite still. His hurried right hand parcelled out the herbs before him into imaginary beds of flowers in a garden ; and his efforts to control and steady his breathing shook the lips from which the colour rushed to his heart. The buzz of the great flies was loud again.

" Miss Manette, have you seen the prisoner before ? "

" Yes, sir."

" Where ? "

" On board of the packet-ship just now referred to, sir, and on the same occasion."

" You are the young lady just now referred to ? "

" Oh ! most unhappily, I am ! "

The plaintive tone of her compassion merged into the less musical voice of the Judge, as he said, something fiercely : " Answer the questions put to you, and make no remark upon them."

" Miss Manette, had you any conversation with the prisoner on that passage across the Channel ? "

" Yes, sir."

" Recall it."

In the midst of a profound stillness, she faintly began : —

" When the gentleman came on board — "

" Do you mean the prisoner ? " inquired the Judge, knitting his brows.

" Yes, my Lord."

" Then say the prisoner."

" When the prisoner came on board, he noticed that my father," turning her eyes lovingly to him as he stood beside her, " was much fatigued and in a very weak state of health. My father was so reduced, that I was afraid to take him out of the air, and I had made a bed for him on the deck near the cabin steps, and I sat on the deck at his side to take care of him. There were no other passengers that night, but we four. The prisoner was so good as to beg permission to advise me how I could shelter my father from the wind and weather better than I had done. I had not known how to do it well, not understanding how the wind would set when we were out of the harbour. He did it for me. He expressed great gentleness and kindness for my father's state, and I am sure he felt it. That was the manner of our beginning to speak together."

"Let me interrupt you for a moment. Had he come on board alone ? "

"No."

"How many were with him ? "

"Two French gentlemen."

"Had they conferred together ? "

"They had conferred together until the last moment, when it was necessary for the French gentlemen to be landed in their boat."

"Had any papers been handed about among them, similar to these lists ? "

"Some papers had been handed about among them, but I don't know what papers."

"Like these in shape and size ? "

"Possibly, but indeed I don't know, although they stood whispering very near to me ; because they stood at the top of the cabin steps to have the light of the lamp that was hanging there ; it was a dull lamp, and they spoke very low, and I did not hear what they said, and saw only that they looked at papers."

"Now, to the prisoner's conversation, Miss Manette."

"The prisoner was as open in his confidence with me — which arose out of my helpless situation — as he was kind, and good, and useful to my father. I hope," bursting into tears, "I may not repay him by doing him harm to-day."

Buzzing from the blue-flies.

" Miss Manette, if the prisoner does not perfectly understand that you give the evidence which it is your duty to give — which you must give — and which you cannot escape from giving — with great unwillingness, he is the only person present in that condition. Please to go on."

"He told me that he was travelling on business of a delicate and difficult nature, which might get people into trouble, and that he was therefore travelling under an assumed name. He said that this business had, within a few days, taken him to France, and might, at intervals, take him backwards and forwards between France and England for a long time to come."

"Did he say anything about America, Miss Manette? Be particular."

"He tried to explain to me how that quarrel had arisen, and he said that, so far as he could judge, it was a wrong and foolish one on England's part. He added, in a jesting way, that perhaps George Washington might gain almost as great a name in history as George the Third. But there was no harm in his way of saying this: it was said laughingly, and to beguile the time."

Any strongly marked expression of face on the part of a chief actor in a scene of great interest to whom many eyes are directed will be unconsciously imitated by the spectators. Her forehead was painfully anxious and intent as she gave this evidence, and, in the pauses when she stopped for the Judge to write it down, watched its effect upon the counsel for and against. Among the lookers-on there was the same expression in all quarters of the court; insomuch, that a great majority of the foreheads there might have been mirrors reflecting the witness, when the Judge looked up from his notes to glare at that tremendous heresy about George Washington.

Mr. Attorney-General now signified to my Lord, that he deemed it necessary, as a matter of precaution and form, to call the young lady's father, Doctor Manette. Who was called accordingly.

"Doctor Manette, look upon the prisoner. Have you ever seen him before?"

"Once. When he called at my lodgings in London. Some three years, or three years and a half ago."

"Can you identify him as your fellow-passenger on board the packet, or speak to his conversation with your daughter?"

"Sir, I can do neither."

"Is there any particular and special reason for your being unable to do either?"

He answered, in a low voice, "There is."

"Has it been your misfortune to undergo a long imprisonment, without trial, or even accusation, in your native country, Doctor Manette?"

He answered, in a tone that went to every heart, "A long imprisonment."

"Were you newly released on the occasion in question?"

"They tell me so."

"Have you no remembrance of the occasion ?"

"None. My mind is a blank, from some time — I cannot even say what time — when I employed myself, in my captivity, in making shoes, to the time when I found myself living in London with my dear daughter here. She had become familiar to me, when a gracious God restored my faculties ; but I am quite unable even to say how she had become familiar. I have no remembrance of the process."

Mr. Attorney-General sat down, and the father and daughter sat down together.

A singular circumstance then arose in the case. The object in hand being, to show that the prisoner went down, with some fellow-plotter untracked, in the Dover mail on that Friday night in November five years ago, and got out of the mail in the night, as a blind, at a place where he did not remain, but from which he travelled back some dozen miles or more, to a garrison and dockyard, and there collected information ; a witness was called to identify him as having been at the precise time required, in the coffee-room of an hotel in that garrison and dockyard town, waiting for another person. The prisoner's counsel was cross-examining this witness with no result, except that he had never seen the prisoner on any other occasion, when the wigged gentleman, who had all this time been looking at the ceiling of the court, wrote a word or two on a little piece of paper, screwed it up, and tossed it to him. Opening this piece of paper in the next pause, the counsel looked with great attention and curiosity at the prisoner.

"You say again you are quite sure that it *was* the prisoner ?" The witness was quite sure.

"Did you ever see anybody very like the prisoner ?"

Not so like (the witness said), as that he could be mistaken.

"Look well upon that gentleman, my learned friend there," pointing to him who had tossed the paper over, "and then look well upon the prisoner. How say you? Are they very like each other ?"

Allowing for my learned friend's appearance being careless and slovenly, if not debauched, they were sufficiently like each other to surprise, not only the witness, but everybody present, when they were thus brought into comparison. My Lord being prayed to bid my learned friend lay aside his wig, and giving no very gracious consent, the likeness became much more remark-

able. My Lord inquired of Mr. Stryver (the prisoner's counsel),
whether they were next to try Mr. Carton (name of my learned
friend) for treason ? But Mr. Stryver replied to my Lord, no;
but he would ask the witness to tell him whether what happened once, might happen twice; whether he would have been
so confident if he had seen this illustration of his rashness
sooner; whether he would be so confident, having seen it; and
more. The upshot of which was, to smash this witness like
a crockery vessel, and shiver his part of the case to useless
lumber.

Mr. Cruncher had by this time taken quite a lunch of rust
off his fingers, in his following of the evidence. He had now
to attend while Mr. Stryver fitted the prisoner's case on the
jury like a compact suit of clothes; showing them how the
patriot, Barsad, was a hired spy and traitor, an unblushing traf-
ficker in blood, and one of the greatest scoundrels upon earth
since accursed Judas — which he certainly did look rather like.
How the virtuous servant, Cly, was his friend and partner, and
was worthy to be; how the watchful eyes of those forgers and
false swearers had rested on the prisoner as a victim, because
some family affairs in France, he being of French extraction,
did require his making those passages across the Channel —
though what those affairs were, a consideration for others who
were near and dear to him forbade him, even for his life, to disclose. How the evidence that had been warped and wrested
from the young lady, whose anguish in giving it they had wit-
nessed, came to nothing, involving the mere little innocent
gallantries and politenesses likely to pass between any young
gentleman and young lady so thrown together, — with the
exception of that reference to George Washington, which was
altogether too extravagant and impossible, to be regarded in any
other light than as a monstrous joke. How it would be a weakness in the government to break down in this attempt to practise
for popularity on the lowest national antipathies and fears, and
therefore Mr. Attorney-General had made the most of it; how,
nevertheless, it rested upon nothing, save that vile and infamous
character of evidence too often disfiguring such cases, and of
which the State Trials of this country were full. But there
My Lord interposed (with as grave a face as if it had not been
true), saying that he could not sit upon that Bench and suffer
those allusions.

Mr. Stryver then called his few witnesses, and Mr. Cruncher had next to attend while Mr. Attorney-General turned the whole suit of clothes Mr. Stryver had fitted on the jury, inside out; showing how Barsad and Cly were even a hundred times better than he had thought them, and the prisoner a hundred times worse. Lastly, came My Lord himself, turning the suit of clothes, now inside out, now outside in, but on the whole decidedly trimming and shaping them into grave-clothes for the prisoner.

And now, the jury turned to consider, and the great flies swarmed again.

Mr. Carton, who had so long sat looking at the ceiling of the court, changed neither his place nor his attitude, even in this excitement. While his learned friend, Mr. Stryver, massing his papers before him, whispered with those who sat near, and from time to time glanced anxiously at the jury; while all the spectators moved more or less, and grouped themselves anew; while even My Lord himself arose from his seat, and slowly paced up and down his platform, not unattended by a suspicion in the minds of the audience that his state was feverish; this one man sat leaning back, with his torn gown half off him, his untidy wig put on just as it had happened to light on his head after its removal, his hands in his pockets, and his eyes on the ceiling as they had been all day. Something especially reckless in his demeanour, not only gave him a disreputable look, but so diminished the strong resemblance he undoubtedly bore to the prisoner (which his momentary earnestness, when they were compared together, had strengthened), that many of the lookers-on, taking note of him now, said to one another they would hardly have thought the two were so alike. Mr. Cruncher made the observation to his next neighbour, and added, "I'd hold half a guinea that *he* don't get no law-work to do. Don't look like the sort of one to get any, do he?"

Yet, this Mr. Carton took in more of the details of the scene than he appeared to take in; for now, when Miss Manette's head dropped upon her father's breast, he was the first to see it, and to say audibly, "Officer! look to that young lady. Help the gentleman to take her out. Don't you see she will fall!"

There was much commiseration for her as she was removed, and much sympathy with her father. It had evidently been a great distress to him to have the days of his imprisonment recalled. He had shown strong internal agitation when he was questioned, and that pondering or brooding look, which made him old, had been upon him, like a heavy cloud, ever since. As he passed out, the jury, who had turned back and paused a moment, spoke, through their foreman.

They were not agreed, and wished to retire. My Lord (perhaps with George Washington on his mind) showed some surprise that they were not agreed, but signified his pleasure that they should retire under watch and ward, and retired himself. The trial had lasted all day, and the lamps in the court were now being lighted. It began to be rumoured that the jury would be out a long while. The spectators dropped off to get refreshment, and the prisoner withdrew to the back of the dock, and sat down.

Mr. Lorry, who had gone out when the young lady and her father went out, now reappeared, and beckoned to Jerry, who, in the slackened interest, could easily get near him.

" Jerry, if you wish to take something to eat, you can. But keep in the way. You will be sure to hear when the jury come in. Don't be a moment behind them, for I want you to take the verdict back to the bank. You are the quickest messenger I know, and will get to Temple Bar long before I can."

Jerry had just enough forehead to knuckle, and he knuckled it in acknowledgment of this communication and a shilling. Mr. Carton came up at the moment, and touched Mr. Lorry on the arm.

" How is the young lady ? "

" She is greatly distressed ; but her father is comforting her, and she feels the better for being out of court."

" I 'll tell the prisoner so. It won't do for a respectable bank-gentleman like you to be seen speaking to him publicly, you know."

Mr. Lorry reddened, as if he were conscious of having debated the point in his mind, and Mr. Carton made his way to the outside of the bar. The way out of court lay in that direction, and Jerry followed him, all eyes, ears, and spikes.

" Mr. Darnay ! "

The prisoner came forward directly.

" You will naturally be anxious to hear of the witness, Miss

Manette. She will do very well. You have seen the worst of her agitation."

"I am deeply sorry to have been the cause of it. Could you tell her so for me, with my fervent acknowledgments?"

"Yes, I could. I will, if you ask it."

Mr. Carton's manner was so careless as to be almost insolent. He stood, half turned from the prisoner, lounging with his elbow against the bar.

"I do ask it. Accept my cordial thanks."

"What," said Carton, still only half turned towards him, "do you expect, Mr. Darnay?"

"The worst."

"It's the wisest thing to expect, and the likeliest. But I think their withdrawing is in your favour."

Loitering on the way out of court not being allowed, Jerry heard no more; but left them — so like each other in feature, so unlike each other in manner — standing side by side, both reflected in the glass above them.

An hour and a half limped heavily away in the thief-and-rascal-crowded passages below, even though assisted off with mutton-pies and ale. The hoarse messenger, uncomfortably seated on a form after taking that refection, had dropped into a doze, when a loud murmur and a rapid tide of people setting up the stairs that led to the court carried him along with them.

"Jerry! Jerry!" Mr. Lorry was already calling at the door when he got there.

"Here, sir! It's a fight to get back again. Here I am, sir!"

Mr. Lorry handed him a paper through the throng. "Quick! Have you got it?"

"Yes, sir."

Hastily written on the paper was the word "ACQUITTED."

"If you had sent the message, 'Recalled to life,' again," muttered Jerry, as he turned, "I should have known what you meant, this time."

He had no opportunity of saying, or so much as thinking, anything else, until he was clear of the Old Bailey; for the crowd came pouring out with a vehemence that nearly took him off his legs, and a loud buzz swept into the street as if the baffled blue-flies were dispersing in search of other carrion.

CHAPTER IV

CONGRATULATORY

FROM the dimly-lighted passages of the court, the last sediment of the human stew that had been boiling there all day was straining off, when Doctor Manette, Lucie Manette his daughter, Mr. Lorry, the solicitor for the defence, and its counsel Mr. Stryver, stood gathered around Mr. Charles Darney — just released — congratulating him on his escape from death.

It would have been difficult by a far brighter light to recognise in Doctor Manette, intellectual of face and upright of bearing, the shoemaker of the garret in Paris. Yet, no one could have looked at him twice, without looking again : even though the opportunity of observation had not extended to the mournful cadence of his low grave voice, and to the abstraction that overclouded him fitfully, without any apparent reason. While one external cause, and that a reference to his long lingering agony, would always — as on the trial — evoke this condition from the depths of his soul, it was also in its nature to arise of itself, and to draw a gloom over him, as incomprehensible to those unacquainted with his story as if they had seen the shadow of the actual Bastille thrown upon him by a summer sun, when the substance was three hundred miles away.

Only his daughter had the power of charming this black brooding from his mind. She was the golden thread that united him to a Past beyond his misery, and to a Present beyond his misery : and the sound of her voice, the light of her face, the touch of her hand, had a strong beneficial influence with him almost always. Not absolutely always, for she could recall some occasions on which her power had failed ; but they were few and slight, and she believed them over.

Mr. Darnay had kissed her hand fervently and gratefully, and had turned to Mr. Stryver, whom he warmly thanked. Mr. Stryver, a man of little more than thirty, but looking twenty years older than he was, stout, loud, red, bluff, and free from any drawback of delicacy, had a pushing way of shouldering himself (morally and physically) into companies and conversations, that argued well for his shouldering his way up in life.

He still had his wig and gown on, and he said, squaring himself at his late client to that degree that he squeezed the innocent Mr. Lorry clean out of the group: "I am glad to have brought you off with honour, Mr. Darnay. It was an infamous prosecution, grossly infamous; but not the less likely to succeed, on that account."

"You have laid me under an obligation to you for life — in two senses," said his late client, taking his hand.

"I have done my best for you, Mr. Darnay; and my best is as good as another man's, I believe."

It clearly being incumbent on somebody to say, "Much better," Mr. Lorry said it; perhaps not quite disinterestedly, but with the interested object of squeezing himself back again.

"You think so?" said Mr. Stryver. "Well! you have been present all day, and you ought to know. You are a man of business, too."

"And as such," quoth Mr. Lorry, whom the counsel learned in the law had now shouldered back into the group, just as he had previously shouldered him out of it — "as such, I will appeal to Doctor Manette, to break up this conference and order us all to our homes. Miss Lucie looks ill, Mr. Darnay has had a terrible day, and we are worn out."

"Speak for yourself, Mr. Lorry," said Stryver; "I have a night's work to do yet. Speak for yourself."

"I speak for myself," answered Mr. Lorry, "and for Mr. Darnay, and for Miss Lucie, and — Miss Lucie, do you not think I may speak for us all?" He asked her the question pointedly, and with a glance at her father.

His face had become frozen, as it were, in a very curious look at Darnay: an intent look, deepening into a frown of dislike and distrust, not even unmixed with fear. With this strange expression on him his thoughts had wandered away.

"My father," said Lucie, softly laying her hand on his.

He slowly shook the shadow off, and turned to her.

"Shall we go home, my father?"

With a long breath, he answered, "Yes."

The friends of the acquitted prisoner had dispersed, under the impression — which he himself had originated — that he would not be released that night. The lights were nearly all extinguished in the passages, the iron gates were being closed with a jar and a rattle, and the dismal place was deserted until to-morrow morning's interest of gallows, pillory, whipping-post, and branding-iron, should repeople it. Walking between her father and Mr. Darnay, Lucie Manette passed into the open air. A hackney-coach was called, and the father and daughter departed in it.

Mr. Stryver had left them in the passages, to shoulder his way back to the robing-room. Another person who had not joined the group, or interchanged a word with any one of them, but who had been leaning against the wall where its shadow was darkest, had silently strolled out after the rest, and had looked on until the coach drove away. He now stepped up to where Mr. Lorry and Mr. Darnay stood upon the pavement.

"So, Mr. Lorry ! Men of business may speak to Mr. Darnay now ? "

Nobody had made any acknowledgment of Mr. Carton's part in the day's proceedings ; nobody had known of it. He was unrobed, and was none the better for it in appearance.

"If you knew what a conflict goes on in the business mind, when the business mind is divided between good-natured impulse and business appearances, you would be amused, Mr. Darnay."

Mr. Lorry reddened, and said warmly, " You have mentioned that before, sir. We men of business, who serve a House, are not our own masters. We have to think of the House more than ourselves."

" *I* know, *I* know," rejoined Mr. Carton carelessly. " Don't be nettled, Mr. Lorry. You are as good as another, I have no doubt ; better, I dare say."

" And indeed, sir," pursued Mr. Lorry, not minding him, " I really don't know what you have to do with the matter. If you 'll excuse me, as very much your elder, for saying so, I really don't know that it is your business."

" Business ! Bless you, *I* have no business," said Mr. Carton.

" It is a pity you have not, sir."

" I think so too."

"If you had," pursued Mr. Lorry, "perhaps you would attend to it."

"Lord love you, no! — I should n't," said Mr. Carton.

"Well, sir!" cried Mr. Lorry, thoroughly heated by his indifference, "business is a very good thing, and a very respectable thing. And, sir, if business imposes its restraints and its silences and impediments, Mr. Darnay, as a young gentleman of generosity, knows how to make allowance for that circumstance. Mr. Darnay, good night, God bless you, sir! I hope you have been this day preserved for a prosperous and happy life. — Chair there!"

Perhaps a little angry with himself, as well as with the barrister, Mr. Lorry bustled into the chair, and was carried off to Tellson's. Carton, who smelt of port wine, and did not appear to be quite sober, laughed then, and turned to Darnay: —

"This is a strange chance that throws you and me together. This must be a strange night to you, standing alone here with your counterpart on these street stones?"

"I hardly seem yet," returned Charles Darnay, "to belong to this world again."

"I don't wonder at it; it's not so long since you were pretty far advanced on your way to another. You speak faintly."

"I begin to think I *am* faint."

"Then why the devil don't you dine? I dined, myself, while those numskulls were deliberating which world you should belong to — this, or some other. Let me show you the nearest tavern to dine well at."

Drawing his arm through his own, he took him down Ludgate Hill to Fleet Street, and so, up a covered way, into a tavern. Here, they were shown into a little room, where Charles Darnay was soon recruiting his strength with a good plain dinner and good wine: while Carton sat opposite to him at the same table, with his separate bottle of port before him, and his fully half-insolent manner upon him.

"Do you feel, yet, that you belong to this terrestrial scheme again, Mr. Darnay?"

"I am frightfully confused regarding time and place; but I am so far mended as to feel that."

"It must be an immense satisfaction!"

He said it bitterly, and filled up his glass again: which was a large one.

"As to me, the greatest desire I have is to forget that I belong to it. It has no good in it for me — except wine like this — nor I for it. So we are not much alike in that particular. Indeed, I begin to think we are not much alike in any particular, you and I."

Confused by the emotion of the day, and feeling his being there with this Double of coarse deportment to be like a dream, Charles Darnay was at a loss how to answer; finally, answered not at all.

"Now your dinner is done," Carton presently said, "why don't you call a health, Mr. Darnay; why don't you give your toast?"

"What health? What toast?"

"Why, it's on the tip of your tongue. It ought to be, it must be, I'll swear it's there."

"Miss Manette, then!"

"Miss Manette, then!"

Looking his companion full in his face while he drank the toast, Carton flung his glass over his shoulder against the wall, where it shivered to pieces; then rang the bell, and ordered in another.

"That's a fair young lady to hand to a coach in the dark, Mr. Darnay!" he said, filling his new goblet.

A slight frown and a laconic "Yes," were the answer.

"That's a fair young lady to be pitied by and wept for by! How does it feel? Is it worth being tried for one's life, to be the object of such sympathy and compassion, Mr. Darnay?"

Again Darnay answered not a word.

"She was mightily pleased to have your message, when I gave it her. Not that she showed she was pleased, but I suppose she was."

The allusion served as a timely reminder to Darnay that this disagreeable companion had, of his own free will, assisted him in the strait of the day. He turned the dialogue to that point, and thanked him for it.

"I neither want any thanks, nor merit any," was the careless rejoinder. "It was nothing to do, in the first place; and I don't know why I did it, in the second. Mr. Darnay, let me ask you a question."

"Willingly, and a small return for your good offices."

"Do you think I particularly like you?"

"Really, Mr. Carton," returned the other, oddly disconcerted, "I have not asked myself the question."

"But ask yourself the question now."

"You have acted as if you do; but I don't think you do."

"*I* don't think I do," said Carton. "I begin to have a very good opinion of your understanding."

"Nevertheless," pursued Darnay, rising to ring the bell, "there is nothing in that, I hope, to prevent my calling the reckoning, and our parting without ill-blood on either side."

Carton rejoining, "Nothing in life!" Darnay rang. "Do you call the whole reckoning?" said Carton. On his answering in the affirmative, "Then bring me another pint of this same wine, drawer, and come and wake me at ten."

The bill being paid, Charles Darnay rose and wished him good night. Without returning the wish, Carton rose too with something of a threat or defiance in his manner, and said, "A last word, Mr. Darnay: you think I am drunk?"

"I think you have been drinking, Mr. Carton."

"Think? You know I have been drinking."

"Since I must say so, I know it."

"Then you shall likewise know why. I am a disappointed drudge, sir. I care for no man on earth, and no man on earth cares for me."

"Much to be regretted. You might have used your talents better."

"May be so, Mr. Darnay; may be not. Don't let your sober face elate you, however; you don't know what it may come to. Good night!"

When he was left alone, this strange being took up a candle, went to a glass that hung against the wall, and surveyed himself minutely in it.

"Do you particularly like the man?" he muttered, at his own image; "why should you particularly like a man who resembles you? There is nothing in you to like; you know that. Ah, confound you! What a change you have made in yourself! A good reason for taking to a man, that he shows you what you have fallen away from, and what you might have been! Change places with him, and would you have been looked at by those blue eyes as he was, and commiserated by that agitated face as he was? Come on, and have it out in plain words! You hate the fellow."

He resorted to his pint of wine for consolation, drank it all in a few minutes, and fell asleep on his arms, with his hair straggling over the table, and a long winding-sheet in the candle dripping down upon him.

CHAPTER V

THE JACKAL

THOSE were drinking days, and most men drank hard. So very great is the improvement Time has brought about in such habits, that a moderate statement of the quantity of wine and punch which one man would swallow in the course of a night, without any detriment to his reputation as a perfect gentleman, would seem, in these days, a ridiculous exaggeration. The learned profession of the Law was certainly not behind any other learned profession in its Bacchanalian propensities; neither was Mr. Stryver, already fast shouldering his way to a large and lucrative practice, behind his compeers in this particular, any more than in the drier parts of the legal race.

A favourite at the Old Bailey, and eke at the Sessions, Mr. Stryver had begun cautiously to hew away the lower staves of the ladder on which he mounted. Sessions and Old Bailey had now to summon their favourite, specially, to their longing arms; and shouldering itself towards the visage of the Lord Chief Justice in the Court of King's Bench, the florid countenance of Mr. Stryver might be daily seen, bursting out of the bed of wigs, like a great sunflower pushing its way at the sun from among a rank garden-full of flaring companions.

It had once been noted at the Bar, that while Mr. Stryver was a glib man, and an unscrupulous, and a ready, and a bold, he had not that faculty of extracting the essence from a heap of statements, which is among the most striking and necessary of the advocate's accomplishments. But a remarkable improvement came upon him as to this. The more business he got, the greater his power seemed to grow of getting at its pith and marrow; and however late at night he sat carousing with Sydney Carton, he always had his points at his fingers' ends in the morning.

Sydney Carton, idlest and most unpromising of men, was Stryver's great ally. What the two drank together, between Hilary

Term and Michaelmas, might have floated a king's ship.   Stryver never had a case in hand, anywhere, but Carton was there,
with his hands in his pockets, staring at the ceiling of the
court ; they went the same Circuit, and even there they prolonged
their usual orgies late into the night, and Carton was rumoured
to be seen at broad day, going home stealthily and unsteadily
to his lodgings, like a dissipated cat.   At last, it began to get
about, among such as were interested in the matter, that
although Sydney Carton would never be a lion, he was an
amazingly good jackal, and that he rendered suit and service to
Stryver in that humble capacity.

"Ten o'clock, sir," said the man at the tavern, whom he had
charged to wake him — "ten o'clock, sir."

"*What's* the matter ?"

"Ten o'clock, sir."

"What do you mean ?   Ten o'clock at night ?"

"Yes, sir.   Your honour told me to call you."

"Oh! I remember.   Very well, very well."

After a few dull efforts to get to sleep again, which the man
dexterously combated by stirring the fire continuously for five
minutes, he got up, tossed his hat on, and walked out.   He
turned into the Temple, and, having revived himself by twice
pacing the pavements of King's Bench walk and Paper-build-
ings, turned into the Stryver chambers.

The Stryver clerk, who never assisted at these conferences,
had gone home, and the Stryver principal opened the door.
He had his slippers on, and a loose bedgown, and his throat was
bare for his greater ease.   He had that rather wild, strained,
seared marking about the eyes, which may be observed in all
free livers of his class, from the portrait of Jeffries downward,
and which can be traced, under various disguises of Art, through
the portraits of every Drinking Age.

"You are a little late, Memory," said Stryver.

"About the usual time; it may be a quarter of an hour
later."

They went into a dingy room lined with books and littered
with papers, where there was a blazing fire.   A kettle steamed
upon the hob, and in the midst of the wreck of papers a table
shone, with plenty of wine upon it, and brandy, and rum, and
sugar, and lemons.

"You have had your bottle, I perceive, Sydney."

"Two to-night, I think. I have been dining with the day's client; or seeing him dine — it's all one!"

"That was a rare point, Sydney, that you brought to bear upon the identification. How did you come by it? When did it strike you?"

"I thought he was rather a handsome fellow, and I thought I should have been much the same sort of fellow, if I had had any luck."

Mr. Stryver laughed, till he shook his precocious paunch. "You and your luck, Sydney! Get to work, get to work."

Sullenly enough, the jackal loosened his dress, went into an adjoining room, and came back with a large jug of cold water, a basin, and a towel or two. Steeping the towels in the water, and partially wringing them out, he folded them on his head in a manner hideous to behold, sat down at the table, and said, "Now I am ready!"

"Not much boiling down to be done to-night, Memory," said Mr. Stryver gaily, as he looked among his papers.

"How much?"

"Only two sets of them."

"Give me the worst first."

"There they are, Sydney. Fire away!"

The lion then composed himself on his back on a sofa on one side of the drinking-table, while the jackal sat at his own paper-bestrewn table proper, on the other side of it, with the bottles and glasses ready to his hand. Both resorted to the drinking-table without stint, but each in a different way: the lion for the most part reclining with his hands in his waistband, locking at the fire, or occasionally flirting with some lighter document; the jackal, with knitted brows and intent face, so deep in his task, that his eyes did not even follow the hand he stretched out for his glass — which often groped about, for a minute or more, before it found the glass for his lips. Two or three times, the matter in hand became so knotty, that the jackal found it imperative on him to get up, and steep his towels anew. From these pilgrimages to the jug and basin, he returned with such eccentricities of damp head-gear as no words can describe; which were made the more ludicrous by his anxious gravity.

At length the jackal had got together a compact repast for the lion, and proceeded to offer it to him. The lion took it with care and caution, made his selections from it, and his remarks upon it, and the jackal assisted both. When the repast was fully discussed, the lion put his hands in his waistband again, and lay down to meditate. The jackal then invigorated himself with a bumper for his throttle, and a fresh application to his head, and applied himself to the collection of a second meal; this was administered to the lion in the same manner, and was not disposed of until the clocks struck three in the morning.

"And now we have done, Sydney, fill a bumper of punch," said Mr. Stryver.

The jackal removed the towels from his head, which had been steaming again, shook himself, yawned, shivered, and complied.

"You were very sound, Sydney, in the matter of those crown witnesses to-day. Every question told."

"I always am sound; am I not?"

"I don't gainsay it. What has roughened your temper? Put some punch to it and smooth it again."

With a deprecatory grunt, the jackal again complied.

"The old Sydney Carton of old Shrewsbury School," said Stryver, nodding his head over him as he reviewed him in the present and the past, "the old seesaw Sydney. Up one minute and down the next; now in spirits and now in despondency!"

"Ah!" returned the other, sighing: "yes! The same Sydney, with the same luck. Even then, I did exercises for other boys, and seldom did my own."

"And why not?"

"God knows. It was my way, I suppose."

He sat, with his hands in his pockets and his legs stretched out before him, looking at the fire.

"Carton," said his friend, squaring himself at him with a bullying air, as if the fire-grate had been the furnace in which sustained endeavour was forged, and the one delicate thing to be done for the old Sydney Carton of old Shrewsbury School was to shoulder him into it, "your way is, and always was, a lame way. You summon no energy and purpose. Look at me."

"Oh, botheration!" returned Sydney, with a lighter and more good-humoured laugh, "don't *you* be moral!"

"How have I done what I have done?" said Stryver; "how do I do what I do?"

"Partly through paying me to help you, I suppose. But it's

VALLEY VIEW SCHOOL   ORDER BLANK

Gelatin Desserts (2 Bags in Box) $ .20

_____ Boxes   Strawberry

_____ "   Raspberry

_____ "   Wild Cherry

_____ "   Lemon

_____ "   Loganberry

_____ "   Red Currant

_____ "   Pineapple-Orange

_____ "   Blackberry

Creamy Puddings (2 Bags in Box) $ .20

_____ Boxes   Chocolate

_____ "   Coconut Custard

_____ "   Butterscotch

_____ "   Lemon Pie Filling

Total Number Boxes_____ Amount_____

_____ Purchaser

_____ Pupil

+	E	M	Me
16	12	5	12
27	24	10	18
33	36	20	30
17	51	29	57
53	58	51	73
5	93	56	93
76	100	72	—
81	107	80	102
4	126	90	111
—	128	—	124
7			

91	111	74	116

9	—	4	— 14
18	—	7	34
30		27	41
39		33	55
44		47	72
52		69	—

not worth your while to apostrophise me, or the air, about it; what you want to do, you do. You were always in the front rank, and I was always behind."

"I had to get into the front rank; I was not born there, was I?"

"I was not present at the ceremony; but my opinion is you were," said Carton. At this he laughed again, and they both laughed.

"Before Shrewsbury, and at Shrewsbury, and ever since Shrewsbury," pursued Carton, "you have fallen into your rank, and I have fallen into mine. Even when we were fellow-students in the Student-Quarter of Paris, picking up French, and French law, and other French crumbs that we did n't get much good of, you were always somewhere, and I was always — nowhere."

"And whose fault was that?"

"Upon my soul, I am not sure that it was not yours. You were always driving and riving and shouldering and pressing, to that restless degree that I had no chance for my life but in rust and repose. It's a gloomy thing, however, to talk about one's own past, with the day breaking. Turn me in some other direction before I go."

"Well, then! Pledge me to the pretty witness," said Stryver, holding up his glass. "Are you turned in a pleasant direction?"

Apparently not, for he became gloomy again.

"Pretty witness," he muttered, looking down into his glass. "I have had enough of witnesses to-day and to-night; who's your pretty witness?"

"The picturesque doctor's daughter, Miss Manette."

"*She* pretty!"

"Is she not?"

"No."

"Why, man alive, she was the admiration of the whole Court!"

"Rot the admiration of the whole Court! Who made the Old Bailey a judge of beauty? She was a golden-haired doll!"

"Do you know, Sydney," said Mr. Stryver, looking at him with sharp eyes, and slowly drawing a hand across his florid face, — "do you know, I rather thought, at the time, that you sympathised with the golden-haired doll, and were quick to see what happened to the golden-haired doll ? "

"Quick to see what happened! If a girl, doll or no doll, swoons within a yard or two of a man's nose, he can see it without a perspective-glass. I pledge you, but I deny the beauty. And now I'll have no more drink; I'll get to bed."

When his host followed him out on the staircase with a candle, to light him down the stairs, the day was coldly looking in through its grimy windows. When he got out of the house, the air was cold and sad, the dull sky overcast, the river dark and dim, the whole scene like a lifeless desert. And wreaths of dust were spinning round and round before the morning blast, as if the desert sand had risen far away, and the first spray of it in its advance had begun to overwhelm the city.

Waste forces within him, and a desert all around, this man stood still on his way across a silent terrace, and saw for a moment, lying in the wilderness before him, a mirage of honourable ambition, self-denial, and perseverance. In the fair city of this vision, there were airy galleries from which the loves and graces looked upon him, gardens in which the fruits of life hung ripening, waters of Hope that sparkled in his sight. A moment, and it was gone. Climbing to a high chamber in a well of houses, he threw himself down in his clothes on a neglected bed, and its pillow was wet with wasted tears.

Sadly, sadly, the sun rose; it rose upon no sadder sight than the man of good abilities and good emotions, incapable of their directed exercise, incapable of his own help and his own happiness, sensible of the blight on him, and resigning himself to let it eat him away.

CHAPTER VI

HUNDREDS OF PEOPLE

THE quiet lodgings of Doctor Manette were in a quiet street corner not far from Soho Square. On the afternoon of a certain fine Sunday when the waves of four months had rolled over the trial for treason, and carried it, as to the public interest and memory, far out to sea, Mr. Jarvis Lorry walked along the sunny streets from Clerkenwell where he lived, on his way to dine with the doctor. After several relapses into business absorption, Mr. Lorry had become the doctor's friend, and the quiet street corner was the sunny part of his life.

On this certain fine Sunday, Mr. Lorry walked towards Soho, early in the afternoon, for three reasons of habit. Firstly, because, on fine Sundays, he often walked out, before dinner, with the doctor and Lucie; secondly, because, on unfavourable Sundays, he was accustomed to be with them as the family friend, talking, reading, looking out of window, and generally getting through the day; thirdly, because he happened to have his own little shrewd doubts to solve, and knew how the ways of the doctor's household pointed to that time as a likely time for solving them.

A quainter corner than the corner where the doctor lived was not to be found in London. There was no way through it, and the front windows of the doctor's lodgings commanded a pleasant little vista of street that had a congenial air of retirement on it. There were few buildings, then, north of the Oxford Road, and forest trees flourished, and wild flowers grew, and the hawthorn blossomed, in the now vanished fields. As a consequence, country airs circulated in Soho with vigorous freedom, instead of languishing into the parish like stray paupers without a settlement; and there was many a good south wall, not far off, on which the peaches ripened in their season.

The summer light struck into the corner brilliantly in the

earlier part of the day; but when the streets grew hot, the corner was in shadow, though not in shadow so remote but that you could see beyond it into a glare of brightness. It was a cool spot, staid but cheerful, a wonderful place for echoes, and a very harbour from the raging streets.

There ought to have been a tranquil bark in such an anchorage, and there was. The doctor occupied two floors of a large, still house, where several callings purported to be pursued by day, but whereof little was audible any day, and which was shunned by all of them at night. In a building at the back, attainable by a courtyard where a plane-tree rustled its green leaves, church organs claimed to be made, and silver to be chased, and likewise gold to be beaten by some mysterious giant who had a golden arm starting out of the wall of the front hall — as if he had beaten himself precious, and menaced a similar conversion of all visitors. Very little of these trades, or of a lonely lodger rumoured to live up stairs, or of a dim coach-trimming maker asserted to have a counting-house below, was ever heard or seen. Occasionally, a stray workman putting his coat on traversed the hall, or a stranger peered about there, or a distant clink was heard across the courtyard, or a thump from the golden giant. These, however, were only the exceptions required to prove the rule that the sparrows in the plane-tree behind the house, and the echoes in the corner before it, had their own way from Sunday morning unto Saturday night.

Doctor Manette received such patients here as his old reputation, and its revival in the floating whispers of his story, brought him. His scientific knowledge, and his vigilance and skill in conducting ingenious experiments, brought him otherwise into moderate request, and he earned as much as he wanted.

These things were within Mr. Jarvis Lorry's knowledge, thoughts, and notice, when he rang the door-bell of the tranquil house in the corner, on the fine Sunday afternoon.

" Doctor Manette at home ? "

Expected home.

" Miss Lucie at home ? "

Expected home.

" Miss Pross at home ? "

Possibly at home, but of a certainty impossible for handmaid to anticipate intentions of Miss Pross, as to admission or denial of the fact.

"As I am at home myself," said Mr. Lorry, "I'll go up stairs."

Although the doctor's daughter had known nothing of the country of her birth, she appeared to have innately derived from it that ability to make much of little means, which is one of its most useful and most agreeable characteristics. Simple as the furniture was, it was set off by so many little adornments, of no value but for their taste and fancy, that its effect was delightful. The disposition of everything in the rooms, from the largest object to the least; the arrangement of colours, the elegant variety and contrast obtained by thrift in trifles, by delicate hands, clear eyes, and good sense, were at once so pleasant in themselves, and so expressive of their originator, that, as Mr. Lorry stood looking about him, the very chairs and tables seemed to ask him, with something of that peculiar expression which he knew so well by this time, whether he approved ?

There were three rooms on a floor, and, the doors by which they communicated being put open that the air might pass freely through them all, Mr. Lorry, smilingly observant of that fanciful resemblance which he detected all around him, walked from one to another. The first was the best room, and in it were Lucie's birds, and flowers, and books, and desk, and worktable, and box of water-colours; the second was the doctor's consulting-room, used also as the dining-room; the third, changingly speckled by the rustle of the plane-tree in the yard, was the doctor's bedroom, and there, in a corner, stood the disused shoemaker's bench and tray of tools, much as it had stood on the fifth floor of the dismal house by the wine-shop, in the suburb of Saint Antoine in Paris.

"I wonder," said Mr. Lorry, pausing in his looking about, "that he keeps that reminder of his sufferings by him !"

"And why wonder at that ?" was the abrupt inquiry that made him start.

It proceeded from Miss Pross, the wild red woman, strong of hand, whose acquaintance he had first made at the Royal George Hotel at Dover, and had since improved.

"I should have thought" — Mr. Lorry began.

"Pooh ! You'd have thought !" said Miss Pross; and Mr. Lorry left off.

"How do you do ?" inquired that lady then — sharply, and yet as if to express that she bore him no malice.

"I am pretty well, I thank you," answered Mr. Lorry, with meekness, "how are you?"

"Nothing to boast of," said Miss Pross.

"Indeed?"

"Ah! indeed!" said Miss Pross. "I am very much put out about my Ladybird."

"Indeed?"

"For gracious' sake say something else besides 'indeed,' or you'll fidget me to death," said Miss Pross, whose character (dissociated from stature) was shortness.

"Really then?" said Mr. Lorry as an amendment.

"Really, is bad enough," returned Miss Pross, "but better. Yes, I am very much put out."

"May I ask the cause?"

"I don't want dozens of people who are not at all worthy of Ladybird to come here looking after her," said Miss Pross.

"*Do* dozens come for that purpose?"

"Hundreds," said Miss Pross.

It was characteristic of this lady (as of some other people before her time and since) that whenever her original proposition was questioned, she exaggerated it.

"Dear me!" said Mr. Lorry, as the safest remark he could think of.

"I have lived with the darling — or the darling has lived with me, and paid me for it; which she certainly should never have done, you may take your affidavit, if I could have afforded to keep either myself or her for nothing — since she was ten years old. And it's really very hard," said Miss Pross.

Not seeing with precision what was very hard, Mr. Lorry shook his head; using that important part of himself as a sort of fairy cloak that would fit anything.

"All sorts of people, who are not in the least degree worthy of the pet, are always turning up," said Miss Pross. "When you began it — "

"*I* began it, Miss Pross?"

"Did n't you? Who brought her father to life?"

"Oh! If *that* was beginning it" — said Mr. Lorry.

"It was n't ending it, I suppose? I say, when you began it, it was hard enough; not that I have any fault to find with Doctor Manette, except that he is not worthy of such a daughter, which is no imputation on him, for it was not to be expected that anybody should be, under any circumstances. But it really is doubly and trebly hard to have crowds and multitudes of people turning up after him (I could have forgiven him), to take Ladybird's affections away from me."

Mr. Lorry knew Miss Pross to be very jealous, but he also knew her by this time to be, beneath the surface of her eccentricity, one of those unselfish creatures — found only among women — who will, for pure love and admiration, bind themselves willing slaves to youth when they have lost it, to beauty that they never had, to accomplishments that they were never fortunate enough to gain, to bright hopes that never shone upon their own sombre lives. He knew enough of the world to know that there is nothing in it better than the faithful service of the heart; so rendered and so free from any mercenary taint, he had such an exalted respect for it, that, in the retributive arrangements made by his own mind, — we all make such arrangements, more or less, — he stationed Miss Pross much nearer to the lower Angels than many ladies immeasurably better got up both by Nature and Art, who had balances at Tellson's.

"There never was, nor will be, but one man worthy of Ladybird," said Miss Pross; "and that was my brother Solomon, if he had n't made a mistake in life."

Here again : Mr. Lorry's inquiries into Miss Pross's personal history had established the fact that her brother Solomon was a heartless scoundrel who had stripped her of everything she possessed, as a stake to speculate with, and had abandoned her in her poverty for evermore, with no touch of compunction. Miss Pross's fidelity of belief in Solomon (deducting a mere trifle for this slight mistake) was quite a serious matter with Mr. Lorry, and had its weight in his good opinion of her.

"As we happen to be alone for the moment, and are both people of business," he said, when they had got back to the drawing-room, and had sat down there in friendly relations, "let me ask you — does the doctor, in talking with Lucie, never refer to the shoemaking time, yet ? "

"Never."

"And yet keeps that bench and those tools beside him ? "

"Ah ! " returned Miss Pross, shaking her head. "But I don't say he don't refer to it within himself."

"Do you believe that he thinks of it much ? "

"I do," said Miss Pross.

"Do you imagine" — Mr. Lorry had begun, when Miss Pross took him up short with : —

"Never imagine anything. Have no imagination at all."

"I stand corrected ; do you suppose — you go so far as to suppose, sometimes ? "

"Now and then," said Miss Pross.

"Do you suppose," Mr. Lorry went on, with a laughing twinkle in his bright eye, as it looked kindly at her, "that Doctor Manette has any theory of his own, preserved through all those years, relative to the cause of his being so oppressed ; perhaps, even to the name of his oppressor ? "

"I don't suppose anything about it but what Ladybird tells me."

"And that is — "

"That she thinks he has."

"Now don't be angry at my asking all these questions ; because I am a mere dull man of business, and you are a woman of business."

"Dull ? " Miss Pross inquired, with placidity.

Rather wishing his modest adjective away, Mr. Lorry replied, "No, no, no. Surely not. To return to business : Is it not remarkable that Doctor Manette, unquestionably innocent of any crime as we are well assured he is, should never touch upon that question ? I will not say with me, though he had business relations with me many years ago and we are now intimate ; I will say with the fair daughter to whom he is so devotedly attached, and who is so devotedly attached to him ? Believe me, Miss Pross, I don't approach the topic with you out of curiosity, but out of zealous interest."

"Well ! To the best of my understanding, and bad's the best you'll tell me," said Miss Pross, softened by the tone of the apology, " he is afraid of the whole subject."

"Afraid ? "

"It's plain enough, I should think, why he may be. It's a dreadful remembrance. Besides that, his loss of himself grew out of it. Not knowing how he lost himself, or how he recovered himself, he may never feel certain of not losing himself again. That alone wouldn't make the subject pleasant, I should think."

It was a profounder remark than Mr. Lorry had looked for.

"True," said he, "and fearful to reflect upon. Yet a doubt lurks in my mind, Miss Pross, whether it is good for Doctor Manette to have that suppression always shut up within him. Indeed, it is this doubt and the uneasiness it sometimes causes me that has led me to our present confidence."

"Can't be helped," said Miss Pross, shaking her head. "Touch that string, and he instantly changes for the worse. Better leave it alone. In short, must leave it alone, like or no like. Sometimes, he gets up in the dead of the night, and will be heard, by us overhead there, walking up and down, walking up and down, in his room. Ladybird has learnt to know then, that his mind is walking up and down, walking up and down, in his old prison. She hurries to him, and they go on together, walking up and down, walking up and down, until he is composed. But he never says a word of the true reason of his restlessness to her, and she finds it best not to hint at it to him. In silence they go walking up and down together, walking up and down together, till her love and company have brought him to himself."

Notwithstanding Miss Pross's denial of her own imagination, there was a perception of the pain of being monotonously haunted by one sad idea, in her repetition of the phrase, walking up and down, which testified to her possessing such a thing.

The corner has been mentioned as a wonderful corner for echoes; it had begun to echo so resoundingly to the tread of coming feet, that it seemed as though the very mention of that weary pacing to and fro had set it going.

"Here they are!" said Miss Pross, rising to break up the conference; "and now we shall have hundreds of people pretty soon!"

It was such a curious corner in its acoustical properties, such a peculiar Ear of a place, that as Mr. Lorry stood at the open window, looking for the father and daughter whose steps he heard, he fancied they would never approach. Not only would the echoes die away, as though the steps had gone, but echoes of other steps that never came would be heard in their stead, and would die away for good when they seemed close at hand. However, father and daughter did at last appear, and Miss Pross was ready at the street door to receive them.

Miss Pross was a pleasant sight, albeit wild, and red and grim, taking off her darling's bonnet when she came up stairs, and touching it up with the ends of her handkerchief, and blowing the dust off it, and folding her mantle ready for laying by, and smoothing her rich hair with as much pride as she could possibly have taken in her own hair if she had been the vainest and handsomest of women. Her darling was a pleasant sight, too, embracing her and thanking her, and protesting against her taking so much trouble for her — which last she only dared to do playfully, or Miss Pross, sorely hurt, would have retired to her own chamber and cried. The doctor was a pleasant sight, too, looking on at them, and telling Miss Pross how she spoilt Lucie, in accents and with eyes that had as much spoiling in them as Miss Pross had, and would have had more if it were possible. Mr. Lorry was a pleasant sight, too, beaming at all this in his little wig, and thanking his bachelor stars for having lighted him in his declining years to a Home. But no hundreds of people came to see the sights, and Mr. Lorry looked in vain for the fulfilment of Miss Pross's prediction.

Dinner-time, and still no hundreds of people. In the arrangements of the little household, Miss Pross took charge of the lower regions, and always acquitted herself marvellously. Her dinners, of a very modest quality, were so well cooked and so well served, and so neat in their contrivances, half English and half French, that nothing could be better. Miss Pross's friendship being of the thoroughly practical kind, she had ravaged Soho and the adjacent provinces, in search of impoverished French, who, tempted by shillings and half-crowns, would impart culinary mysteries to her. From these decayed sons and daughters of Gaul, she had acquired such wonderful arts, that the woman and girl who formed the staff of domestics regarded her as quite a Sorceress, or Cinderella's Godmother, who would send out for a fowl, a rabbit, a vegetable or two from the garden, and change them into anything she pleased.

On Sundays, Miss Pross dined at the doctor's table, but on other days persisted in taking her meals, at unknown periods, either in the lower regions, or in her own room on the second floor — a blue chamber, to which no one but her Ladybird ever gained admittance. On this occasion Miss Pross, responding to Ladybird's pleasant face and pleasant efforts to please her, unbent exceedingly; so the dinner was very pleasant, too.

It was an oppressive day, and, after dinner, Lucie proposed that the wine should be carried out under the plane-tree, and

they should sit there in the air. As everything turned upon
her and revolved about her, they went out under the plane-tree,
and she carried the wine down for the special benefit of Mr.
Lorry. She had installed herself some time before, as Mr.
Lorry's cup-bearer; and while they sat under the plane-tree,
talking, she kept his glass replenished. Mysterious backs and
ends of houses peeped at them as they talked, and the plane-
tree whispered to them in its own way above their heads.

Still, the Hundreds of people did not present themselves.
Mr. Darnay presented himself while they were sitting under
the plane-tree, but he was only One.

Doctor Manette received him kindly and so did Lucie. But
Miss Pross suddenly became afflicted with a twitching in the
head and body, and retired into the house. She was not unfrequently the victim of this disorder, and she called it, in familiar
conversation, "a fit of the jerks."

The doctor was in his best condition, and looked specially
young. The resemblance between him and Lucie was very
strong at such times, and as they sat side by side, she leaning
on his shoulder, and he resting his arm on the back of her chair,
it was very agreeable to trace the likeness.

He had been talking all day, on many subjects and with
unusual vivacity. "Pray, Doctor Manette," said Mr. Darnay,
as they sat under the plane-tree, — and he said it in the natural
pursuit of the topic in hand, which happened to be the old
buildings of London, — "have you seen much of the Tower?"

"Lucie and I have been there, but only casually. We have
seen enough of it, to know that it teems with interest; little
more."

"*I* have been there, as you remember," said Darnay, with a
smile, though reddening a little angrily, "in another character, and not in a character that gives facilities for seeing much
of it. They told me a curious thing when I was there."

"What was that?" Lucie asked.

"In making some alterations, the workmen came upon an
old dungeon, which had been, for many years, built up and forgotten. Every stone of its inner wall was covered with inscrip-
tions which had been carved by prisoners — dates, names, com-
plaints, and prayers. Upon a corner stone in an angle of the
wall, one prisoner who seemed to have gone to execution had
cut, as his last work, three letters. They were done with some

very poor instrument, and hurriedly, with an unsteady hand. At first, they were read as D I C; but on being more carefully examined, the last letter was found to be G. There was no record or legend of any prisoner with those initials, and many fruitless guesses were made what the name could have been. At length, it was suggested that the letters were not initials, but the complete word, DIG. The floor was examined very carefully under the inscription, and in the earth beneath a stone, or tile, or some fragment of paving, were found the ashes of a paper, mingled with the ashes of a small leathern case or bag. What the unknown prisoner had written will never be read, but he had written something, and hidden it away to keep it from the jailer."

"My father!" exclaimed Lucie, "you are ill!"

He had suddenly started up, with his hand to his head. His manner and his look quite terrified them all.

"No, my dear, not ill. There are large drops of rain falling, and they made me start. We had better go in."

He recovered himself almost instantly. Rain was really falling in large drops, and he showed the back of his hand with rain-drops on it. But he said not a single word in reference to the discovery that had been told of, and, as they went into the house, the business eye of Mr. Lorry either detected, or fancied it detected, on his face, as it turned towards Charles Darnay, the same singular look that had been upon it when it turned towards him in the passages of the Court House.

He recovered himself so quickly, however, that Mr. Lorry had doubts of his business eye. The arm of the golden giant in the hall was not more steady than he was, when he stopped under it to remark to them that he was not yet proof against slight surprises (if he ever would be), and that the rain had startled him.

Tea-time, and Miss Pross making tea, with another fit cf the jerks upon her, and yet no Hundreds of people. Mr. Carton had lounged in, but he made only Two.

The night was so very sultry, that although they sat with doors and windows open, they were overpowered by heat. When the tea-table was done with, they all moved to one of the windows, and looked out into the heavy twilight. Lucie sat by her father; Darnay sat beside her; Carton leaned against a window. The curtains were long and white, and

some of the thunder-gusts that whirled into the corner caught
them up to the ceiling, and waved them like spectral wings.

"The rain-drops are still falling, large, heavy, and few," said
Doctor Manette. "It comes slowly."

"It comes surely," said Carton.

They spoke low, as people watching and waiting mostly do;
as people in a dark room, watching and waiting for Lightning,
always do.

There was a great hurry in the streets, of people speeding
away to get shelter before the storm broke; the wonderful
corner for echoes resounded with the echoes of footsteps coming
and going, yet not a footstep was there.

"A multitude of people, and yet a solitude!" said Darnay,
when they had listened for a while.

"Is it not impressive, Mr. Darnay?" asked Lucie. "Sometimes I have sat here of an evening, until I have fancied — but
even the shade of a foolish fancy makes me shudder to-night,
when all is so black and solemn — "

"Let us shudder too. We may know what it is."

"It will seem nothing to you. Such whims are only impressive as we originate them, I think; they are not to be
communicated. I have sometimes sat alone here of an evening,
listening, until I have made the echoes out to be the echoes of
all the footsteps that are coming by and by into our lives."

"There is a great crowd coming one day into our lives, if
that be so," Sydney Carton struck in, in his moody way.

The footsteps were incessant, and the hurry of them became
more and more rapid. The corner echoed and re-echoed with
the tread of feet; some, as it seemed, under the windows;
some, as it seemed, in the room; some coming, some going,
some breaking off, some stopping altogether; all in the distant
streets, and not one within sight.

"Are all these footsteps destined to come to all of us, Miss
Manette, or are we to divide them among us?"

"I don't know, Mr. Darnay; I told you it was a foolish
fancy, but you asked for it. When I have yielded myself to
it, I have been alone, and then I have imagined them the footsteps of the people who are to come into my life, and my
father's."

"I take them into mine!" said Carton. "I ask no questions
and make no stipulations. There is a great crowd bearing down

upon us, Miss Manette, and I see them! — by the Lightning." He added the last words after there had been a vivid flash which had shown him lounging in the window.

"And I hear them!" he added again, after a peal of thunder. "Here they come, fast, fierce, and furious!"

It was the rush and roar of rain that he typified, and it stopped him, for no voice could be heard in it. A memorable storm of thunder and lightning broke with that sweep of water, and there was not a moment's interval in crash, and fire, and rain, until after the moon rose at midnight.

The great bell of Saint Paul's was striking One in the cleared air, when Mr. Lorry, escorted by Jerry, high-booted and bearing a lantern, set forth on his return passage to Clerkenwell. There were solitary patches of road on the way between Soho and Clerkenwell, and Mr. Lorry, mindful of footpads, always retained Jerry for this service, though it was usually performed a good two hours earlier.

"What a night it has been! Almost a night, Jerry," said Mr. Lorry, "to bring the dead out of their graves."

"I never see the night myself, master, — nor yet I don't expect to it, — what would do that," answered Jerry.

"Good night, Mr. Carton," said the man of business. "Good night, Mr. Darnay. Shall we ever see such a night again, together!"

Perhaps. Perhaps, see the great crowd of people with its rush and roar, bearing down upon them, too.

CHAPTER VII

MONSEIGNEUR IN TOWN

MONSEIGNEUR, one of the great lords in power at the Court, held his fortnightly reception in his grand hotel in Paris. Monseigneur was in his inner room, his sanctuary of sanctuaries, the Holiest of Holiests to the crowd of worshippers in the suite of rooms without. Monseigneur was about to take his chocolate. Monseigneur could swallow a great many things with ease, and was by some few sullen minds supposed to be rather rapidly swallowing France; but his morning's chocolate could not so much as get into the throat of Monseigneur without the aid of four strong men besides the Cook.

Yes. It took four men, all four ablaze with gorgeous decoration, and the Chief of them unable to exist with fewer than two gold watches in his pocket, emulative of the noble and chaste fashion set by Monseigneur, to conduct the happy chocolate to Monseigneur's lips. One lacquey carried the chocolate-pot into the sacred presence; a second, milled and frothed the chocolate with the little instrument he bore for that function; a third, presented the favoured napkin; a fourth (he of the two gold watches), poured the chocolate out. It was impossible for Monseigneur to dispense with one of these attendants on the chocolate and hold his high place under the admiring heavens. Deep would have been the blot upon his escutcheon if his chocolate had been ignobly waited on by only three men; he must have died of two.

Monseigneur had been out at a little supper last night, where the Comedy and the Grand Opera were charmingly represented. Monseigneur was out at a little supper most nights, with fascinating company. So polite and so impressible was Monseigneur, that the Comedy and the Grand Opera had far more influence with him in the tiresome articles of state affairs and state secrets, than the needs of all France. A happy circumstance for France, as the like always is for all countries similarly favoured!—

always was for England (by way of example), in the regretted days of the merry Stuart who sold it.

Monseigneur had one truly noble idea of general public business, which was, to let everything go on in its own way; of particular public business, Monseigneur had the other truly noble idea that it must all go his way — tend to his own power and pocket. Of his pleasures, general and particular, Monseigneur had the other truly noble idea, that the world was made for them. The text of his order (altered from the original by only a pronoun, which is not much) ran : " The earth and the fulness thereof are mine, saith Monseigneur."

Yet, Monseigneur had slowly found that vulgar embarrassments crept into his affairs, both private and public; and he had, as to both classes of affairs, allied himself per force with a Farmer-General. As to finances public, because Monseigneur could not make anything at all of them, and must consequently let them out to somebody who could; as to finances private, because Farmer-Generals were rich, and Monseigneur, after generations of great luxury and expense, was growing poor. Hence, Monseigneur had taken his sister from a convent, while there was yet time to ward off the impending veil, the cheapest garment she could wear, and had bestowed her as a prize upon a very rich Farmer-General, poor in family. Which Farmer-General, carrying an appropriate cane with a golden apple on the top of it, was now among the company in the outer rooms, much prostrated before by mankind — always excepting superior mankind of the blood of Monseigneur, who, his own wife included, looked down upon him with the loftiest contempt.

A sumptuous man was the Farmer-General. Thirty horses stood in his stables, twenty-four male domestics sat in his halls, six body-women waited on his wife. As one who pretended to do nothing but plunder and forage where he could, the Farmer-General — howsoever his matrimonial relations conduced to social morality — was at least the greatest reality among the personages who attended at the hotel of Monseigneur that day.

For the rooms, though a beautiful scene to look at, and adorned with every device of decoration that the taste and skill of the time could achieve, were, in truth, not a sound business; considered with any reference to the scarecrows in the rags and nightcaps elsewhere (and not so far off, either, but that the watching towers of Notre-Dame, almost equidistant from the two extremes, could see them both), they would have been an exceedingly uncomfortable business — if that could have been anybody's business, at the house of Monseigneur. Military officers destitute of military knowledge; naval officers with no idea of a ship; civil officers without a notion of affairs; brazen ecclesiastics, of the worst world worldly, with sensual eyes, loose tongues, and looser lives; all totally unfit for their several callings, all lying horribly in pretending to belong to them, but all nearly or remotely of the order of Monseigneur, and therefore foisted on all public employments from which anything was to be got; these were to be told off by the score and the score. People not immediately connected with Monseigneur or the State, yet equally unconnected with anything that was real, or with lives passed in travelling by any straight road to any true earthly end, were no less abundant. Doctors, who made great fortunes out of dainty remedies for imaginary disorders that never existed, smiled upon their courtly patients in the ante-chambers of Monseigneur. Projectors who had discovered every kind of remedy for the little evils with which the State was touched, except the remedy of setting to work in earnest to root out a single sin, poured their distracting babble into any ears they could lay hold of, at the reception of Monseigneur. Unbelieving Philosophers who were remodelling the world with words, and making card-towers of Babel to scale the skies with, talked with Unbelieving Chemists who had an eye on the transmutation of metals, at this wonderful gathering accumulated by Monseigneur. Exquisite gentlemen of the finest breeding, which was at that remarkable time — and has been since — to be known by its fruits of indifference to every natural subject of human interest, were in the most exemplary state of exhaustion, at the hotel of Monseigneur. Such homes had these various notabilities left behind them in the fine world of Paris, that the Spies among the assembled devotees of Monseigneur — forming a goodly half of the polite company — would have found it hard to discover among the angels of that sphere one solitary wife, who, in her manners and appearance, owned to being a Mother. Indeed, except for the mere act of bringing a troublesome creature into this world — which does not go far towards the realisation of the name of mother — there was no such thing known to the fashion. Peasant women kept the unfashionable babies close, and brought them up ; and charming grandmammas of sixty dressed and supped as at twenty.

The leprosy of unreality disfigured every human creature in attendance upon Monseigneur. In the outermost room were half a dozen exceptional people who had had, for a few years, some vague misgiving in them that things in general were going rather wrong. As a promising way of setting them right, half of the half dozen had become members of a fantastic sect of Convulsionists, and were even then considering within themselves whether they should foam, rage, roar, and turn cataleptic on the spot — thereby setting up a highly intelligible finger-post to the Future, for Monseigneur's guidance. Besides these Dervishes, were other three who had rushed into another sect, which mended matters with a jargon about " the Centre of Truth : " holding that Man had got out of the Centre of truth — which did not need much demonstration — but had not got out of the Circumference, and that he was to be kept from flying out of the Circumference, and was even to be shoved back into the Centre, by fasting and seeing of spirits. Among these, accordingly, much discoursing with spirits went on — and it did a world of good which never became manifest.

But the comfort was, that all the company at the grand hotel of Monseigneur were perfectly dressed. If the Day of Judgment had only been ascertained to be a dress day, everybody there would have been eternally correct. Such frizzling and powdering and sticking up of hair, such delicate complexions artificially preserved and mended, such gallant swords to look at, and such delicate honour to the sense of smell, would surely keep anything going, for ever and ever. The exquisite gentlemen of the finest breeding wore little pendent trinkets that chinked as they languidly moved ; these golden fetters rang like precious little bells ; and what with that ringing, and with the rustle of silk and brocade and fine linen, there was a flutter in the air that fanned Saint Antoine and his devouring hunger far away.

Dress was the one unfailing talisman and charm used for keeping all things in their places. Everybody was dressed for a Fancy Ball that was never to leave off. From the Palace of the Tuileries, through Monseigneur and the whole Court, through the Chambers, the Tribunals of Justice, and all society (except the scarecrows), the Fancy Ball descended to the Common Executioner : who, in pursuance of the charm, was required to officiate "frizzled, powdered, in a gold-laced coat, pumps, and white silk stockings." At the gallows and the wheel — the axe was a rarity — Monsieur Paris, as it was the episcopal mode among his brother Professors of the provinces, Monsieur Orleans, and the rest, to call him, presided in this dainty dress. And who among the company at Monseigneur's reception in that seventeen hundred and eightieth year of our Lord, could possibly doubt, that a system rooted in a frizzled hangman, powdered, gold-laced, pumped, and white-silk stockinged, would see the very stars out!

Monseigneur, having eased his four men of their burdens and taken his chocolate, caused the doors of the Holiest of Holiests to be thrown open, and issued forth. Then, what submission, what cringing and fawning, what servility, what abject humiliation! As to bowing down in body and spirit, nothing in that way was left for Heaven — which may have been one among other reasons why the worshippers of Monseigneur never troubled it.

Bestowing a word of promise here and a smile there, a whisper on one happy slave and a wave of the hand on another, Monseigneur affably passed through his rooms to the remote region of the Circumference of Truth. There, Monseigneur turned, and came back again, and so in due course of time got himself shut up in his sanctuary by the chocolate sprites, and was seen no more.

The show being over, the flutter in the air became quite a little storm, and the precious little bells went ringing down stairs. There was soon but one person left of all the crowd, and he, with his hat under his arm and his snuff-box in his hand, slowly passed among the mirrors on his way out.

"I devote you," said this person, stopping at the last door on his way, and turning in the direction of the sanctuary, "to the Devil!"

With that, he shook the snuff from his fingers as if he had shaken the dust from his feet, and quietly walked down stairs.

He was a man of about sixty, handsomely dressed, haughty in manner, and with a face like a fine mask. A face of a transparent paleness; every feature in it clearly defined; one set expression on it. The nose, beautifully formed otherwise, was very slightly pinched at the top of each nostril. In those two compressions, or dints, the only little change that the face ever showed, resided. They persisted in changing colour sometimes, and they would be occasionally dilated and contracted by something like a faint pulsation; then they gave a look of treachery and cruelty to the whole countenance. Examined with attention, its capacity of helping such a look was to be found in the line of the mouth, and the lines of the orbits of the eyes, being much too horizontal and thin; still, in the effect the face made it was a handsome face, and a remarkable one.

Its owner went down stairs into the courtyard, got into his carriage, and drove away. Not many people had talked with him at the reception; he had stood in a little space apart, and Monseigneur might have been warmer in his manner. It appeared, under the circumstances, rather agreeable to him to see the common people dispersed before his horses, and often barely escaping from being run down. His man drove as if he were charging an enemy, and the furious recklessness of the man brought no check into the face, or to the lips, of the master. The complaint had sometimes made itself audible, even in that deaf city and dumb age, that, in the narrow streets without footways, the fierce patrician custom of hard driving endangered and maimed the mere vulgar in a barbarous manner. But few cared enough for that to think of it a second time, and in this matter, as in all others, the common wretches were left to get out of their difficulties as they could.

With a wild rattle and clatter, and an inhuman abandonment of consideration not easy to be understood in these days, the carriage dashed through streets and swept round corners, with women screaming before it, and men clutching each other and clutching children out of its way. At last, swooping at a street corner by a fountain, one of its wheels came to a sickening little jolt, and there was a loud cry from a number of voices, and the horses reared and plunged.

But for the latter inconvenience, the carriage probably would not have stopped; carriages were often known to drive on, and leave their wounded behind, and why not? But the frightened valet had got down in a hurry, and there were twenty hands at the horses' bridles.

"What has gone wrong?" said Monsieur, calmly looking out.

A tall man in a nightcap had caught up a bundle from among the feet of the horses, and had laid it on the basement of the fountain, and was down in the mud and wet, howling over it like a wild animal.

"Pardon, Monsieur the Marquis!" said a ragged and submissive man, "it is a child."

"Why does he make that abominable noise? Is it his child?"

"Excuse me, Monsieur the Marquis — it is a pity — yes."

The fountain was a little removed; for the street opened, where it was, into a space some ten or twelve yards square. As the tall man suddenly got up from the ground, and came running at the carriage, Monsieur the Marquis clapped his hand for an instant on his sword-hilt.

"Killed!" shrieked the man, in wild desperation, extending both arms at their length above his head, and staring at him. "Dead!"

The people closed round, and looked at Monsieur the Marquis. There was nothing revealed by the many eyes that looked at him but watchfulness and eagerness; there was no visible menacing or anger. Neither did the people say anything; after the first cry, they had been silent, and they remained so. The voice of the submissive man who had spoken was flat and tame in its extreme submission. Monsieur the Marquis ran his eyes over them all, as if they had been mere rats come out of their holes.

He took out his purse.

"It is extraordinary to me," said he, "that you people cannot take care of yourselves and your children. One or the other of you is for ever in the way. How do I know what injury you have done my horses. See! Give him that."

He threw out a gold coin for the valet to pick up, and all the heads craned forward that all the eyes might look down at it as it fell. The tall man called out again with a most unearthly cry, "Dead!"

He was arrested by the quick arrival of another man, for whom the rest made way. On seeing him, the miserable creature fell upon his shoulder, sobbing and crying, and pointing to the fountain, where some women were stooping over the motionless bundle, and moving gently about it. They were as silent, however, as the men.

"I know all, I know all," said the last comer. "Be a brave man, my Gaspard! It is better for the poor little plaything to

die so, than to live.   It has died in a moment without pain.
Could it have lived an hour as happily ? "

" You are a philosopher, you there," said the Marquis, smiling.   " How do they call you ? "

" They call me Defarge."

" Of what trade ? "

" Monsieur the Marquis, vender of wine."

" Pick up that, philosopher and vender of wine," said the
Marquis, throwing him another gold coin, " and spend it as you
will.   The horses there; are they right ? "

Without deigning to look at the assemblage a second time,
Monsieur the Marquis leaned back in his seat, and was just
being driven away with the air of a gentleman who had accidentally broken some common thing, and had paid for it and
could afford to pay for it; when his ease was suddenly disturbed
by a coin flying into his carriage, and ringing on its floor.

" Hold ! " said Monsieur the Marquis.   " Hold the horses !
Who threw that ? "

He looked to the spot where Defarge the vender of wine had
stood a moment before ; but the wretched father was grovelling
on his face on the pavement in that spot, and the figure that
stood beside him was the figure of a dark stout woman, knitting.

" You dogs ! " said the Marquis, but smoothly, and with an
unchanged front, except as to the spots on his nose : " I would
ride over any of you very willingly, and exterminate you from
the earth.   If I knew which rascal threw at the carriage, and
if that brigand were sufficiently near it, he should be crushed
under the wheels."

So cowed was their condition, and so long and hard their
experience of what such a man could do to them, within the
law and beyond it, that not a voice, or a hand, or even an eye
was raised.   Among the men, not one.   But the woman who
stood knitting looked up steadily, and looked the Marquis in
the face.   It was not for his dignity to notice it; his contemp-
tuous eyes passed over her, and over all the other rats ; and he
leaned back in his seat again, and gave the word " Go on ! "

He was driven on, and other carriages came whirling by in
quick succession ; the Minister, the State-Projector, the Farmer-
General, the Doctor, the Lawyer, the Ecclesiastic, the Grand
Opera, the Comedy, the whole Fancy Ball in a bright continuous
flow, came whirling by.   The rats had crept out of their holes

to look on, and they remained looking on for hours; soldiers and police often passing between them and the spectacle, and making a barrier behind which they slunk, and through which they peeped. The father had long ago taken up his bundle and hidden himself away with it, when the women, who had tended the bundle while it lay on the base of the fountain, sat there watching the running of the water and the rolling of the Fancy Ball — when the one woman who had stood conspicuous, knitting, still knitted on with the steadfastness of Fate. The water of the fountain ran, the swift river ran, the day ran into evening, so much life in the city ran into death according to rule, time and tide waited for no man, the rats were sleeping close together in their dark holes again, the Fancy Ball was lighted up at supper, all things ran their course.

CHAPTER VIII

MONSEIGNEUR IN THE COUNTRY

A BEAUTIFUL landscape, with the corn bright in it but not abundant. Patches of poor rye where corn should have been, patches of poor peas and beans, patches of most coarse vegetable substitutes for wheat. On inanimate nature, as on the men and women who cultivated it, a prevalent tendency towards an appearance of vegetating unwillingly — a dejected disposition to give up, and wither away.

Monsieur the Marquis in his travelling-carriage (which might have been lighter), conducted by four post-horses and two postilions, fagged up a steep hill. A blush on the countenance of Monsieur the Marquis was no impeachment of his high breeding; it was not from within; it was occasioned by an external circumstance beyond his control — the setting sun.

The sunset struck so brilliantly into the travelling-carriage when it gained the hilltop, that its occupant was steeped in crimson. "It will die out," said Monsieur the Marquis, glancing at his hands, "directly."

In effect, the sun was so low that it dipped at the moment. When the heavy drag had been adjusted to the wheel, and the carriage slid down hill, with a cinderous smell, in a cloud of dust, the red glow departed quickly; the sun and the Marquis going down together, there was no glow left when the drag was taken off.

But there remained a broken country, bold and open, a little village at the bottom of the hill, a broad sweep and rise beyond it, a church-tower, a windmill, a forest for the chase, and a crag with a fortress on it used as a prison. Round upon all these darkening objects as the night drew on, the Marquis looked, with the air of one who was coming near home.

The village had its one poor street, with its poor brewery, poor tannery, poor tavern, poor stable-yard for relays of post-horses, poor fountain, all usual poor appointments. It had its poor people too. All its people were poor, and many of them were sitting at their doors, shredding spare onions and the like for supper, while many were at the fountain, washing leaves, and grasses, and any such small yieldings of the earth that could be eaten. Expressive signs of what made them poor were not wanting; the tax for the state, the tax for the church, the tax for the lord tax local and tax general, were to be paid here and to be paid there, according to solemn inscription in the little village, until the wonder was, that there was any village left unswallowed.

Few children were to be seen, and no dogs. As to the men and women, their choice on earth was stated in the prospect — Life on the lowest terms that could sustain it, down in the little village under the mill; or captivity and Death in the dominant prison on the crag.

Heralded by a courier in advance, and by the cracking of his postilions' whips, which twined snake-like about their heads in the evening air, as if he came attended by the Furies, Monsieur the Marquis drew up in his travelling-carriage at the posting-house gate. It was hard by the fountain, and the peasants suspended their operations to look at him. He looked at them, and saw in them, without knowing it, the slow sure filing down of misery-worn face and figure, that was to make the meagreness of Frenchmen an English superstition which should survive the truth through the best part of a hundred years.

Monsieur the Marquis cast his eyes over the submissive faces that drooped before him, as the like of himself had drooped before Monseigneur of the Court — only the difference was, that these faces drooped merely to suffer and not to propitiate — when a grizzled mender of the roads joined the group.

"Bring me hither that fellow!" said the Marquis to the courier.

The fellow was brought, cap in hand, and the other fellows closed round to look and listen, in the manner of the people at the Paris fountain.

"I passed you on the road?"

"Monseigneur, it is true. I had the honour of being passed on the road."

"Coming up the hill, and at the top of the hill, both?"

"Monseigneur, it is true."

"What did you look at, so fixedly?"

"Monseigneur, I looked at the man."

He stooped a little, and with his tattered blue cap pointed under the carriage. All his fellows stooped to look under the carriage.

"What man, pig? And why look there?"

"Pardon, Monseigneur; he swung by the chain of the shoe — the drag."

"Who?" demanded the traveller.

"Monseigneur, the man."

"May the Devil carry away these idiots! How do you call the man? You know all the men of this part of the country. Who was he?"

"Your clemency, Monseigneur! He was not of this part of the country. Of all the days of my life, I never saw him."

"Swinging by the chain? To be suffocated?"

"With your gracious permission, that was the wonder of it, Monseigneur. His head hanging over — like this!"

He turned himself sideways to the carriage, and leaned back, with his face thrown up to the sky, and his head hanging down; then recovered himself, fumbled with his cap, and made a bow.

"What was he like?"

"Monseigneur he was whiter than the miller. All covered with dust, white as a spectre, tall as a spectre!"

The picture produced an immense sensation in the little crowd; but all eyes, without comparing notes with other eyes, looked at Monsieur the Marquis. Perhaps, to observe whether he had any spectre on his conscience.

"Truly, you did well," said the Marquis, felicitously sensible that such vermin were not to ruffle him, "to see a thief accompanying my carriage, and not open that great mouth of yours. Bah! Put him aside, Monsieur Gabelle!"

Monsieur Gabelle was the Postmaster, and some other taxing functionary, united; he had come out with great obsequiousness to assist at this examination, and had held the examined by the drapery of his arm in an official manner.

"Bah! Go aside!" said Monsieur Gabelle.

"Lay hands on this stranger if he seeks to lodge in your village to-night, and be sure that his business is honest, Gabelle."

"Monseigneur, I am flattered to devote myself to your orders."

"Did he run away, fellow? — where is that Accursed?"

The accursed was already under the carriage with some half dozen particular friends, pointing out the chain with his blue cap. Some half dozen other particular friends promptly haled him out, and presented him breathless to Monsieur the Marquis.

"Did the man run away, Dolt, when we stopped for the drag?"

"Monseigneur, he precipitated himself over the hillside, head first, as a person plunges into the river."

"See to it, Gabelle. Go on!"

The half dozen who were peering at the chain were still among the wheels, like sheep; the wheels turned so suddenly that they were lucky to save their skins and bones; they had very little else to save, or they might not have been so fortunate.

The burst with which the carriage started out of the village and up the rise beyond was soon checked by the steepness of the hill. Gradually it subsided to a foot pace, swinging and lumbering upward among the many sweet scents of a summer night. The postilions, with a thousand gossamer gnats circling about them in lieu of the Furies, quietly mended the points to the lashes of their whips; the valet walked by the horses; the courier was audible, trotting on ahead into the dim distance.

At the steepest point of the hill there was a little burial-ground, with a Cross and a new large figure of Our Saviour on it; it was a poor figure in wood, done by some inexperienced rustic carver, but he had studied the figure from the life — his own life, may be — for it was dreadfully spare and thin.

To this distressful emblem of a great distress that had long been growing worse, and was not at its worst, a woman was kneeling. She turned her head as the carriage came up to her, rose quickly, and presented herself at the carriage-door.

"It is you, Monseigneur! Monseigneur, a petition."

With an exclamation of impatience, but with his unchangeable face, Monseigneur looked out.

"How, then! What is it? Always petitions!"

"Monseigneur. For the love of the great God! My husband, the forester."

"What of your husband, the forester? Always the same with you people. He cannot pay something?"

"He has paid all, Monseigneur. He is dead."

" Well! He is quiet. Can I restore him to you ? "

" Alas, no, Monseigneur ! But he lies yonder, under a little heap of poor grass."

" Well ? "

" Monseigneur, there are so many little heaps of poor grass ? "

" Again, well ? "

She looked an old woman, but was young. Her manner was one of passionate grief ; by turns she clasped her veinous and knotted hands together with wild energy, and laid one of them on the carriage-door — tenderly, caressingly, as if it had been a human breast, and could be expected to feel the appealing touch.

" Monseigneur, hear me ! Monseigneur, hear my petition ! My husband died of want ; so many die of want ; so many more will die of want."

" Again, well ? Can I feed them ? "

" Monseigneur, the good God knows ; but I don't ask it. My petition is, that a morsel of stone or wood, with my husband's name, may be placed over him to show where he lies. Otherwise, the place will be quickly forgotten, it will never be found when I am dead of the same malady, I shall be laid under some other heap of poor grass. Monseigneur, they are so many, they increase so fast, there is so much want. Monseigneur ! Monseigneur ! "

The valet had put her away from the door, the carriage had broken into a brisk trot, the postilions had quickened the pace, she was left far behind, and Monseigneur, again escorted by the Furies, was rapidly diminishing the league or two of distance that remained between him and his château.

The sweet scents of the summer night rose all around him, and rose, as the rain falls, impartially, on the dusty, ragged, and toil-worn group at the fountain not far away ; to whom the mender of roads, with the aid of the blue cap without which he was nothing, still enlarged upon his man like a spectre, as long as they could bear it. By degrees, as they could bear no more, they dropped off one by one, and lights twinkled in little casements ; which lights, as the casements darkened, and more stars came out, seemed to have shot up into the sky instead of having been extinguished

The shadow of a large high-roofed house, and of many overhanging trees, was upon Monsieur the Marquis by that time; and the shadow was exchanged for the light of a flambeau, as his carriage stopped, and the great door of his château was opened to him.

"Monsieur Charles, whom I expect; is he arrived from England?"

"Monseigneur, not yet."

CHAPTER IX

THE GORGON'S HEAD

IT was a heavy mass of building, that château of Monsieur the Marquis, with a large stone courtyard before it, and two stone sweeps of staircase meeting in a stone terrace before the principal door. A stony business altogether, with heavy stone balustrades, and stone urns, and stone flowers, and stone faces of men, and stone heads of lions, in all directions. As if the Gorgon's head had surveyed it, when it was finished, two centuries ago.

Up the broad flight of shallow steps, Monsieur the Marquis, flambeau preceded, went from his carriage, sufficiently disturbing the darkness to elicit loud remonstrance from an owl in the roof of the great pile of stable-building away among the trees. All else was so quiet, that the flambeau carried up the steps, and the other flambeau held at the great door, burnt as if they were in a close room of state, instead of being in the open night-air. Other sound than the owl's voice there was none, save the falling of a fountain into its stone basin ; for it was one of those dark nights that hold their breath by the hour together, and then heave a long low sigh, and hold their breath again.

The great door clanged behind him, and Monsieur the Marquis crossed a hall grim with certain old boar-spears, swords, and knives of the chase ; grimmer with certain heavy riding-rods and riding-whips, of which many a peasant, gone to his benefactor Death, had felt the weight when his lord was angry.

Avoiding the larger rooms, which were dark and made fast for the night, Monsieur the Marquis, with his flambeau-bearer going on before, went up the staircase to a door in a corridor. This thrown open admitted him to his own private apartment of three rooms ; his bed-chamber and two others. High vaulted rooms with cool uncarpeted floors, great dogs upon the hearths for the burning of wood in winter-time, and all luxuries befitting the state of a marquis in a luxurious age and country. The fashion of the last Louis but one, of the line that was never to break — the fourteenth Louis — was conspicuous in their rich furniture; but it was diversified by many objects that were illustrations of old pages in the history of France.

A supper-table was laid for two, in the third of the rooms; a round room, in one of the château's four extinguisher-topped towers. A small lofty room, with its window wide open, and the wooden jalousie-blinds closed, so that the dark night only showed in slight horizontal lines of black, alternating with their broad lines of stone colour.

"My nephew," said the Marquis, glancing at the supper preparation; "they said he was not arrived."

Nor was he; but he had been expected with Monseigneur.

"Ah! It is not probable he will arrive to-night; nevertheless, leave the table as it is. I shall be ready in a quarter of an hour."

In a quarter of an hour, Monseigneur was ready, and sat down alone to his sumptuous and choice supper. His chair was opposite to the window, and he had taken his soup, and was raising his glass of Bordeaux to his lips, when he put it down.

"What is that?" he calmly asked, looking with attention at the horizontal lines of black and stone colour.

"Monseigneur? That?"

"Outside the blinds. Open the blinds."

It was done.

"Well?"

"Monseigneur, it is nothing. The trees and the night and all that are here."

The servant who spoke had thrown the blinds wide, had looked out into the vacant darkness, and stood, with that blank behind him, looking round for instructions.

"Good," said the imperturbable master. "Close them again."

That was done too, and the Marquis went on with his supper. He was halfway through it, when he again stopped with his glass in his hand, hearing the sound of wheels. It came on briskly, and came up to the front of the château.

"Ask who is arrived."

It was the nephew of Monseigneur. He had been some few leagues behind Monseigneur, early in the afternoon. He had diminished the distance rapidly, but not so rapidly as to come up with Monseigneur on the road. He had heard of Monseigneur, at the posting-houses, as being before him.

He was to be told (said Monseigneur) that supper awaited him then and there, and that he was prayed to come to it. In a little while, he came. He had been known in England as Charles Darnay.

Monseigneur received him in a courtly manner, but they did not shake hands.

" You left Paris yesterday, sir ? " he said to Monseigneur, as he took his seat at table.

" Yesterday. And you ? "

" I come direct."

" From London ? "

" Yes."

" You have been a long time coming," said the Marquis, with a smile.

" On the contrary ; I come direct."

" Pardon me ! I mean, not a long time on the journey ; a long time intending the journey."

" I have been detained by " — the nephew stopped a moment in his answer — " various business."

" Without doubt," said the polished uncle.

So long as a servant was present, no other words passed between them. When coffee had been served and they were alone together, the nephew, looking at the uncle and meeting the eyes of the face that was like a fine mask, opened a conversation.

" I have come back, sir, as you anticipate, pursuing the object that took me away. It carried me into great and unexpected peril ; but it is a sacred object, and if it had carried me to death I hope it would have sustained me."

" Not to death," said the uncle ; " it is not necessary to say, to death."

" I doubt, sir," returned the nephew, " whether, if it had carried me to the utmost brink of death, you would have cared to stop me there."

The deepened marks in the nose, and the lengthening of the fine straight lines in the cruel face, looked ominous as to that ;

the uncle made a graceful gesture of protest, which was so clearly a slight form of good breeding that it was not reassuring.

"Indeed, sir," pursued the nephew, "for anything I know, you may have expressly worked to give a more suspicious appearance to the suspicious circumstances that surrounded me."

"No, no, no," said the uncle pleasantly.

"But, however that may be," resumed the nephew, glancing at him with deep distrust, "I know that your diplomacy would stop me by any means, and would know no scruple as to means."

"My friend, I told you so," said the uncle, with a fine pulsation in the two marks. "Do me the favour to recall that I told you so, long ago."

"I recall it."

"Thank you," said the Marquis — very sweetly indeed.

His tone lingered in the air, almost like the tone of a musical instrument.

"In effect, sir," pursued the nephew, "I believe it to be at once your bad fortune, and my good fortune, that has kept me out of a prison in France here."

"I do not quite understand," returned the uncle, sipping his coffee. "Dare I ask you to explain?"

"I believe that if you were not in disgrace with the Court, and had not been overshadowed by that cloud for years past, a letter *de cachet* would have sent me to some fortress indefinitely."

"It is possible," said the uncle, with great calmness. "For the honour of the family, I could even resolve to incommode you to that extent. Pray excuse me!"

"I perceive that, happily for me, the Reception of the day before yesterday was, as usual, a cold one," observed the nephew.

"I would not say happily, my friend," returned the uncle, with refined politeness; "I would not be sure of that. A good opportunity for consideration, surrounded by the advantages of solitude, might influence your destiny to far greater advantage than you influence it for yourself. But it is useless to discuss the question. I am, as you say, at a disadvantage. These little instruments of correction, these gentle aids to the power and honour of families, these slight favours that might so incommode you, are only to be obtained now by interest and importunity. They are sought by so many, and they are granted (comparatively) to so few! It used not to be so, but France in all such things is changed for the worst. Our not remote ancestors held the right of life and death over the surrounding vulgar. From this room, many such dogs have been taken out to be hanged ; in the next room (my bedroom), one fellow, to our knowledge, was poniarded on the spot for professing some insolent delicacy respecting his daughter — *his* daughter ! We have lost many privileges ; a new philosophy has become the mode ; and the assertion of our station, in these days, might (I do not go so far as to say would, but might) cause us real inconvenience. All very bad, very bad ! "

The Marquis took a gentle little pinch of snuff, and shook his head ; as elegantly despondent as he could becomingly be of a country still containing himself, that great means of regeneration.

" We have so asserted our station, both in the old time and in the modern time also," said the nephew gloomily, " that I believe our name to be more detested than any name in France."

" Let us hope so," said the uncle. " Detestation of the high is the involuntary homage of the low."

" There is not," pursued the nephew, in his former tone, " a face I can look at, in all this country round about us, which looks at me with any deference on it but the dark deference of fear and slavery."

" A compliment," said the Marquis, " to the grandeur of the family, merited by the manner in which the family has sustained its grandeur. Hah ! " And he took another gentle little pinch of snuff, and lightly crossed his legs.

But when his nephew. leaning an elbow on the table, covered his eyes thoughtfully and dejectedly with his hand, the fine mask looked at him sideways with a stronger concentration of keenness, closeness, and dislike, than was comportable with its wearer's assumption of indifference.

" Repression is the only lasting philosophy. The dark deference of fear and slavery, my friend," observed the Marquis, " will keep the dogs obedient to the whip as long as this roof," looking up to it, " shuts out the sky."

That might not be so long as the Marquis supposed. If a picture of the château as it was to be a very few years hence, and of fifty like it as they too were to be a very few years hence, could have been shown to him that night, he might have been at a loss to claim his own from the ghastly, fire-charred, plunder-wrecked ruins. As for the roof he vaunted, he might have found *that* shutting out the sky in a new way — to wit for ever, from the eyes of the bodies into which its lead was fired, out of the barrels of a hundred thousand muskets.

"Meanwhile," said the Marquis, "I will preserve the honour and repose of the family, if you will not. But you must be fatigued. Shall we terminate our conference for the night ? "

"A moment more."

"An hour, if you please."

"Sir," said the nephew, "we have done wrong, and are reaping the fruits of wrong."

"*We* have done wrong ? " repeated the Marquis, with an inquiring smile, and delicately pointing, first to his nephew, then to himself.

"Our family ; our honourable family, whose honour is of so much account to both of us, in such different ways. Even in my father's time, we did a world of wrong, injuring every human creature who came between us and our pleasure, whatever it was. Why need I speak of my father's time, when it is equally yours ? Can I separate my father's twin-brother, joint inheritor, and next successor, from himself ? "

"Death has done that ! " said the Marquis.

"And has left me," answered the nephew, "bound to a system that is frightful to me, responsible for it, but powerless in it ; seeking to execute the last request of my dear mother's lips, and obey the last look of my dear mother's eyes, which implored me to have mercy and to redress ; and tortured by seeking assistance and power in vain."

"Seeking them from me, my nephew," said the Marquis, touching him on the breast with his forefinger, — they were now standing by the hearth, — "you will for ever seek them in vain, be assured."

Every fine straight line in the clear whiteness of his face was cruelly, craftily, and closely compressed, while he stood looking quietly at his nephew, with his snuff-box in his hand. Once again he touched him on the breast, as though his finger were the fine point of a small sword, with which, in delicate finesse, he ran him through the body, and said, —

"My friend, I will die, perpetuating the system under which I have lived."

When he had said it, he took a culminating pinch of snuff, and put his box in his pocket.

"Better to be a rational creature," he added then, after ringing a small bell on the table, " and accept your natural destiny. But you are lost, Monsieur Charles, I see."

" This property and France are lost to me," said the nephew sadly ; " I renounce them."

" Are they both yours to renounce ?   France may be, but is the property ?   It is scarcely worth mentioning; but is it yet ? "

" I had no intention, in the words I used, to claim it yet. If it passed to me from you to-morrow — "

" Which I have the vanity to hope is not probable."

" — or twenty years hence — "

" You do me too much honour," said the Marquis ; " still, I prefer that supposition."

" — I would abandon it, and live otherwise and elsewhere. It is little to relinquish.   What is it but a wilderness of misery and ruin ! "

" Hah ! " said the Marquis, glancing round the luxurious room.

" To the eye it is fair enough, here ; but seen in its integrity, under the sky, and by the daylight, it is a crumbling tower of waste, mismanagement, extortion, debt, mortgage, oppression, hunger, nakedness, and suffering."

" Hah ! " said the Marquis again, in a well-satisfied manner.

" If it ever becomes mine, it shall be put into some hands better qualified to free it slowly (if such a thing is possible) from the weight that drags it down, so that the miserable people who cannot leave it, and who have been long wrung to the last point of endurance, may, in another generation, suffer less ; but it is not for me.   There is a curse on it, and on all this land."

" And you ? " said the uncle.   " Forgive my curiosity; do you, under your new philosophy, graciously intend to live ? "

" I must do, to live, what others of my countrymen, even with nobility at their backs, may have to do some day — work."

" In England, for example ? "

" Yes.   The family honour, sir, is safe for me in this country. The family name can suffer from me in no other, for I bear it in no other."

The ringing of the bell had caused the adjoining bed-chamber to be lighted.   It now shone brightly, through the door of communication.   The Marquis looked that way, and listened for the retreating step of his valet.

"England is very attractive to you, seeing how indifferently you have prospered there," he observed then, turning his calm face to his nephew with a smile.

"I have already said, that for my prospering there, I am sensible I may be indebted to you, sir. For the rest, it is my Refuge."

"They say, those boastful English, that it is the Refuge of many. You know a compatriot who has found a Refuge there? A doctor?"

"Yes."

"With a daughter?"

"Yes."

"Yes," said the Marquis. "You are fatigued. Good night!"

As he bent his head in his most courtly manner, there was a secrecy in his smiling face, and he conveyed an air of mystery to those words, which struck the eyes and ears of his nephew forcibly. At the same time, the thin straight lines of the setting of the eyes, and the thin straight lips, and the markings in the nose, curved with a sarcasm that looked handsomely diabolic.

"Yes," repeated the Marquis. "A doctor with a daughter. Yes. So commences the new philosophy! You are fatigued. Good night!"

It would have been of as much avail to interrogate any stone face outside the château as to interrogate that face of his. The nephew looked at him, in vain, in passing on to the door.

"Good night!" said the uncle. "I look to the pleasure of seeing you again in the morning. Good repose! Light Monsieur my nephew to his chamber there! — And burn Monsieur my nephew in his bed, if you will," he added to himself, before he rang his little bell again, and summoned his valet to his own bedroom.

The valet come and gone, Monsieur the Marquis walked to and fro in his loose chamber-robe, to prepare himself gently for sleep, that hot still night. Rustling about the room, his softly slippered feet making no noise on the floor, he moved like a refined tiger — looked like some enchanted marquis of the impenitently wicked sort, in story, whose periodical change into tiger form was either just going off, or just coming on.

He moved from end to end of his voluptuous bedroom, looking again at the scraps of the day's journey that came unbidden into his mind : the slow toil up the hill at sunset, the setting sun, the descent, the mill, the prison on the crag, the little village in the hollow, the peasants at the fountain, and the mender of roads with his blue cap pointing out the chain under the carriage. That fountain suggested the Paris fountain, the little bundle lying on the step, the women bending over it, and the tall man with his arms up, crying, " Dead ! "

" I am cool now," said Monsieur the Marquis, " and may go to bed."

So, leaving only one light burning on the large hearth, he let his thin gauze curtains fall around him, and heard the night break its silence with a long sigh as he composed himself to sleep.

The stone faces on the outer walls stared blindly at the black night for three heavy hours; for three heavy hours, the horses in the stables rattled at their racks, the dogs barked, and the owl made a noise with very little resemblance in it to the noise conventionally assigned to the owl by men-poets. But it is the obstinate custom of such creatures hardly ever to say what is set down for them.

For three heavy hours, the stone faces of the château, lion and human, stared blindly at the night. Dead darkness lay on all the landscape, dead darkness added its own hush to the hushing dust on all the roads. The burial-place had got to the pass that its little heaps of poor grass were undistinguishable from one another ; the figure on the Cross might have come down, for anything that could be seen of it. In the village, taxers and taxed were fast asleep. Dreaming, perhaps, of banquets, as the starved usually do, and of ease and rest, as the driven slave and the yoked ox may, its lean inhabitants slept soundly, and were fed and freed.

The fountain in the village flowed unseen and unheard, and the fountain at the château dropped unseen and unheard — both melting away, like the minutes that were falling from the spring of Time — through three dark hours. Then, the grey water of both began to be ghostly in the light, and the eyes of the stone faces of the château were opened.

Lighter and lighter, until at last the sun touched the tops of the still trees, and poured its radiance over the hill. In the glow, the water of the château fountain seemed to turn to blood, and the stone faces crimsoned. The carol of the birds was loud and high, and, on the weather-beaten sill of the great.window of the bed-chamber of Monsieur the Marquis, one little bird sang its sweetest song with all its might.   At this, the nearest stone face seemed to stare amazed, and, with open mouth and dropped under-jaw, looked awe-stricken.

Now, the sun was full up, and movement began in the village.   Casement windows opened, crazy doors were unbarred, and people came forth shivering — chilled, as yet, by the new sweet air.   Then began the rarely lightened toil of the day among the village population.   Some, to the fountain ; some, to the fields ; men and women here, to dig and delve ; men and women there, to see to the poor live-stock, and lead the bony cows out, to such pasture as could be found by the roadside.   In the church and at the Cross, a kneeling figure or two ; attendant on the latter prayers, the led cow, trying for a break-fast among the weeds at its foot.

The château awoke later, as became its quality, but awoke gradually and surely.   First, the lonely boar-spears and knives of the chase had been reddened as of old ; then, had gleamed trenchant in the morning sunshine ; now, doors and windows were thrown open, horses in their stables looked round over their shoulders at the light and freshness pouring in at doorways, leaves sparkled and rustled at iron-grated windows, dogs pulled hard at their chains, and reared impatiently to be loosed.

All these trivial incidents belonged to the routine of life, and the return of morning.   Surely, not so the ringing of the great bell of the château, nor the running up and down the stairs, nor the hurried figures on the terrace, nor the booting and tramping here and there and everywhere, nor the quick saddling of horses and riding away ?

What winds conveyed this hurry to the grizzled mender of roads, already at work on the hilltop beyond the village, with his day's dinner (not much to carry) lying in a bundle that it was worth no crow's while to peck at, on a heap of stones ? Had the birds, carrying some grains of it to a distance, dropped one over him as they sow chance seeds ?   Whether or no, the mender of roads ran, on the sultry morning, as if for his life, down the hill, knee-high in dust, and never stopped till he got to the fountain.

All the people of the village were at the fountain, standing about in their depressed manner, and whispering low, but showing no other emotions than grim curiosity and surprise. The led cows, hastily brought in and tethered to anything that would hold them, were looking stupidly on, or lying down chewing the cud of nothing particularly repaying their trouble, which they had picked up in their interrupted saunter. Some of the people of the château, and some of those of the posting-house, and all the taxing authorities, were armed more or less, and were crowded on the other side of the little street in a purposeless way, that was highly fraught with nothing. Already, the mender of roads had penetrated into the midst of a group of fifty particular friends, and was smiting himself in the breast with his blue cap. What did all this portend, and what portended the swift hoisting-up of Monsieur Gabelle behind a servant on horseback, and the conveying away of the said Gabelle (double-laden though the horse was), at a gallop, like a new version of the German ballad of Leonora ?

It portended that there was one stone face too many, up at the château.

The Gorgon had surveyed the building again in the night, and had added the one stone face wanting ; the stone face for which it had waited through about two hundred years.

It lay back on the pillow of Monsieur the Marquis. It was like a fine mask, suddenly startled, made angry, and petrified. Driven home into the heart of the stone figure attached to it was a knife. Round its hilt was a frill of paper, on which was scrawled : —

" *Drive him fast to his tomb. This, from* JACQUES."

CHAPTER X

TWO PROMISES

MORE months, to the number of twelve, had come and gone, and Mr. Charles Darnay was established in England as a higher teacher of the French language who was conversant with French literature. In this age, he would have been a Professor; in that age, he was a Tutor. He read with young men who could find any leisure and interest for the study of a living tongue spoken all over the world, and he cultivated a taste for its stores of knowledge and fancy. He could write of them, besides, in sound English, and render them into sound English. Such masters were not at that time easily found; Princes that had been, and Kings that were to be, were not yet of the Teacher class, and no ruined nobility had dropped out of Tellson's ledgers, to turn cooks and carpenters. As a tutor, whose attainments made the student's way unusually pleasant and profitable, and as an elegant translator who brought something to his work besides mere dictionary knowledge, young Mr. Darnay soon became known and encouraged. He was well acquainted, moreover, with the circumstances of his country, and those were of ever growing interest. So, with great perseverance and untiring industry, he prospered.

In London, he had expected neither to walk on pavements of gold, nor to lie on beds of roses; if he had had any such exalted expectation, he would not have prospered. He had expected labour, and he found it, and did it, and made the best of it. In this, his prosperity consisted.

A certain portion of his time was passed at Cambridge, where he read with undergraduates as a sort of tolerated smuggler who drove a contraband trade in European languages, instead of conveying Greek and Latin through the Custom House. The rest of his time he passed in London.

Now, from the days when it was always summer in Eden to these days when it is mostly winter in fallen latitudes, the

world of a man has invariably gone one way — Charles Darnay's
way — the way of the love of a woman.

He had loved Lucie Manette from the hour of his danger.
He had never heard a sound so sweet and dear as the sound
of her compassionate voice; he had never seen a face so tenderly beautiful as hers when it was confronted with his own on
the edge of the grave that had been dug for him.   But he had
not yet spoken to her on the subject; the assassination at the
deserted château far away beyond the heaving water and the
long, long, dusty roads — the solid stone château which had
itself become the mere mist of a dream — had been done a year,
and he had never yet, by so much as a single spoken word, dis-
closed to her the state of his heart.

That he had his reasons for this, he knew full well.   It was
again a summer day when, lately arrived in London from his
college occupation, he turned into the quiet corner in Soho,
bent on seeking an opportunity of opening his mind to Doctor
Manette.   It was the close of the summer day, and he knew
Lucie to be out with Miss Pross.

He found the doctor reading in his armchair at a window.
The energy which had at once supported him under his old
sufferings and aggravated their sharpness had been gradually
restored to him.   He was now a very energetic man indeed,
with great firmness of purpose, strength of resolution, and
vigour of action.   In his recovered energy he was sometimes
a little fitful and sudden, as he had at first been in the exercise
of his other recovered faculties; but this had never been
frequently observable, and had grown more and more rare.

He studied much, slept little, sustained a great deal of fatigue
with ease, and was equably cheerful.   To him, now entered
Charles Darnay, at sight of whom he laid aside his book and
held out his hand.

"Charles Darnay! I rejoice to see you. We have been
counting on your return these three or four days past. Mr.
Stryver and Sydney Carton were both here yesterday, and both
made you out to be more than due."

"I am obliged to them for their interest in the matter," he
answered, a little coldly as to them, though very warmly as to
the doctor.   "Miss Manette — "

"Is well," said the doctor, as he stopped short, "and your
return will delight us all. She has gone out on some household matters, but will soon be home."

"Doctor Manette, I knew she was from home. I took the opportunity of her being from home, to beg to speak to you."

There was a blank silence.

"Yes?" said the doctor, with evident constraint. "Bring your chair here, and speak on."

He complied as to the chair, but appeared to find the speaking on less easy.

"I have had the happiness, Doctor Manette, of being so intimate here," so he at length began, "for some year and a half, that I hope the topic on which I am about to touch may not —"

He was stayed by the doctor's putting out his hand to stop him. When he had kept it so a little while, he said, drawing it back: —

"Is Lucie the topic?"

"She is."

"It is hard for me to speak of her, at any time. It is very hard for me to hear her spoken of in that tone of yours, Charles Darnay."

"It is a tone of fervent admiration, true homage, and deep love, Doctor Manette!" he said deferentially.

There was another blank silence before her father rejoined: —

"I believe it. I do you justice; I believe it."

His constraint was so manifest, and it was so manifest, too, that it originated in an unwillingness to approach the subject, that Charles Darnay hesitated.

"Shall I go on, sir?"

Another blank.

"Yes, go on."

"You anticipate what I would say, though you cannot know how earnestly I say it, how earnestly I feel it, without knowing my secret heart, and the hopes and fears and anxieties with which it has long been laden. Dear Doctor Manette, I love your daughter fondly, dearly, disinterestedly, devotedly. If ever there were love in the world, I love her. You have loved yourself; let your old love speak for me!"

The doctor sat with his face turned away, and his eyes bent on the ground. At the last words, he stretched out his hand again, hurriedly, and cried: —

"Not that, sir! Let that be! I adjure you, do not recall that!"

His cry was so like a cry of actual pain, that it rang in Charles Darnay's ears long after he had ceased. He motioned with the hand he had extended, and it seemed to be an appeal to Darnay to pause. The latter so received it, and remained silent.

"I ask your pardon," said the doctor, in a subdued tone, after some moments. "I do not doubt your loving Lucie; you may be satisfied of it."

He turned towards him in his chair, but did not look at him, or raise his eyes. His chin dropped upon his hand, and his white hair overshadowed his face.

"Have you spoken to Lucie?"

"No."

"Nor written?"

"Never."

"It would be ungenerous to affect not to know that your self-denial is to be referred to your consideration for her father. Her father thanks you."

He offered his hand; but his eyes did not go with it.

"I know," said Darnay respectfully, — "how can I fail to know, Doctor Manette, I who have seen you together from day to day, — that between you and Miss Manette there is an affection so unusual, so touching, so belonging to the circumstances in which it has been nurtured, that it can have few parallels, even in the tenderness between a father and child. I know, Doctor Manette, — how can I fail to know, — that, mingled with the affection and duty of a daughter who has become a woman, there is, in her heart towards you, all the love and reliance of infancy itself. I know that, as in her childhood she had no parent, so she is now devoted to you with all the constancy and fervour of her present years and character, united to the trustfulness and attachment of the early days in which you were lost to her. I know perfectly well that if you had been restored to her from the world beyond this life, you could hardly be invested, in her sight, with a more sacred character than that in which you are always with her. I know that when she is clinging to you, the hands of baby, girl, and woman, all in one, are round your neck. I know that in loving you she sees and loves her mother at her own age, sees and loves you at my age, loves her mother broken-hearted, loves you through your dreadful trial and in your blessed restoration. I have known this, night and day, since I have known you in your home."

Her father sat silent, with his face bent down. His breathing was a little quickened; but he repressed all other signs of agitation.

"Dear Doctor Manette, always knowing this, always seeing her and you with this hallowed light about you, I have forborne, and forborne, as long as it was in the nature of man to do it. I have felt, and do even now feel, that to bring my love — even mine — between you is to touch your history with something not quite so good as itself. But I love her. Heaven is my witness that I love her!"

"I believe it," answered her father mournfully. "I have thought so, before now. I believe it."

"But do not believe," said Darnay, upon whose ear the mournful voice struck with a reproachful sound, "that if my fortune were so cast, as that, being one day so happy as to make her my wife, I must at any time put any separation between her and you, I could or would breathe a word of what I now say. Besides that I should know it to be hopeless, I should know it to be a baseness. If I had any such possibility, even at a remote distance of years, harboured in my thoughts and hidden in my heart — if it ever had been there — if it ever could be there, — I could not now touch this honoured hand."

He laid his own upon it as he spoke.

"No, dear Doctor Manette. Like you, a voluntary exile from France; like you, driven from it by its distractions, oppressions, and miseries; like you, striving to live away from it by my own exertions, and trusting in a happier future; I look only to sharing your fortunes, sharing your life and home, and being faithful to you to the death. Not to divide with Lucie her privilege as your child, companion, and friend; but to come in aid of it, and bind her closer to you, if such a thing can be."

His touch still lingered on her father's hand. Answering the touch for a moment, but not coldly, her father rested his hands upon the arms of his chair, and looked up for the first time since the beginning of the conference. A struggle was evidently in his face — a struggle with that occasional look which had a tendency in it to dark doubt and dread.

"You speak so feelingly and so manfully, Charles Darnay, that I thank you with all my heart, and will open all my heart — or nearly so. Have you any reason to believe that Lucie loves you?"

"None. As yet, none."

"Is it the immediate object of this confidence, that you may at once ascertain that, with my knowledge ? "

"Not even so. I might not have the hopefulness to do it for weeks ; I might (mistaken or not mistaken) have that hopefulness to-morrow."

"Do you seek any guidance from me ? "

"I ask none, sir. But I have thought it possible that you might have it in your power, if you should deem it right, to give me some."

"Do you seek any promise from me ? "

"I do seek that."

"What is it ? "

"I well understand that, without you, I could have no hope. I well understand that even if Miss Manette held me at this moment in her innocent heart, — do not think I have the presumption to assume so much, — I could retain no place in it against her love for her father."

"If that be so, do you see what, on the other hand, is involved in it ? "

"I understand equally well, that a word from her father in any suitor's favour would outweigh herself and all the world. For which reason, Doctor Manette," said Darnay, modestly but firmly, "I would not ask that word, to save my life."

"I am sure of it. Charles Darnay, mysteries arise out of close love, as well as out of wide division; in the former case, they are subtle and delicate, and difficult to penetrate. My daughter Lucie is, in this one respect, such a mystery to me; I can make no guess at the state of her heart."

"May I ask, sir, if you think she is" — As he hesitated, her father supplied the rest.

"Is sought by any other suitor ? "

"It is what I meant to say."

Her father considered a little before he answered : —

"You have seen Mr. Carton here, yourself. Mr. Stryver is here too, occasionally. If it be at all, it can only be by one of these."

"Or both," said Darnay.

"I had not thought of both; I should not think either, likely. You want a promise from me. Tell me what it is."

"It is, that if Miss Manette should bring to you at any time, on her own part, such a confidence as I have ventured to lay before you, you will bear testimony to what I have said, and to your belief in it. I hope you may be able to think so well of me as to urge no influence against me. I say nothing more of my stake in this; this is what I ask. The condition on which I ask it, and which you have an undoubted right to require, I will observe immediately."

"I give the promise," said the doctor, "without any condition. I believe your object to be, purely and truthfully, as you have stated it. I believe your intention is to perpetuate, and not to weaken, the ties between me and my other and far dearer self. If she should ever tell me that you are essential to her perfect happiness, I will give her to you. If there were — Charles Darnay, if there were — "

The young man had taken his hand gratefully; their hands were joined as the doctor spoke.

" — any fancies, any reasons, any apprehensions, anything whatsoever, new or old, against the man she really loved, — the direct responsibility thereof not lying on his head, — they should all be obliterated for her sake. She is everything to me; more to me than suffering, more to me than wrong, more to me — Well! This is idle talk."

So strange was the way in which he faded into silence, and so strange his fixed look when he had ceased to speak, that Darnay felt his own hand turn cold in the hand that slowly released and dropped it.

"You said something to me," said Doctor Manette, breaking into a smile. "What was it you said to me?"

He was at a loss how to answer, until he remembered having spoken of a condition. Relieved as his mind reverted to that, he answered: —

"Your confidence in me ought to be returned with full confidence on my part. My present name, though but slightly changed from my mother's, is not, as you will remember, my own. I wish to tell you what that is, and why I am in England."

"Stop!" said the Doctor of Beauvais.

"I wish it, that I may the better deserve your confidence, and have no secret from you."

"Stop!"

For an instant, the doctor even had his two hands at his ears;

for another instant, even had his two hands laid on Darnay's lips.

"Tell me when I ask you, not now. If your suit should prosper, if Lucie should love you, you shall tell me on your marriage morning. Do you promise ? "

"Willingly."

"Give me your hand. She will be home directly, and it is better she should not see us together to-night. Go ! God bless you ! "

It was dark when Charles Darnay left him, and it was an hour later and darker when Lucie came home ; she hurried into the room alone — for Miss Pross had gone straight up stairs — and was surprised to find his reading-chair empty.

"My father ! " she called to him. "Father dear ! "

Nothing was said in answer, but she heard a low hammering sound in his bedroom. Passing lightly across the intermediate room, she looked in at his door and came running back frightened, crying to herself, with her blood all chilled, "What shall I do ! What shall I do ! "

Her uncertainty lasted but a moment ; she hurried back, and tapped at his door, and softly called to him. The noise ceased at the sound of her voice, and he presently came out to her, and they walked up and down together for a long time.

She came down from her bed, to look at him in his sleep that night. He slept heavily, and his tray of shoemaking tools and his old unfinished work were all as usual.

CHAPTER XI

A COMPANION PICTURE

"Sydney," said Mr. Stryver, on that self-same night, or morning, to his jackal, "mix another bowl of punch; I have something to say to you."

Sydney had been working double tides that night, and the night before, and the night before that, and a good many nights in succession, making a grand clearance among Mr. Stryver's papers before the setting in of the long vacation. The clearance was effected at last; the Stryver arrears were handsomely fetched up; everything was got rid of until November should come with its fogs atmospheric and fogs legal, and bring grist to the mill again.

Sydney was none the livelier and none the soberer for so much application. It had taken a deal of extra wet-towelling to pull him through the night; a correspondingly extra quantity of wine had preceded the towelling; and he was in a very damaged condition, as he now pulled his turban off and threw it into the basin in which he had steeped it at intervals for the last six hours.

"Are you mixing that other bowl of punch?" said Stryver the portly, with his hands in his waistband, glancing round from the sofa where he lay on his back.

"I am."

"Now, look here! I am going to tell you something that will rather surprise you, and that perhaps will make you think me not quite as shrewd as you usually do think me. I intend to marry."

"*Do* you?"

"Yes. And not for money. What do you say now?"

"I don't feel disposed to say much. Who is she?"

"Guess."

"Do I know her?"

"Guess."

" I am not going to guess, at five o'clock in the morning with my brains frying and sputtering in my head. If you want me to guess, you must ask me to dinner."

" Well then, I'll tell you," said Stryver, coming slowly into a sitting posture. " Sydney, I rather despair of making myself intelligible to you, because you are such an insensible dog."

" And you," returned Sydney, busy concocting the punch, " are such a sensitive and poetical spirit."

" Come !" rejoined Stryver, laughing boastfully, " though I don't prefer any claim to being the soul of Romance (for I hope I know better), still, I am a tenderer sort of fellow than *you.*"

" You are a luckier, if you mean that."

" I don't mean that. I mean, I am a man of more — more — "

" Say gallantry, while you are about it," suggested Carton.

" Well! I'll say gallantry. My meaning is, that I am a man," said Stryver, inflating himself at his friend as he made the punch, " who cares more to be agreeable, who takes more pains to be agreeable, who knows better how to be agreeable, in a woman's society, than you do."

" Go on," said Sydney Carton.

" No; but before I go on," said Stryver, shaking his head in his bullying way, " I'll have this out with you. You have been at Doctor Manette's house as much as I have, or more than I have. Why, I have been ashamed of your moroseness there ! Your manners have been of that silent and sullen and hang-dog kind, that, upon my life and soul, I have been ashamed of you, Sydney ! "

" It should be very beneficial to a man in your practice at the bar, to be ashamed of anything," returned Sydney; " you ought to be much obliged to me."

" You shall not get off in that way," rejoined Stryver, shouldering the rejoinder at him; " no, Sydney, it's my duty to tell you — and I tell you to your face to do you good — that you are a de-vilish ill-conditioned fellow in that sort of society. You are a disagreeable fellow."

Sydney drank a bumper of the punch he had made, and laughed.

" Look at me !" said Stryver, squaring himself; " I have less need to make myself agreeable than you have, being more independent in circumstances. Why do I do it ? "

" I never saw you do it yet," muttered Carton.

" I do it because it 's politic ; I do it on principle. And look at me ! I get on."

" You don't get on with your account of your matrimonial intentions," answered Carton, with a careless air ; " I wish you would keep to that. As to me — will you never understand that I am incorrigible ? "

He asked the question with some appearance of scorn.

" You have no business to be incorrigible," was his friend's answer, delivered in no very soothing tone.

" I have no business to be, at all, that I know of," said Sydney Carton. " Who is the lady ? "

" Now, don't let my announcement of the name make you uncomfortable, Sydney," said Mr. Stryver, preparing him with ostentatious friendliness for the disclosure he was about to make, " because I know you don't mean half you say ; and if you meant it all, it would be of no importance. I make this little preface, because you once mentioned the young lady to me in slighting terms."

" I did ? "

" Certainly ; and in these chambers."

Sydney Carton looked at his punch and looked at his complacent friend ; drank his punch and looked at his complacent friend.

" You made mention of the young lady as a golden-haired doll. The young lady is Miss Manette. If you had been a fellow of any sensitiveness or delicacy of feeling in that kind of way, Sydney, I might have been a little resentful of your employing such a designation ; but you are not. You want that sense altogether ; therefore, I am no more annoyed when I think of the expression, than I should be annoyed by a man's opinion of a picture of mine, who had no eye for pictures ; or of a piece of music of mine, who had no ear for music."

Sydney Carton drank the punch at a great rate ; drank it by bumpers, looking at his friend.

" Now you know all about it, Syd," said Mr. Stryver. " I don't care about fortune ; she is a charming creature, and I have made up my mind to please myself : on the whole, I think I can afford to please myself. She will have in me a man already pretty well off, and a rapidly rising man, and a man of some distinction ; it is a piece of good fortune for her, but she is worthy of good fortune. Are you astonished ? "

Carton, still drinking the punch, rejoined, "Why should I be astonished?"

"You approve?"

Carton, still drinking the punch, rejoined, "Why should I not approve?"

"Well!" said his friend Stryver, "you take it more easily than I fancied you would, and are less mercenary on my behalf than I thought you would be; though, to be sure, you know well enough by this time that your ancient chum is a man of a pretty strong will. Yes, Sydney, I have had enough of this style of life, with no other as a change from it; I feel that it is a pleasant thing for a man to have a home when he feels inclined to go to it (when he does n't, he can stay away), and I feel that Miss Manette will tell well in any station, and will always do me credit. So I have made up my mind. And now, Sydney, old boy, I want to say a word to *you* about *your* prospects. You are in a bad way, you know; you really are in a bad way. You don't know the value of money, you live hard, you'll knock up one of these days, and be ill and poor; you really ought to think about a nurse."

The prosperous patronage with which he said it made him look twice as big as he was, and four times as offensive.

"Now, let me recommend you," pursued Stryver, "to look it in the face. I have looked it in the face, in my different way; look it in the face, you, in your different way. Marry. Provide somebody to take care of you. Never mind your having no enjoyment of women's society, nor understanding of it, nor tact for it. Find out somebody. Find out some respectable woman with a little property, — somebody in the landlady way, or lodging-letting way, — and marry her, against a rainy day. That's the kind of thing for *you*. Now think of it, Sydney."

"I'll think of it," said Sydney.

CHAPTER XII

THE FELLOW OF DELICACY

MR. STRYVER, having made up his mind to that magnanimous bestowal of good fortune on the doctor's daughter, resolved to make her happiness known to her before he left town for the Long Vacation. After some mental debating of the point, he came to the conclusion that it would be as well to get all the preliminaries done with, and they could then arrange at their leisure whether he should give her his hand a week or two before Michaelmas Term, or in the little Christmas vacation between it and Hilary.

As to the strength of his case, he had not a doubt about it, but clearly saw his way to the verdict. Argued with the jury on substantial worldly grounds — the only grounds ever worth taking into account — it was a plain case, and had not a weak spot in it. He called himself for the plaintiff, there was no getting over his evidence, the counsel for the defendant threw up his brief, and the jury did not even turn to consider. After trying it, Stryver C. J. was satisfied that no plainer case could be.

Accordingly, Mr. Stryver inaugurated the Long Vacation with a formal proposal to take Miss Manette to Vauxhall Gardens ; that failing, to Ranelagh ; that unaccountably failing too, it behoved him to present himself in Soho, and there declare his noble mind.

Towards Soho, therefore, Mr. Stryver shouldered his way from the Temple, while the bloom of the Long Vacation's infancy was still upon it. Anybody who had seen him projecting himself into Soho while he was yet on Saint Dunstan's side of Temple Bar, bursting in his full-blown way along the pavement, to the jostlement of all weaker people, might have seen how safe and strong he was.

His way taking him past Tellson's, and he both banking at Tellson's and knowing Mr. Lorry as the intimate friend of

the Manettes, it entered Mr. Stryver's mind to enter the bank,
and reveal to Mr. Lorry the brightness of the Soho horizon. So,
he pushed open the door with the weak rattle in its throat,
stumbled down the two steps, got past the two ancient cashiers,
and shouldered himself into the musty back closet where Mr.
Lorry sat at great books ruled for figures, with perpendicular
iron bars to his window as if that were ruled for figures too, and
everything under the clouds were a sum.

"Halloa!" said Mr. Stryver. "How do you do? I hope
you are well!"

It was Stryver's grand peculiarity that he always seemed too
big for any place, or space. He was so much too big for Tellson's, that old clerks in distant corners looked up with looks
of remonstrance, as though he squeezed them against the wall.
The House itself, magnificently reading the paper quite in the
far-off perspective, lowered displeased, as if the Stryver head
had been butted into its responsible waistcoat.

The discreet Mr. Lorry said, in a sample tone of the voice
he would recommend under the circumstances, "How do you
do, Mr. Stryver? How do you do, sir?" and shook hands.
There was a peculiarity in his manner of shaking hands, always
to be seen in any clerk at Tellson's who shook hands with a
customer when the House pervaded the air. He shook in a
self-abnegating way, as one who shook for Tellson and Co.

"Can I do anything for you, Mr. Stryver?" asked Mr.
Lorry, in his business character.

"Why, no, thank you; this is a private visit to yourself,
Mr. Lorry; I have come for a private word."

"Oh, indeed!" said Mr. Lorry, bending down his ear, while
his eye strayed to the House afar off.

"I am going," said Mr. Stryver, leaning his arms confi-
dentially on the desk, — whereupon, although it was a large
double one, there appeared to be not half desk enough for him, —
"I am going to make an offer of myself in marriage to your
agreeable little friend Miss Manette, Mr. Lorry."

"Oh, dear me!" cried Mr. Lorry, rubbing his chin, and
looking at his visitor dubiously.

"Oh, dear me, sir?" repeated Stryver, drawing back. "Oh,
dear you, sir? What may your meaning be, Mr. Lorry?"

"My meaning," answered the man of business, "is, of
course, friendly and appreciative, and that it does you the

greatest credit, and — in short, my meaning is everything you could desire. But — really, you know, Mr. Stryver "— Mr. Lorry paused, and shook his head at him in the oddest manner, as if he were compelled against his will to add, internally, "you know there really is so much too much of you ! "

"Well ! " said Stryver, slapping the desk with his contentious hand, opening his eyes wider, and taking a long breath, "if I understand you, Mr. Lorry, I'll be hanged ! "

Mr. Lorry adjusted his little wig at both ears as a means towards that end, and bit the feather of a pen.

" D—n it all, sir ! " said Stryver, staring at him, "am I not eligible ? "

"Oh, dear, yes ! Yes. Oh, yes, you're eligible ! " said Mr. Lorry. " If you say eligible, you are eligible."

" Am I not prosperous ? " asked Stryver.

"Oh ! if you come to prosperous, you are prosperous," said Mr. Lorry.

" And advancing ? "

" If you come to advancing, you know," said Mr. Lorry, delighted to be able to make another admission, " nobody can doubt that."

" Then what on earth is your meaning, Mr. Lorry ? " demanded Stryver, perceptibly crestfallen.

"Well ! I— Were you going there now ? " asked Mr. Lorry.

" Straight ! " said Stryver, with a plump of his fist on the desk.

"Then I think I would n't, if I was you."

" Why ? " said Stryver. " Now, I'll put you in a corner," forensically shaking a forefinger at him. " You are a man of business and bound to have a reason. State your reason. Why would n't you go ? "

" Because," said Mr. Lorry, " I would n't go on such an object without having some cause to believe that I should succeed."

" D—n ME ! " cried Stryver, " but this beats everything."

Mr. Lorry glanced at the distant House, and glanced at the angry Stryver.

" Here's a man of business — a man of years — a man of experience — *in* a Bank," said Stryver; " and having summed up three leading reasons for complete success, he says there's no reason at all! Says it with his head on!" Mr. Stryver remarked upon the peculiarity as if it would have been infinitely less remarkable if he had said it with his head off.

"When I speak of success, I speak of success with the young lady; and when I speak of causes and reasons to make success probable, I speak of causes and reasons that will tell as such with the young lady. The young lady, my good sir," said Mr. Lorry, mildly tapping the Stryver arm, — "the young lady. The young lady goes before all."

"Then you mean to tell me, Mr. Lorry," said Stryver, squaring his elbows, "that it is your deliberate opinion that the young lady at present in question is a mincing Fool?"

"Not exactly so. I mean to tell you, Mr. Stryver," said Mr. Lorry, reddening, "that I will hear no disrespectful word of that young lady from any lips; and that if I knew any man — which I hope I do not — whose taste was so coarse, and whose temper was so overbearing, that he could not restrain himself from speaking disrespectfully of that young lady at this desk, not even Tellson's should prevent my giving him a piece of my mind."

The necessity of being angry in a suppressed tone had put Mr. Stryver's blood-vessels into a dangerous state when it was his turn to be angry; Mr. Lorry's veins, methodical as their courses could usually be, were in no better state now it was his turn.

"That is what I mean to tell you, sir," said Mr. Lorry. "Pray let there be no mistake about it."

Mr. Stryver sucked the end of a ruler for a little while, and then stood hitting a tune out of his teeth with it, which probably gave him the toothache. He broke the awkward silence by saying : —

"This is something new to me, Mr. Lorry. You deliberately advise me not to go up to Soho and offer myself — myself, Stryver of the King's Bench bar?"

"Do you ask me for my advice, Mr. Stryver?"

"Yes, I do."

"Very good. Then I give it, and you have repeated it correctly."

"And all I can say of it is," laughed Stryver with a vexed laugh, "that this — ha, ha! — beats everything past, present, and to come."

" Now understand me," pursued Mr. Lorry. " As a man of business, I am not justified in saying anything about this matter, for, as a man of business, I know nothing of it. But, as an old fellow, who has carried Miss Manette in his arms who is the trusted friend of Miss Manette and of her father too, and who has a great affection for them both, I have spoken. The confidence is not of my seeking, recollect. Now, you think I may not be right ? "

" Not I ! " said Stryver, whistling. " I can't undertake to find third parties in common sense ; I can only find it for myself. I suppose sense in certain quarters ; you suppose mincing bread-and-butter nonsense. It 's new to me, but you are right, I dare say."

" What I suppose, Mr. Stryver, I claim to characterise for myself. And understand me, sir," said Mr. Lorry, quickly flushing again. " I will not — not even at Tellson's — have it characterised for me by any gentleman breathing."

" There ! I beg your pardon ! " said Stryver.

" Granted. Thank you. Well, Mr. Stryver, I was about to say : it might be painful to you to find yourself mistaken, it might be painful to Doctor Manette to have the task of being explicit with you, it might be very painful to Miss Manette to have the task of being explicit with you. You know the terms upon which I have the honour and happiness to stand with the family. If you please, committing you in no way, representing you in no way, I will undertake to correct my advice by the exercise of a little new observation and judgment expressly brought to bear upon it. If you should then be dissatisfied with it, you can but test its soundness for yourself ; if, on the other hand, you should be satisfied with it, and it should be what it now is, it may spare all sides what is best spared. What do you say ? "

" How long would you keep me in town ? "

" Oh ! It is only a question of a few hours. I could go to Soho in the evening, and come to your chambers afterwards."

" Then I say yes," said Stryver ; " I won't go up there now, I am not so hot upon it as that comes to ; I say yes, and I shall expect you to look in to-night. Good morning."

Then Mr. Stryver turned and burst out of the Bank, causing such a concussion of air on his passage through, that to stand

up against it bowing behind the two counters required the
utmost remaining strength of the two ancient clerks. Those
venerable and feeble persons were always seen by the public
in the act of bowing, and were popularly believed, when they
had bowed a customer out, still to keep on bowing in the empty
office until they bowed another customer in.

The barrister was keen enough to divine that the banker would
not have gone so far in his expression of opinion on any less
solid ground than moral certainty. Unprepared as he was for
the large pill he had to swallow, he got it down. "And now,"
said Mr. Stryver, shaking his forensic forefinger at the Temple
in general, when it was down, "my way out of this is to put
you all in the wrong."

It was a bit of the art of an Old Bailey tactician, in which
he found great relief. "You shall not put me in the wrong,
young lady," said Mr. Stryver; "I'll do that for you."

Accordingly, when Mr. Lorry called that night as late as ten
o'clock, Mr. Stryver, among a quantity of books and papers
littered out for the purpose, seemed to have nothing less on his
mind than the subject of the morning. He even showed surprise when he saw Mr. Lorry, and was altogether in an absent
and preoccupied state.

"Well!" said that good-natured emissary, after a full half
hour of bootless attempts to bring him round to the question,
"I have been to Soho."

"To Soho?" repeated Mr. Stryver coldly. "Oh, to be
sure! What am I thinking of!"

"And I have no doubt," said Mr. Lorry, "that I was right
in the conversation we had. My opinion is confirmed, and I
reiterate my advice."

"I assure you," returned Mr. Stryver, in the friendliest way,
"that I am sorry for it on your account, and sorry for it on
the poor father's account. I know this must always be a sore
subject with the family; let us say no more about it."

"I don't understand you," said Mr. Lorry.

"I dare say not," rejoined Mr. Stryver, nodding his head in
a smoothing and final way; "no matter, no matter."

"But it does matter," Mr. Lorry urged.

"No, it does n't; I assure you it does n't. Having supposed
that there was sense where there is no sense, and a laudable
ambition where there is not a laudable ambition, I am well out

of my mistake, and no harm is done. Young women have committed similar follies often before, and have repented them in poverty and obscurity often before. In an unselfish aspect, I am sorry that the thing is dropped, because it would have been a bad thing for me in a worldly point of view; in a selfish aspect, I am glad that the thing has dropped, because it would have been a bad thing for me in a worldly point of view — it is hardly necessary to say I could have gained nothing by it. There is no harm at all done. I have not proposed to the young lady, and, between ourselves, I am by no means certain, on reflection, that I ever should have committed myself to that extent. Mr. Lorry, you cannot control the mincing vanities and giddinesses of empty-headed girls; you must not expect to do it, or you will always be disappointed. Now, pray say no more about it. I tell you, I regret it on account of others, but I am satisfied on my own account. And I am really very much obliged to you for allowing me to sound you, and for giving me your advice; you know the young lady better than I do; you were right, it never would have done."

Mr. Lorry was so taken aback, that he looked quite stupidly at Mr. Stryver shouldering him towards the door, with an appearance of showering generosity, forbearance, and good-will, on his erring head. " Make the best of it, my dear sir," said Stryver; "say no more about it; thank you again for allowing me to sound you; good night! "

Mr. Lorry was out in the night before he knew where he was. Mr. Stryver was lying back on his sofa, winking at his ceiling.

CHAPTER XIII

THE FELLOW OF NO DELICACY

If Sydney Carton ever shone anywhere, he certainly never shone in the house of Doctor Manette. He had been there often, during a whole year, and had always been the same moody and morose lounger there. When he cared to talk, he talked well; but the cloud of caring for nothing, which over-shadowed him with such a fatal darkness, was very rarely pierced by the light within him.

And yet he did care something for the streets that environed that house, and for the senseless stones that made their pavements. Many a night he vaguely and unhappily wandered there, when wine had brought no transitory gladness to him; many a dreary daybreak revealed his solitary figure lingering there, and still lingering there when the first beams of the sun brought into strong relief removed beauties of architecture in spires of churches and lofty buildings, as perhaps the quiet time brought some sense of better things, else forgotten and unattainable, into his mind. Of late, the neglected bed in the Temple court had known him more scantily than ever; and often when he had thrown himself upon it no longer than a few minutes, he had got up again, and haunted that neighbourhood.

On a day in August, when Mr. Stryver (after notifying to his jackal that "he had thought better of that marrying matter") had carried his delicacy into Devonshire, and when the sight and scent of flowers in the city streets had some waifs of goodness in them for the worst, of health for the sickliest, and of youth for the oldest, Sydney's feet still trod those stones. From being irresolute and purposeless, his feet became animated by an intention, and, in the working out of that intention, they took him to the doctor's door.

He was shown up stairs, and found Lucie at her work, alone. She had never been quite at her ease with him, and received him with some little embarrassment as he seated himself near

her table.   But looking up at his face in the interchange of the
first few common-places, she observed a change in it.

"I fear you are not well, Mr. Carton!"

"No. But the life I lead, Miss Manette, is not conducive to
health. What is to be expected of, or by, such profligates?"

"Is it not — forgive me; I have begun the question on my
lips — a pity to live no better life?"

"God knows it is a shame!"

"Then why not change it?"

Looking gently at him again, she was surprised and saddened
to see that there were tears in his eyes. There were tears in
his voice, too, as he answered: —

"It is too late for that. I shall never be better than I am.
I shall sink lower, and be worse."

He leaned an elbow on her table, and covered his eyes with
his hand. The table trembled in the silence that followed.

She had never seen him softened, and was much distressed.
He knew her to be so, without looking at her, and said: —

"Pray forgive me, Miss Manette. I break down before the
knowledge of what I want to say to you. Will you hear
me?"

"If it will do you any good. Mr. Carton, if it would make
you happier, it would make me very glad!"

"God bless you for your sweet compassion!"

He unshaded his face after a little while, and spoke steadily.

"Don't be afraid to hear me. Don't shrink from anything I
say. I am like one who died young. All my life might have
been."

"No, Mr. Carton. I am sure that the best part of it might
still be; I am sure that you might be much, much worthier of
yourself."

"Say of you, Miss Manette, and although I know better, —
although in the mystery of my own wretched heart I know better, — I shall never forget it!"

She was pale and trembling. He came to her relief with a
fixed despair of himself which made the interview unlike any
other that could have been holden.

"If it had been possible, Miss Manette, that you could have
returned the love of the man you see before you, — self-flung
away, wasted, drunken, poor creature of misuse as you know
him to be, — he would have been conscious this day and hour,

in spite of his happiness, that he would bring you to misery,
bring you to sorrow and repentance, blight you, disgrace you,
pull you down with him. I know very well that you can have
no tenderness for me; I ask for none; I am even thankful
that it cannot be."

"Without it, can I not save you, Mr. Carton? Can I not
recall you — forgive me again! — to a better course? Can I in
no way repay your confidence? I know this is a confidence,"
she modestly said, after a little hesitation, and in earnest tears,
"I know you would say this to no one else. Can I turn it to
no good account for yourself, Mr. Carton?"

He shook his head.

"To none. No, Miss Manette, to none. If you will hear
me through a very little more, all you can ever do for me is
done. I wish you to know that you have been the last dream
of my soul. In my degradation, I have not been so degraded
but that the sight of you with your father, and of this home,
made such a home by you, has stirred old shadows that I
thought had died out of me. Since I knew you, I have been
troubled by a remorse that I thought would never reproach me
again, and I have heard whispers from old voices impelling
me upward, that I thought were silent for ever. I have had
unformed ideas of striving afresh, beginning anew, shaking off
sloth and sensuality, and fighting out the abandoned fight. A
dream, all a dream, that ends in nothing, and leaves the sleeper
where he lay down, but I wish you to know that you in-
spired it."

"Will nothing of it remain? Oh, Mr. Carton, think again!
Try again!"

"No, Miss Manette; all through it, I have known myself
to be quite undeserving. And yet I have had the weakness,
and have still the weakness, to wish you to know with what a
sudden mastery you kindled me, heap of ashes that I am, into
fire — a fire, however, inseparable in its nature from myself,
quickening nothing, lighting nothing, doing no service, idly
burning away."

"Since it is my misfortune, Mr. Carton, to have made you
more unhappy than you were before you knew me — "

"Don't say that, Miss Manette, for you would have reclaimed
me, if anything could. You will not be the cause of my becoming worse."

"Since the state of your mind that you describe is, at all events, attributable to some influence of mine, — this is what I mean, if I can make it plain, — can I use no influence to serve you? Have I no power for good, with you, at all?"

"The utmost good that I am capable of now, Miss Manette, I have come here to realise. Let me carry through the rest of my misdirected life, the remembrance that I opened my heart to you, last of all the world; and that there was something left in me at this time which you could deplore and pity."

"Which I entreated you to believe, again and again, most fervently, with all my heart, was capable of better things, Mr. Carton!"

"Entreat me to believe it no more, Miss Manette. I have proved myself, and I know better. I distress you; I draw fast to an end. Will you let me believe, when I recall this day, that the last confidence of my life was reposed in your pure and innocent breast, and that it lies there alone, and will be shared by no one?"

"If that will be a consolation to you, yes."

"Not even by the dearest one ever to be known to you?"

"Mr. Carton," she answered, after an agitated pause, "the secret is yours, not mine; and I promise to respect it."

"Thank you. And again, God bless you."

He put her hand to his lips, and moved towards the door.

"Be under no apprehension, Miss Manette, of my ever resuming this conversation by so much as a passing word. I will never refer to it again. If I were dead, that could not be surer than it is henceforth. In the hour of my death, I shall hold sacred the one good remembrance — and shall thank and bless you for it — that my last avowal of myself was made to you, and that my name, and faults, and miseries, were gently carried in your heart. May it otherwise be light and happy!"

He was so unlike what he had ever shown himself to be, and it was so sad to think how much he had thrown away, and how much he every day kept down and perverted, that Lucie Manette wept mournfully for him as he stood looking back at her.

"Be comforted!" he said, "I am not worth such feeling, Miss Manette. An hour or two hence, and the low companions and low habits that I scorn, but yield to, will render me less worth such tears as those, than any wretch who creeps along the streets. Be comforted! But within myself, I shall always be, towards you, what I am now, though outwardly I shall be what you have heretofore seen me. The last supplication but one I make to you, is, that you will believe this of me."

"I will, Mr. Carton."

"My last supplication of all, is this; and with it, I will relieve you of a visitor with whom I well know you have nothing in unison, and between whom and you there is an impassable space. It is useless to say it, I know, but it rises out of my soul. For you, and for any dear to you, I would do anything. If my career were of that better kind that there was any opportunity or capacity of sacrifice in it, I would embrace any sacrifice for you and for those dear to you. Try to hold me in your mind, at some quiet times, as ardent and sincere in this one thing. The time will come, the time will not be long in coming, when new ties will be formed about you — ties that will bind you yet more tenderly and strongly to the home you so adorn — the dearest ties that will ever grace and gladden you. O Miss Manette, when the little picture of a happy father's face looks up in yours, when you see your own bright beauty springing up anew at your feet, think now and then that there is a man who would give his life, to keep a life you love beside you!"

He said, "Farewell!" said, "A last God bless you!" and left her.

CHAPTER XIV

THE HONEST TRADESMAN

To the eyes of Mr. Jeremiah Cruncher, sitting on his stool in Fleet Street with his grisly urchin beside him, a vast number and variety of objects in movement were every day presented. Who could sit upon anything in Fleet Street during the busy hours of the day, and not be dazed and deafened by two immense processions, one ever tending westward with the sun, the other ever tending eastward from the sun, both ever tending to the plains beyond the range of red and purple where the sun goes down !

With his straw in his mouth, Mr. Cruncher sat watching the two streams, like the heathen rustic who has for several centuries been on duty watching one stream — saving that Jerry had no expectation of their ever running dry. Nor would it have been an expectation of a hopeful kind, since a small part of his income was derived from the pilotage of timid women (mostly of a full habit and past the middle term of life) from Tellson's side of the tides to the opposite shore. Brief as such companionship was in every separate instance, Mr. Cruncher never failed to become so interested in the lady as to express a strong desire to have the honour of drinking her very good health. And it was from the gifts bestowed upon him towards the execution of this benevolent purpose, that he recruited his finances, as just now observed.

Time was, when a poet sat upon a stool in a public place, and mused in the sight of men. Mr. Cruncher, sitting on a stool in a public place, but not being a poet, mused as little as possible, and looked about him.

It fell out that he was thus engaged in a season when crowds were few, and belated women few, and when his affairs in general were so unprosperous as to awaken a strong suspicion in his breast that Mrs. Cruncher must have been " flopping " in some pointed manner, when an unusual concourse pouring down

Fleet Street westward attracted his attention. Looking that way, Mr. Cruncher made out that some kind of funeral was coming along, and that there was popular objection to this funeral, which engendered uproar.

"Young Jerry," said Mr. Cruncher, turning to his offspring, "it's a buryin'."

"Hooroar, father!" cried Young Jerry.

The young gentleman uttered this exultant sound with mysterious significance. The elder gentleman took the cry so ill, that he watched his opportunity, and smote the young gentleman on the ear.

"What d' ye mean? What are you hooroaring at? What do you want to convey to your own father, you young Rip? This boy is getting too many for *me!*" said Mr. Cruncher, surveying him. "Him and his hooroars! Don't let me hear no more of you, or you shall feel some more of me. D' ye hear?"

"I warn't doing no harm," Young Jerry protested, rubbing his cheek.

"Drop it then," said Mr. Cruncher; "I won't have none of *your* no harms. Get a top of that there seat, and look at the crowd."

His son obeyed, and the crowd approached; they were bawling and hissing round a dingy hearse and dingy mourning-coach, in which mourning-coach there was only one mourner, dressed in the dingy trappings that were considered essential to the dignity of the position. The position appeared by no means to please him, however, with an increasing rabble surrounding the coach, deriding him, making grimaces at him, and incessantly groaning and calling out: "Yah! Spies! Tst! Yaha! Spies!" with many compliments too numerous and forcible to repeat.

Funerals had at all times a remarkable attraction for Mr. Cruncher; he always pricked up his senses, and became excited, when a funeral passed Tellson's. Naturally, therefore, a funeral with this uncommon attendance excited him greatly, and he asked of the first man who ran against him: —

"What is it, brother? What's it about?"

"*I* don't know," said the man. "Spies! Yaha! Tst! Spies!"

He asked another man, "Who is it?"

" *I* don't know," returned the man : clapping his hands to his mouth nevertheless, and vociferating in a surprising heat and with the greatest ardour, " Spies ! Yaha ! Tst, tst ! Spi-ies ! "

At length, a person better informed on the merits of the case, tumbled against him, and from this person he learned that the funeral was the funeral of one Roger Cly.

" Was He a spy ? " asked Mr. Cruncher.

" Old Bailey spy," returned his informant.   " Yaha ! Tst ! Yah ! Old Bailey Spi-i-ies ! "

" Why, to be sure ! " exclaimed Jerry, recalling the Trial at which he had assisted.   " I 've seen him.   Dead, is he ? "

" Dead as mutton," returned the other, " and can't be too dead. Have 'em out, there ! Spies ! Pull 'em out, there ! Spies ! "

The idea was so acceptable in the prevalent absence of any idea, that the crowd caught it up with eagerness, and loudly repeating the suggestion to have 'em out, and to pull 'em out, mobbed the two vehicles so closely that they came to a stop. On the crowd's opening the coach doors, the one mourner scuffled out of himself and was in their hands for a moment ; but he was so alert, and made such good use of his time, that in another moment he was scouring away up a by-street, after shedding his cloak, hat, long hatband, white pocket-handker-chief, and other symbolical tears.

These, the people tore to pieces, and scattered far and wide with great enjoyment, while the tradesmen hurriedly shut up their shops ; for a crowd in those times stopped at nothing, and was a monster much dreaded.   They had already got the length of opening the hearse to take the coffin out, when some brighter genius proposed instead, its being escorted to its destination amidst general rejoicing. Practical suggestions being much needed, this suggestion, too, was received with acclamation, and the coach was immediately filled with eight inside and a dozen out, while as many people got on the roof of the hearse as could by any exercise of ingenuity stick upon it.   Among the first of these volunteers was Jerry Cruncher himself, who modestly concealed his spiky head from the observation of Tellson's, in the further corner of the mourning-coach.

The officiating undertakers made some protest against these changes in the ceremonies ; but the river being alarmingly near, and several voices remarking on the efficacy of cold immersion in bringing refractory members of the profession to reason, the protest was faint and brief. The remodelled procession started, with a chimney-sweep driving the hearse, — advised by the regular driver, who was perched beside him, under close inspection, for the purpose, — and with a pieman, also attended by his cabinet-minister, driving the mourning-coach. A bear-leader, a popular street character of the time, was impressed as an additional ornament, before the cavalcade had gone far down the Strand; and his bear, who was black and very mangy, gave quite an Undertaking air to that part of the procession in which he walked.

Thus, with beer-drinking, pipe-smoking, song-roaring, and infinite caricaturing of woe, the disorderly procession went its way, recruiting at every step, and all the shops shutting up before it. Its destination was the old church of Saint Pancras, far off in the fields. It got there in course of time; insisted on pouring into the burial-ground; finally, accomplished the interment of the deceased Roger Cly in its own way, and highly to its own satisfaction.

The dead man disposed of, and the crowd being under the necessity of providing some other entertainment for itself, another brighter genius (or perhaps the same) conceived the humour of impeaching casual passers-by, as Old Bailey spies, and wreaking vengeance on them. Chase was given to some scores of inoffensive persons who had never been near the Old Bailey in their lives, in the realisation of this fancy, and they were roughly hustled and maltreated. The transition to the sport of window-breaking, and thence to the plundering of public-houses, was easy and natural. At last, after several hours, when sundry summer-houses had been pulled down, and some area railings had been torn up, to arm the more belligerent spirits, a rumour got about that the Guards were coming. Before this rumour, the crowd gradually melted away, and perhaps the Guards came, and perhaps they never came, and this was the usual progress of a mob.

Mr. Cruncher did not assist at the closing sports, but had remained behind in the churchyard, to confer and condole with the undertakers. The place had a soothing influence on him. He procured a pipe from a neighbouring public-house, and smoked it, looking in at the railings and maturely considering the spot.

"Jerry," said Mr. Cruncher, apostrophising himself in his usual way, "you see that there Cly that day, and you see with your own eyes that he was a young 'un and a straight made 'un."

Having smoked his pipe out, and ruminated a little longer, he turned himself about, that he might appear, before the hour of closing, on his station at Tellson's. Whether his meditations on mortality had touched his liver, or whether his general health had been previously at all amiss, or whether he desired to show a little attention to an eminent man, is not so much to the purpose, as that he made a short call upon his medical adviser — a distinguished surgeon — on his way back.

Young Jerry relieved his father with dutiful interest, and reported No job in his absence. The Bank closed, the ancient clerks came out, the usual watch was set, and Mr. Cruncher and his son went home to tea.

"Now, I tell you where it is!" said Mr. Cruncher to his wife, on entering. "If, as a honest tradesman, my wenturs goes wrong to-night, I shall make sure that you've been praying agin me, and I shall work you for it just the same as if I seen you do it."

The dejected Mrs. Cruncher shook her head.

"Why, you're at it afore my face!" said Mr. Cruncher, with signs of angry apprehension.

"I am saying nothing."

"Well then, don't meditate nothing. You might as well flop as meditate. You may as well go agin me one way as another. Drop it altogether."

"Yes, Jerry."

"Yes, Jerry," repeated Mr. Cruncher, sitting down to tea. "Ah! It *is* yes, Jerry. That's about it. You may say yes, Jerry."

Mr. Cruncher had no particular meaning in these sulky corroborations, but made use of them, as people not unfrequently do, to express general ironical dissatisfaction.

"You and your yes, Jerry," said Mr. Cruncher, taking a bite out of his bread and butter, and seeming to help it down with a large invisible oyster out of his saucer. "Ah! I think so. I believe you."

"You are going out to-night?" asked his decent wife, when he took another bite.

" Yes, I am."

" May I go with you, father ? " asked his son briskly.

" No, you may n't.   I 'm a going — as your mother knows — a fishing.   That 's where I 'm going to.   Going a fishing."

" Your fishing-rod gets rayther rusty; don't it, father ? "

" Never you mind."

" Shall you bring any fish home, father ? "

" If I don't, you 'll have short commons to-morrow," returned that gentleman, shaking his head; " that 's questions enough for you; I ain't a going out, till you 've been long abed."

He devoted himself during the remainder of the evening to keeping a most vigilant watch on Mrs. Cruncher, and sullenly holding her in conversation that she might be prevented from meditating any petitions to his disadvantage.   With this view, he urged his son to hold her in conversation also, and led the unfortunate woman a hard life by dwelling on any causes of complaint he could bring against her, rather than he would leave her for a moment to her own reflections.   The devoutest person could have rendered no greater homage to the efficacy of an honest prayer than he did in this distrust of his wife.   It was as if a professed unbeliever in ghosts should be frightened by a ghost story.

" And mind you! " said Mr. Cruncher.   " No games to-morrow!   If I, as a honest tradesman, succeed in providing a jinte of meat or two, none of your not touching of it, and sticking to bread.   If I, as a honest tradesman, am able to provide a little beer, none of your declaring on water.   When you go to Rome, do as Rome does.   Rome will be a ugly customer to you, if you don't.   I 'm your Rome, you know."

Then he began grumbling again : —

" With your flying into the face of your own wittles and drink!   I don't know how scarce you may n't make the wittles and drink here, by your flopping tricks and your unfeeling conduct.   Look at your boy: he *is* your'n, ain't he ?   He 's as thin as a lath.   Do you call yourself a mother, and not know that a mother's first duty is to blow her boy out ? "

This touched Young Jerry on a tender place; who adjured his mother to perform her first duty, and, whatever else she did or neglected, above all things to lay especial stress on the discharge of that maternal function so affectingly and delicately indicated by his other parent.

Thus the evening wore away with the Cruncher family, until
Young Jerry was ordered to bed, and his mother, laid under
similar injunctions, obeyed them.   Mr. Cruncher beguiled the
earlier watches of the night with solitary pipes, and did not
start upon his excursion until nearly one o'clock.   Towards that
small and ghostly hour, he rose up from his chair, took a key
out of his pocket, opened a locked cupboard, and brought forth
a sack, a crowbar of convenient size, a rope and chain, and other
fishing-tackle of that nature.   Disposing these articles about
him in skilful manner, he bestowed a parting defiance on Mrs.
Cruncher, extinguished the light, and went out.

Young Jerry, who had only made a feint of undressing when
he went to bed, was not long after his father.   Under cover of
the darkness he followed out of the room, followed down the
stairs, followed down the court, followed out into the streets. He
was in no uneasiness concerning his getting into the house again,
for it was full of lodgers, and the door stood ajar all night.

Impelled by a laudable ambition to study the art and mystery
of his father's honest calling, Young Jerry, keeping as close to
house-fronts, walls, and doorways, as his eyes were close to one
another, held his honoured parent in view.   The honoured
parent steering Northward, had not gone far, when he was
joined by another disciple of Izaak Walton, and the two trudged
on together.

Within half an hour from the first starting, they were beyond
the winking lamps, and the more than winking watchmen, and
were out upon a lonely road.   Another fisherman was picked up
here — and that so silently, that if Young Jerry had been su-
perstitious, he might have supposed the second follower of the
gentle craft to have, all of a sudden, split himself into two.

The three went on, and Young Jerry went on until the three
stopped under a bank overhanging the road.   Upon the top of
the bank was a low brick wall surmounted by an iron railing.
In the shadow of bank and wall, the three turned out of the
road, and up a blind lane, of which the wall — there, risen to
some eight or ten feet high — formed one side.   Crouching
down in a corner, peeping up the lane, the next object that
Young Jerry saw was the form of his honoured parent, pretty
well defined against a watery and clouded moon, nimbly scaling
an iron gate.   He was soon over, and then the second fisherman
got over, and then the third.   They all dropped softly on the

ground within the gate, and lay there a little — listening perhaps. Then, they moved away on their hands and knees.

It was now Young Jerry's turn to approach the gate : which
he did, holding his breath. Crouching down again in a corner
there, and looking in, he made out the three fishermen creeping
through some rank grass ; and all the gravestones in the churchyard — it was a large churchyard that they were in — looking
on like ghosts in white, while the church tower itself looked
on like the ghost of a monstrous giant. They did not creep
far, before they stopped and stood upright. And then they
began to fish.

They fished with a spade, at first. Presently the honoured
parent appeared to be adjusting some instrument like a great
corkscrew. Whatever tools they worked with, they worked
hard, until the awful striking of the church clock so terrified
Young Jerry, that he made off, with his hair as stiff as his
father's.

But his long-cherished desire to know more about these
matters, not only stopped him in his running away, but lured
him back again. They were still fishing perseveringly, when he
peeped in at the gate for the second time ; but now they
seemed to have got a bite. There was a screwing and complaining sound down below, and their bent figures were strained, as
if by a weight. By slow degrees the weight broke away the
earth upon it, and came to the surface. Young Jerry very well
knew what it would be ; but when he saw it, and saw his honoured parent about to wrench it open, he was so frightened,
being new to the sight, that he made off again, and never
stopped until he had run a mile or more.

He would not have stopped then, for anything less necessary
than breath, it being a spectral sort of race that he ran, and one
highly desirable to get to the end of. He had a strong idea
that the coffin he had seen was running after him ; and, pictured as hopping on behind him, bolt upright upon its narrow
end, always on the point of overtaking him and hopping on at
his side — perhaps taking his arm — it was a pursuer to shun.
It was an inconsistent and ubiquitous fiend too, for while it was
making the whole night behind him dreadful, he darted out into
the roadway to avoid dark alleys, fearful of its coming hopping
out of them like a dropsical boy's-Kite without tail and wings.
It hid in doorways too, rubbing its horrible shoulders against

doors, and drawing them up to its ears, as if it were laughing.
It got into shadows on the road, and lay cunningly on its back
to trip him up. All this time, it was incessantly hopping on
behind and gaining on him, so that when the boy got to his
own door he had reason for being half dead. And even then it
would not leave him, but followed him up stairs with a bump
on every stair, scrambled into bed with him, and bumped down,
dead and heavy, on his breast when he fell asleep.

From his oppressed slumber, Young Jerry in his closet was
awakened after daybreak and before sunrise, by the presence of
his father in the family room. Something had gone wrong with
him ; at least, so Young Jerry inferred, from the circumstance
of his holding Mrs. Cruncher by the ears, and knocking the
back of her head against the headboard of the bed.

" I told you I would," said Mr. Cruncher, " and I did."

" Jerry, Jerry, Jerry ! " his wife implored.

" You oppose yourself to the profit of the business," said
Jerry, " and me and my partners suffer. You was to honour
and obey ; why the devil don't you ? "

" I 'll try to be a good wife, Jerry," the poor woman protested, with tears.

" Is it being a good wife to oppose your husband's business ?
Is it honouring your husband to dishonour his business ? Is it
obeying your husband to disobey him on the wital subject of his
business ? "

" You had n't taken to the dreadful business then, Jerry."

" It 's enough for you," retorted Mr. Cruncher, " to be the
wife of a honest tradesman, and not to occupy your female
mind with calculations when he took to his trade or when he
did n't. A honouring and obeying wife would let his trade alone
altogether. Call yourself a religious woman ? If you 're a religious woman, give me a irreligious one ! You have no more
nat'ral sense of duty than the bed of this here Thames River has
of a pile, and similarly it must be knocked into you."

The altercation was conducted in a low tone of voice, and
terminated in the honest tradesman's kicking off his clay-soiled
boots, and lying down at his length on the floor. After taking
a timid peep at him, lying on his back, with his rusty hand
under his head for a pillow, his son lay down too, and fell
asleep again

There was no fish for breakfast, and not much of anything

else. Mr. Cruncher was out of spirits, and out of temper, and kept an iron pot-lid by him as a projectile for the correction of Mrs. Cruncher, in case he should observe any symptoms of her saying Grace. He was brushed and washed at the usual hour, and set off with his son to pursue his ostensible calling.

Young Jerry, walking with the stool under his arm at his father's side along sunny and crowded Fleet Street, was a very different Young Jerry from him of the previous night, running home through darkness and solitude from his grim pursuer. His cunning was fresh with the day, and his qualms were gone with the night — in which particulars it is not improbable that he had compeers in Fleet Street and the City of London, that fine morning.

"Father," said Young Jerry, as they walked along, taking care to keep at arm's length and to have the stool well between them, "what's a Resurrection-Man?"

Mr. Cruncher came to a stop on the pavement before he answered, "How should I know?"

"I thought you knowed everything, father," said the artless boy.

"Hem! Well," returned Mr. Cruncher, going on again, and lifting off his hat to give his spikes free play, "he's a tradesman."

"What's his goods, father?" asked the brisk Young Jerry.

"His goods," said Mr. Cruncher, after turning it over in his mind, "is a branch of Scientific goods."

"Persons' bodies, ain't it, father?" asked the lively boy.

"I believe it is something of that sort," said Mr. Cruncher.

"Oh, father, I should so like to be a Resurrection-Man when I'm quite growed up!"

Mr. Cruncher was soothed, but shook his head in a dubious and moral way. "It depends upon how you dewelop your talents. Be careful to dewelop your talents, and never to say no more than you can help to nobody, and there's no telling at the present time what you may not come to be fit for." As Young Jerry, thus encouraged, went on a few yards in advance, to plant the stool in the shadow of the Bar, Mr. Cruncher added to himself: "Jerry, you honest tradesman, there's hopes wot that boy will yet be a blessing to you, and a recompense to you for his mother!"

CHAPTER XV

KNITTING

THERE had been earlier drinking than usual in the wine-shop of Monsieur Defarge. As early as six o'clock in the morning, sallow faces peeping through its barred windows had descried other faces within, bending over measures of wine. Monsieur Defarge sold a very thin wine at the best of times, but it would seem to have been an unusually thin wine that he sold at this time. A sour wine, moreover, or a souring, for its influence on the mood of those who drank it was to make them gloomy. No vivacious Bacchanalian flame leaped out of the pressed grape of Monsieur Defarge; but a smouldering fire that burnt in the dark lay hidden in the dregs of it.

This had been the third morning in succession on which there had been early drinking at the wine-shop of Monsieur Defarge. It had begun on Monday, and here was Wednesday come. There had been more of early brooding than drinking; for many men had listened and whispered and slunk about there from the time of the opening of the door, who could not have laid a piece of money on the counter to save their souls. These were to the full as interested in the place, however, as if they could have commanded whole barrels of wine; and they glided from seat to seat, and from corner to corner, swallowing talk in lieu of drink, with greedy looks.

Notwithstanding an unusual flow of company, the master of the wine-shop was not visible. He was not missed; for nobody who crossed the threshold looked for him, nobody asked for him, nobody wondered to see only Madame Defarge in her seat, presiding over the distribution of wine, with a bowl of battered small coins before her, as much defaced and beaten out of their original impress as the small coinage of humanity from whose ragged pockets they had come.

A suspended interest and a prevalent absence of mind were perhaps observed by the spies who looked in at the wine-shop, as they looked in at every place, high and low, from the king's palace to the criminal's jail. Games at cards languished, players at dominoes musingly built towers with them, drinkers drew figures on the tables with spilt drops of wine, Madame Defarge herself picked out the pattern on her sleeve with her toothpick, and saw and heard something inaudible and invisible a long way off.

Thus, Saint Antoine in this vinous feature of his, until midday. It was high noontide, when two dusty men passed through his streets and under his swinging lamps, of whom, one was Monsieur Defarge; the other, a mender of roads in a blue cap. All adust and athirst, the two entered the wine-shop. . Their arrival had lighted a kind of fire in the breast of Saint Antoine, fast spreading as they came along, which stirred and flickered in flames of faces at most doors and windows. Yet, no one had followed them, and no man spoke when they entered the wine-shop, though the eyes of every man there were turned upon them.

" Good day, gentlemen ! " said Monsieur Defarge.

It may have been a signal for loosening the general tongue. It elicited an answering chorus of " Good day ! "

" It is bad weather, gentlemen," said Defarge, shaking his head.

Upon which, every man looked at his neighbour, and then all cast down their eyes and sat silent. Except one man, who got up and went out.

" My wife," said Defarge aloud, addressing Madame Defarge, " I have travelled certain leagues with this good mender of roads, called Jacques. I met him — by accident — a day and a half's journey out of Paris. He is a good child, this mender of roads, called Jacques. Give him to drink, my wife ! "

A second man got up and went out. Madame Defarge set wine before the mender of roads called Jacques, who doffed his blue cap to the company, and drank. In the breast of his blouse, he carried some coarse dark bread; he ate of this between whiles, and sat munching and drinking near Madame Defarge's counter. A third man got up and went out.

Defarge refreshed himself with a draught of wine, — but he took less than was given to the stranger, as being himself a man to whom it was no rarity, — and stood waiting until the countryman had made his breakfast. He looked at no one present, and no one now looked at him; not even Madame Defarge, who had taken up her knitting, and was at work.

"Have you finished your repast, friend?" he asked, in due season.

"Yes, thank you."

"Come then! You shall see the apartment that I told you you could occupy. It will suit you to a marvel."

Out of the wine-shop into the street, out of the street into a courtyard, out of the courtyard up a steep staircase, out of the staircase into a garret — formerly the garret where a white-haired man sat on a low bench, stooping forward and very busy, making shoes.

No white-haired man was there now; but the three men were there who had gone out of the wine-shop singly. And between them and the white-haired man afar off was the one small link, that they had once looked in at him through the chinks in the wall.

Defarge closed the door carefully, and spoke in a subdued voice : —

"Jacques One, Jacques Two, Jacques Three! This is the witness encountered by appointment, by me, Jacques Four. He will tell you all. Speak, Jacques Five!"

The mender of roads, blue cap in hand, wiped his swarthy forehead with it, and said, "Where shall I commence, monsieur?"

"Commence," was Monsieur Defarge's not unreasonable reply, "at the commencement."

"I saw him then, messieurs," began the mender of roads, "a year ago this running summer, underneath the carriage of the Marquis, hanging by the chain. Behold the manner of it. I leaving my work on the road, the sun going to bed, the carriage of the Marquis slowly ascending the hill, he hanging by the chain — like this."

Again, the mender of roads went through the old performance; in which he ought to have been perfect by that time, seeing that it had been the infallible resource and indispensable entertainment of his village during a whole year.

Jacques One struck in, and asked if he had ever seen the man before.

"Never," answered the mender of roads, recovering his perpendicular.

Jacques Three demanded how he afterwards recognised him then ?

"By his tall figure," said the mender of roads, softly, and with his finger at his nose. "When Monsieur the Marquis demands that evening, 'Say, what is he like ?' I make response, 'Tall as a spectre.'"

"You should have said, short as a dwarf," returned Jacques Two.

"But what did I know! The deed was not then accomplished, neither did he confide in me. Observe! Under those circumstances even, I do not offer my testimony. Monsieur the Marquis indicates me with his finger, standing near our little fountain, and says, 'To me! Bring that rascal!' My faith, messieurs, I offer nothing."

"He is right there, Jacques," murmured Defarge, to him who had interrupted. "Go on!"

"Good!" said the mender of roads, with an air of mystery. "The tall man is lost, and he is sought — how many months ? Nine, ten, eleven?"

"No matter, the number," said Defarge. "He is well hidden, but at last he is unluckily found. Go on!"

"I am again at work upon the hillside, and the sun is again about to go to bed. I am collecting my tools to descend to my cottage down in the village below, where it is already dark, when I raise my eyes, and see coming over the hill, six soldiers. In the midst of them is a tall man with his arms bound — tied to his sides, like this!"

With the aid of his indispensable cap, he represented a man with his elbows bound fast at his hips, with cords that were knotted behind him.

"I stand aside, messieurs, by my heap of stones, to see the soldiers and their prisoner pass (for it is a solitary road, that, where any spectacle is well worth looking at), and at first, as they approach, I see no more than that they are six soldiers with a tall man bound, and that they are almost black to my sight — except on the side of the sun going to bed, where they have a red edge, messieurs. Also, I see that their long shadows are on the hollow ridge on the opposite side of the road, and are on the hill above it, and are like the shadows of giants. Also, I see that they are covered with dust, and that the dust moves with them as they come, tramp, tramp! But when they advance quite near to me, I recognise the tall man, and he recognises me. Ah, but he would be well content to precipitate himself over the hillside once again, as on the evening when he and I first encountered, close to the same spot!"

He described it as if he were there, and it was evident that he saw it vividly; perhaps he had not seen much in his life.

"I do not show the soldiers that I recognise the tall man; he does not show the soldiers that he recognises me; we do it, and we know it, with our eyes. 'Come on!' says the chief of that company, pointing to the village, 'bring him fast to his tomb!' and they bring him faster. I follow. His arms are swelled because of being bound so tight, his wooden shoes are large and clumsy, and he is lame. Because he is lame, and consequently slow, they drive him with their guns — like this!"

He imitated the action of a man's being impelled forward by the butt-ends of muskets.

"As they descended the hill like madmen running a race, he falls. They laugh and pick him up again. His face is bleeding and covered with dust, but he cannot touch it; thereupon they laugh again. They bring him into the village; all the village runs to look; they take him past the mill, and up to the prison; all the village sees the prison gate open in the darkness of the night, and swallow him — like this!"

He opened his mouth as wide as he could, and shut it with a sounding snap of his teeth. Observant of his unwillingness to mar the effect by opening it again, Defarge said, "Go on, Jacques."

"All the village," pursued the mender of roads, on tiptoe, and in a low voice, "withdraws; all the village whispers by the fountain; all the village sleeps; all the village dreams of that unhappy one, within the locks and bars of the prison on the crag, and never to come out of it, except to perish. In the morning, with my tools upon my shoulder, eating my morsel of black bread as I go, I make a circuit by the prison, on my way to my work. There, I see him, high up, behind the bars of a lofty iron cage, bloody and dusty as last night, looking through. He has no hand free, to wave to me; I dare not call to him; he regards me like a dead man."

Defarge and the three glanced darkly at one another. The looks of all of them were dark, repressed, and revengeful, as they listened to the countryman's story; the manner of all of them, while it was secret, was authoritative too. They had the air of a rough tribunal; Jacques One and Two sitting on the old pallet-bed, each with his chin resting on his hand, and his eyes intent on the road mender; Jacques Three, equally intent, on one knee behind them, with his agitated hand always gliding over the network of fine nerves about his mouth and nose; Defarge standing between them and the narrator, whom he had stationed in the light of the window, by turns looking from him to them and from them to him.

"Go on, Jacques," said Defarge.

"He remains up there, in his iron cage, some days. The village looks at him by stealth, for it is afraid. But it always looks up, from a distance, at the prison on the crag; and in the evening when the work of the day is achieved and it assembles to gossip at the fountain, all faces are turned towards the prison. Formerly, they were turned towards the posting-house; now, they are turned towards the prison. They whisper at the fountain, that although condemned to death he will not be executed; thay say that petitions have been presented in Paris, showing that he was enraged and made mad by the death of his child; they say that a petition has been presented to the king himself. What do I know? It is possible. Perhaps yes, perhaps no."

"Listen, then, Jacques," Number One of that name sternly interposed. "Know that a petition was presented to the king and queen. All here, yourself excepted, saw the king take it, in his carriage in the street, sitting beside the queen. It is Defarge whom you see here, who, at the hazard of his life, darted out before the horses, with the petition in his hand."

"And once again listen, Jacques!" said the kneeling Number Three, his fingers ever wandering over and over those fine nerves, with a strikingly greedy air, as if he hungered for something — that was neither food nor drink; "the guard, horse and foot, surrounded the petitioner, and struck him blows. You hear?"

"I hear, messieurs."

"Go on, then," said Defarge.

"Again; on the other hand, they whisper at the fountain," resumed the countryman, "that he is brought down into our country to be executed on the spot, and that he will very certainly be executed. They even whisper that because he has

slain Monseigneur, and because Monseigneur was the father of
his tenants — serfs — what you will — he will be executed as a
parricide. One old man says at the fountain, that his right
hand, armed with the knife, will be burnt off before his face ;
that, into wounds which will be made in his arms, his breast,
and his legs, there will be poured boiling oil, melted lead, hot
resin, wax, and sulphur ; finally, that he will be torn limb from
limb by four strong horses. That old man says, all this was
actually done to a prisoner who made an attempt on the life of
the last King, Louis Fifteen. But how do I know if he lies ?
I am not a scholar."

"Listen once again then, Jacques ! " said the man with the
restless hand and the craving air.   " The name of that prisoner
was Damiens, and it was all done in open day, in the open
streets of this city of Paris ; and nothing was more noticed in
the vast concourse that saw it done than the crowd of ladies of
quality and fashion, who were full of eager attention to the last
— to the last, Jacques, prolonged until nightfall, when he had
lost two legs and an arm, and still breathed ! And it was
done — why, how old are you ? "

" Thirty-five," said the mender of roads, who looked sixty.

" It was done when you were more than ten years old ; you
might have seen it."

" Enough ! " said Defarge, with grim impatience.   " Long
live the Devil ! Go on."

" Well ! Some whisper this, some whisper that ; they speak
of nothing else ; even the fountain appears to fall to that tune.
At length, on Sunday night when all the village is asleep, come
soldiers, winding down from the prison, and their guns ring on
the stones of the little street. Workmen dig, workmen hammer,
soldiers laugh and sing ; in the morning, by the fountain, there
is raised a gallows forty feet high poisoning the water."

The mender of roads looked *through* rather than *at* the low
ceiling, and pointed as if he saw the gallows somewhere in the
sky.

" All work is stopped, all assemble there, nobody leads the
cows out, the cows are there with the rest. At mid-day, the
roll of drums. Soldiers have marched into the prison in the
night, and he is in the midst of many soldiers. He is bound as
before, and in his mouth there is a gag — tied so, with a tight
string, making him look almost as if he laughed." He suggested

it, by creasing his face with his two thumbs, from the corners of his mouth to his ears. "On the top of the gallows is fixed the knife, blade upwards, with its point in the air. He is hanged there forty feet high — and is left hanging, poisoning the water."

They looked at one another, as he used his blue cap to wipe his face, on which the perspiration had started afresh while he recalled the spectacle.

"It is frightful, messieurs. How can the women and the children draw water! Who can gossip of an evening, under that shadow! Under it, have I said? When I left the village, Monday evening as the sun was going to bed, and looked back from the hill, the shadow struck across the church, across the mill, across the prison — seemed to strike across the earth, messieurs, to where the sky rests upon it!"

The hungry man gnawed one of his fingers as he looked at the other three, and his finger quivered with the craving that was on him.

"That's all, messieurs. I left at sunset (as I had been warned to do), and I walked on, that night and half next day, until I met (as I was warned I should) this comrade. With him, I came on, now riding and now walking, through the rest of yesterday and through last night. And here you see me!"

After a gloomy silence, the first Jacques said, "Good. You have acted and recounted faithfully. Will you wait for us a little, outside the door?"

"Very willingly," said the mender of roads. Whom Defarge escorted to the top of the stairs, and, leaving seated there, returned.

The three had risen, and their heads were together when he came back to the garret.

"How say you, Jacques?" demanded Number One. "To be registered?"

"To be registered, as doomed to destruction," returned Defarge.

"Magnificent!" croaked the man with the craving.

"The château, and all the race?" inquired the first.

"The château, and all the race," returned Defarge. "Extermination."

The hungry man repeated, in a rapturous croak, "Magnificent!" and began gnawing another finger.

"Are you sure," asked Jacques Two, of Defarge, "that no embarrassment can arise from our manner of keeping the register? Without doubt it is safe, for no one beyond ourselves can decipher it; but shall we always be able to decipher it — or, I ought to say, will she?"

"Jacques," returned Defarge, drawing himself up, "if madame my wife undertook to keep the register in her memory alone, she would not lose a word of it — not a syllable of it. Knitted, in her own stitches and her own symbols, it will always be as plain to her as the sun. Confide in Madame Defarge. It would be easier for the weakest poltroon that lives, to erase himself from existence, than to erase one letter of his name or crimes from the knitted register of Madame Defarge."

There was a murmur of confidence and approval, and then the man who hungered, asked: "Is this rustic to be sent back soon? I hope so. He is very simple; is he not a little dangerous?"

"He knows nothing," said Defarge; "at least nothing more than would easily elevate him to a gallows of the same height. I charge myself with him; let him remain with me; I will take care of him, and set him on his road. He wishes to see the fine world — the King, the Queen, and Court; let him see them on Sunday."

"What?" exclaimed the hungry man, staring. "Is it a good sign, that he wishes to see Royalty and Nobility?"

"Jacques," said Defarge; "judiciously show a cat milk, if you wish her to thirst for it. Judiciously show a dog his natural prey, if you wish him to bring it down one day."

Nothing more was said, and the mender of roads, being found already dozing on the topmost stair, was advised to lay himself down on the pallet-bed and take some rest. He needed no persuasion, and was soon asleep.

Worse quarters than Defarge's wine-shop could easily have been found in Paris for a provincial slave of that degree. Saving for a mysterious dread of madame by which he was constantly haunted, his life was very new and agreeable. But madame sat all day at her counter, so expressly unconscious of him, and so particularly determined not to perceive that his being there had any connection with anything below the surface, that he shook in his wooden shoes whenever his eye lighted on her. For he contended with himself that it was impossible to foresee what that lady might pretend next; and he felt assured that if she should take it into her brightly ornamented head to pretend that she had seen him do a murder and afterwards flay the victim, she would infallibly go through with it until the play was played out.

Therefore, when Sunday came, the mender of roads was not enchanted (though he said he was) to find that madame was to accompany monsieur and himself to Versailles. It was additionally disconcerting to have madame knitting all the way there, in a public conveyance; it was additionally disconcerting yet, to have madame in the crowd in the afternoon, still with her knitting in her hands as the crowd waited to see the carriage of the King and Queen.

"You work hard, madame," said a man near her.

"Yes," answered Madame Defarge; "I have a good deal to do."

"What do you make, madame?"

"Many things."

"For instance — "

"For instance," returned Madame Defarge composedly, "shrouds."

The man moved a little further away, as soon as he could, and the mender of roads fanned himself with his blue cap: feeling it mightily close and oppressive. If he needed a King and Queen to restore him, he was fortunate in having his remedy at hand; for soon the large-faced King and the fair-faced Queen came in their golden coach, attended by the shining Bull's Eye of their Court, a glittering multitude of laughing ladies and fine lords; and in jewels and silks and powder and splendour and elegantly spurning figures and handsomely disdainful faces of both sexes, the mender of roads bathed himself, so much to his temporary intoxication, that he cried Long live the King, Long live the Queen, Long live everybody and everything! as if he had never heard of ubiquitous Jacques in his time. Then, there were gardens, courtyards, terraces, fountains, green banks, more King and Queen, more Bull's Eye, more lords and ladies, more Long live they all! until he absolutely wept with sentiment. During the whole of this scene. which lasted some three hours, he had plenty of shouting and weeping and sentimental company, and throughout Defarge held him by the collar, as if to restrain

him from flying at the objects of his brief devotion and tearing
them to pieces.

"Bravo!" said Defarge, clapping him on the back when it
was over, like a patron; "you are a good boy!"

The mender of roads was now coming to himself, and was
mistrustful of having made a mistake in his late demonstrations;
but no.

"You are the fellow we want," said Defarge, in his ear;
"you make these fools believe that it will last for ever. Then,
they are the more insolent, and it is the nearer ended."

"Hey!" cried the mender of roads reflectively; "that's
true."

"These fools know nothing. While they despise your
breath, and would stop it for ever and ever, in you or in a
hundred like you rather than in one of their own horses or
dogs, they only know what your breath tells them. Let it
deceive them, then, a little longer; it cannot deceive them too
much."

Madame Defarge looked superciliously at the client, and
nodded in confirmation.

"As to you," said she, "you would shout and shed tears for
anything, if it made a show and a noise. Say! Would you
not?"

"Truly, madame, I think so. For the moment."

"If you were shown a great heap of dolls, and were set upon
them to pluck them to pieces and despoil them for your own
advantage, you would pick out the richest and gayest. Say!
Would you not?"

"Truly yes, madame."

"Yes. And if you were shown a flock of birds, unable to
fly, and were set upon them to strip them of their feathers for
your own advantage, you would set upon the birds of the finest
feathers; would you not?"

"It is true, madame."

"You have seen both dolls and birds to-day," said Madame
Defarge, with a wave of her hand towards the place where they
had last been apparent; "now, go home!"

CHAPTER XVI

STILL KNITTING

MADAME DEFARGE and monsieur her husband returned amicably to the bosom of Saint Antoine, while a speck in a blue cap toiled through the darkness, and through the dust, and down the weary miles of avenue by the wayside, slowly tending towards that point of the compass where the château of Monsieur the Marquis, now in his grave, listened to the whispering trees.   Such ample leisure had the stone faces, now, for listening to the trees and to the fountain, that the few village scarecrows who, in their quest for herbs to eat and fragments of dead stick to burn, strayed within sight of the great stone courtyard and terrace staircase, had it borne in upon their starved fancy that the expression of the faces was altered.   A rumour just lived in the village — had a faint and bare existence there, as its people had — that when the knife struck home, the faces changed, from faces of pride to faces of anger and pain ; also, that when that dangling figure was hauled up forty feet above the fountain, they changed again, and bore a cruel look of being avenged, which they would henceforth bear for ever.   In the stone face over the great window of the bed-chamber where the murder was done, two fine dints were pointed out in the sculptured nose, which everybody recognised, and which nobody had seen of old ; and on the scarce occasions when two or three ragged peasants emerged from the crowd to take a hurried peep at Monsieur the Marquis petrified, a skinny finger would not have pointed to it for a minute, before they all started away among the moss and leaves, like the more fortunate hares who could find a living there.

Château and hut, stone face and dangling figure, the red stain on the stone floor, and the pure water in the village well — thousands of acres of land — a whole province of France — all France itself — lay under the night sky, concentrated into a faint hair-breadth line.   So does a whole world, with all its greatnesses and littlenesses, lie in a twinkling star. And as mere human knowledge can split a ray of light and analyse the manner of its composition, so, sublimer intelligences may read in the feeble shining of this earth of ours, every thought and act, every vice and virtue, of every responsible creature on it.

The Defarges, husband and wife, came lumbering under the starlight, in their public vehicle, to that gate of Paris whereunto their journey naturally tended. There was the usual stoppage at the barrier guard-house, and the usual lanterns came glancing forth for the usual examination and inquiry. Monsieur Defarge alighted, knowing one or two of the soldiery there, and one of the police. The latter he was intimate with, and affectionately embraced.

When Saint Antoine had again enfolded the Defarges in his dusky wings, and they, having finally alighted near the Saint's boundaries, were picking their way on foot through the black mud and offal of his streets, Madame Defarge spoke to her husband : —

"Say, then, my friend, what did Jacques of the police tell thee ? "

"Very little to-night, but all he knows. There is another spy commissioned for our quarter. There may be many more, for all that he can say, but he knows of one."

"Eh, well ! " said Madame Defarge, raising her eyebrows with a cool business air. "It is necessary to register him. How do they call that man ? "

"He is English."

"So much the better. His name ? "

"Barsad," said Defarge, making it French by pronunciation. But he had been so careful to get it accurately, that he then spelt it with perfect correctness.

"Barsad," repeated madame. "Good. Christian name ? "
"John."

"John Barsad," repeated madame, after murmuring it once to herself. "Good. His appearance; is it known ? "

"Age, about forty years; height, about five feet nine; black hair; complexion dark; generally, rather handsome visage; eyes dark, face thin, long, and sallow; nose aquiline, but not straight, having a peculiar inclination towards the left cheek; expression, therefore, sinister."

"Eh, my faith. It is a portrait ! " said madame, laughing. "He shall be registered to-morrow."

They turned into the wine-shop, which was closed (for it was midnight), and where Madame Defarge immediately took her post at the desk, counted the small moneys that had been taken during her absence, examined the stock, went through the entries in the book, made other entries of her own, checked the serving-man in every possible way, and finally dismissed him to bed. Then she turned out the contents of the bowl of money for the second time, and began knotting them up in her hand-kerchief, in a chain of separate knots, for safe keeping through the night. All this while, Defarge, with his pipe in his mouth, walked up and down, complacently admiring, but never inter-fering; in which condition, indeed, as to the business and his domestic affairs, he walked up and down through life.

The night was hot, and the shop, close shut and surrounded by so foul a neighbourhood, was ill-smelling. Monsieur De-farge's olfactory sense was by no means delicate, but the stock of wine smelt much stronger than it ever tasted, and so did the stock of rum and brandy and aniseed. He whiffed the com-pound of scents away as he put down his smoked-out pipe.

" You are fatigued," said madame, raising her glance as she knotted the money. " There are only the usual odours."

" I am a little tired," her husband acknowledged.

" You are a little depressed, too," said madame, whose quick eyes had never been so intent on the accounts, but they had had a ray or two for him. " Oh, the men, the men ! "

" But, my dear," began Defarge.

" But, my dear ! " repeated madame, nodding firmly : " but, my dear ! You are faint of heart to-night, my dear ! "

" Well, then," said Defarge, as if a thought were wrung out of his breast, " it *is* a long time."

" It is a long time," repeated his wife ; " and when is it not a long time ? Vengeance and retribution require a long time ; it is the rule."

" It does not take a long time to strike a man with Light-ning," said Defarge.

" How long," demanded madame composedly, " does it take to make and store the lightning ? Tell me ? "

Defarge raised his head thoughtfully, as if there were some-thing in that, too.

" It does not take a long time," said madame, " for an earth-quake to swallow a town. Eh, well ! Tell me how long it takes to prepare the earthquake ? "

"A long time, I suppose," said Defarge.

"But when it is ready, it takes place, and grinds to pieces everything before it. In the mean time, it is always preparing, though it is not seen or heard. That is your consolation. Keep it."

She tied a knot with flashing eyes, as if it throttled a foe.

"I tell thee," said madame, extending her right hand, for emphasis, "that although it is a long time on the road, it is on the road and coming. I tell thee it never retreats, and never stops. I tell thee it is always advancing. Look around and consider the lives of all the world that we know, consider the faces of all the world that we know, consider the rage and discontent to which the Jacquerie addresses itself with more and more of certainty every hour. Can such things last? Bah! I mock you."

"My brave wife," returned Defarge, standing before her with his head a little bent, and his hands clasped at his back, like a docile and attentive pupil before his catechist, "I do not question all this. But it has lasted a long time, and it is possible — you know well, my wife, it is possible — that it may not come during our lives."

"Eh, well! How then?" demanded madame, tying another knot, as if there were another enemy strangled.

"Well!" said Defarge, with a half complaining and half apologetic shrug. "We shall not see the triumph."

"We shall have helped it," returned madame, with her extended hand in strong action. "Nothing that we do is done in vain. I believe, with all my soul, that we shall see the triumph. But even if not, even if I knew certainly not, show me the neck of an aristocrat and tyrant, and still I would — "

There madame, with her teeth set, tied a very terrible knot indeed.

"Hold!" cried Defarge, reddening a little as if he felt charged with cowardice; "I too, my dear, will stop at nothing."

"Yes! But it is your weakness that you sometimes need to see your victim and your opportunity, to sustain you. Sustain yourself without that. When the time comes, let loose a tiger and a devil; but wait for the time with the tiger and the devil chained — not shown — yet always ready."

Madame enforced the conclusion of this piece of advice by striking her little counter with her chain of money as if she knocked its brains out, and then gathering the heavy handkerchief under her arm in a serene manner, and observing that it was time to go to bed.

Next noontide saw the admirable woman in her usual place in the wine-shop, knitting away assiduously. A rose lay beside her, and if she now and then glanced at the flower, it was with no infraction of her usual preoccupied air. There were a few customers, drinking or not drinking, standing or seated, sprinkled about. The day was very hot, and heaps of flies, who were extending their inquisitive and adventurous perquisitions into all the glutinous little glasses near madame, fell dead at the bottom. Their decease made no impression on the other flies out promenading, who looked at them in the coolest manner (as if they themselves were elephants, or something as far removed), until they met the same fate. Curious to consider how heedless flies are ! — perhaps they thought as much at Court that sunny summer day.

A figure entering at the door threw a shadow on Madame Defarge which she felt to be a new one. She laid down her knitting, and began to pin her rose in her head-dress, before she looked at the figure.

It was curious. The moment Madame Defarge took up the rose, the customers ceased talking, and began gradually to drop out of the wine-shop.

"Good day, madame," said the new-comer.

"Good day, monsieur."

She said it aloud, but added to herself, as she resumed her knitting : "Hah ! Good day, age about forty, height about five feet nine, black hair, generally rather handsome visage, complexion dark, eyes dark, thin, long and sallow face, aquiline nose but not straight, having a peculiar inclination towards the left cheek which imparts a sinister expression ! Good day, one and all ! "

" Have the goodness to give me a little glass of old cognac, and a mouthful of cool fresh water, madame."

Madame complied with a polite air.

" Marvellous cognac this, madame ! "

It was the first time it had ever been so complimented, and Madame Defarge knew enough of its antecedents to know better. She said, however, that the cognac was flattered, and took up her knitting. The visitor watched her fingers for a few moments, and took the opportunity of observing the place in general.

"You knit with great skill, madame."

"I am accustomed to it."

"A pretty pattern too!"

"*You* think so?" said madame, looking at him with a smile.

"Decidedly. May one ask what it is for?"

"Pastime," said madame, looking at him with a smile, while her fingers moved nimbly.

"Not for use?"

"That depends. I may find a use for it, one day. If I do — well," said madame, drawing a breath and nodding her head with a stern kind of coquetry, "I'll use it!"

It was remarkable; but the taste of Saint Antoine seemed to be decidedly opposed to a rose on the head-dress of Madame Defarge. Two men had entered separately, and had been about to order drink, when, catching sight of that novelty, they faltered, made a pretence of looking about as if for some friend who was not there, and went away. Nor, of those who had been there when this visitor entered, was there one left. They had all dropped off. The spy had kept his eyes open, but had been able to detect no sign. They had lounged away in a poverty-stricken, purposeless, accidental manner, quite natural and unimpeachable.

"JOHN," thought madame, checking off her work as her fingers knitted, and her eyes looked at the stranger. "Stay long enough, and I shall knit 'BARSAD' before you go."

"You have a husband, madame?"

"I have."

"Children?"

"No children."

"Business seems bad?"

"Business is very bad; the people are so poor."

"Ah, the unfortunate, miserable people! So oppressed too — as you say."

"As *you* say," madame retorted, correcting him, and deftly knitting an extra something into his name that boded him no good.

"Pardon me; certainly it was I who said so, but you naturally think so. Of course."

"*I* think?" returned madame, in a high voice. "I and my husband have enough to do to keep this wine-shop open, without thinking. All we think, here, is, how to live. That is the subject *we* think of, and it gives us, from morning to night, enough to think about, without embarrassing our heads concerning others. *I* think for others? No, no."

The spy, who was there to pick up any crumbs he could find or make, did not allow his baffled state to express itself in his sinister face, but stood with an air of gossiping gallantry, leaning his elbow on Madame Defarge's little counter, and occasionally sipping his cognac.

"A bad business this, madame, of Gaspard's execution. Ah! the poor Gaspard!" With a sigh of great compassion.

"My faith!" returned madame, coolly and lightly, "if people use knives for such purposes, they have to pay for it. He knew beforehand what the price of his luxury was; he has paid the price."

"I believe," said the spy, dropping his soft voice to a tone that invited confidence, and expressing an injured revolutionary susceptibility in every muscle of his wicked face, — "I believe there is much compassion and anger in this neighbourhood, touching the poor fellow? Between ourselves."

"Is there?" asked madame vacantly.

"Is there not?"

" — Here is my husband!" said Madame Defarge.

As the keeper of the wine-shop entered at the door, the spy saluted him by touching his hat, and saying, with an engaging smile, "Good day, Jacques!" Defarge stopped short, and stared at him.

"Good day, Jacques!" the spy repeated, with not quite so much confidence, or quite so easy a smile under the stare.

"You deceive yourself, monsieur," returned the keeper of the wine-shop. "You mistake me for another. That is not my name. I am Ernest Defarge."

"It is all the same," said the spy, airily, but discomfited too; "good day!"

"Good day!" answered Defarge drily.

"I was saying to madame, with whom I had the pleasure of chatting when you entered, that they tell me there is — and no wonder ! — much sympathy and anger in Saint Antoine, touching the unhappy fate of poor Gaspard."

"No one has told me so," said Defarge, shaking his head. "I know nothing of it."

Having said it, he passed behind the little counter, and stood with his hand on the back of his wife's chair, looking over that barrier at the person to whom they were both opposed, and whom either of them would have shot with the greatest satisfaction.

The spy, well used to his business, did not change his unconscious attitude, but drained his little glass of cognac, took a sip of fresh water, and asked for another glass of cognac. Madame Defarge poured it out for him, took to her knitting again, and hummed a little song over it.

"You seem to know this quarter well ; that is to say, better than I do ? " observed Defarge.

"Not at all, but I hope to know it better. I am so profoundly interested in its miserable inhabitants."

"Hah ! " muttered Defarge.

"The pleasure of conversing with you, Monsieur Defarge, recalls to me," pursued the spy, "that I have the honour of cherishing some interesting associations with your name."

"Indeed ? " said Defarge, with much indifference.

"Yes, indeed. When Doctor Manette was released, you his old domestic had the charge of him, I know. He was delivered to you. You see I am informed of the circumstances ? "

"Such is the fact, certainly," said Defarge. He had had it conveyed to him, in an accidental touch of his wife's elbow as she knitted and warbled, that he would do best to answer, but always with brevity.

"It was to you," said the spy, "that his daughter came; and it was from your care that his daughter took him, accompanied by a neat brown monsieur; how is he called ? — in a little wig — Lorry — of the bank of Tellson and Company — over to England."

"Such is the fact," repeated Defarge.

"Very interesting remembrances ! " said the spy. "I have known Doctor Manette and his daughter, in England."

"Yes," said Defarge.

"You don't hear much about them now," said the spy.

"No," said Defarge.

"In effect," madame struck in, looking up from her work and her little song, "we never hear about them. We received the news of their safe arrival, and perhaps another letter or perhaps two; but since then, they have gradually taken their road in life — we, ours — and we have held no correspondence."

"Perfectly so, madame," replied the spy. "She is going to be married."

"Going?" echoed madame. "She was pretty enough to have been married long ago. You English are cold, it seems to me."

"Oh! You know I am English?"

"I perceive your tongue is," returned madame; "and what the tongue is, I suppose the man is."

He did not take the identification as a compliment; but he made the best of it, and turned it off with a laugh. After sipping his cognac to the end, he added : —

"Yes, Miss Manette is going to be married. But not to an Englishman; to one who, like herself, is French by birth. And speaking of Gaspard (ah, poor Gaspard! It was cruel, cruel!), it is a curious thing that she is going to marry the nephew of Monsieur the Marquis, for whom Gaspard was exalted to that height of so many feet; in other words, the present Marquis. But he lives unknown in England, he is no Marquis there; he is Mr. Charles Darnay. D'Aulnais is the name of his mother's family."

Madame Defarge knitted steadily, but the intelligence had a palpable effect upon her husband. Do what he would, behind the little counter, as to the striking of a light and the lighting of his pipe, he was troubled, and his hand was not trustworthy. The spy would have been no spy if he had failed to see it, or to record it in his mind.

Having made, at least, this one hit, whatever it might prove to be worth, and no customers coming in to help him to any other, Mr. Barsad paid for what he had drunk, and took his leave; taking occasion to say, in a genteel manner, before he departed, that he looked forward to the pleasure of seeing Monsieur and Madame Defarge again. For some minutes after he had emerged into the outer presence of Saint Antoine, the husband and wife remained exactly as he had left them, lest he should come back.

"Can it be true," said Defarge, in a low voice, looking down at his wife as he stood smoking with his hand on the back of her chair, " what he has said of Ma'amselle Manette ? "

" As he has said it," returned madame, lifting her eyebrows a little, " it is probably false. But it may be true."

" If it is " — Defarge began, and stopped.

" If it is ? " repeated his wife.

" — And if it does come, while we live to see it triumph — I hope, for her sake, Destiny will keep her husband out of France."

" Her husband's destiny," said Madame Defarge, with her usual composure, " will take him where he is to go, and will lead him to the end that is to end him. That is all I know."

" But it is very strange — now, at least is it not very strange " — said Defarge, rather pleading with his wife to induce her to admit it, " that, after all our sympathy for Monsieur her father and herself, her husband's name should be proscribed under your hand at this moment, by the side of that infernal dog's who has just left us ? "

" Stranger things than that will happen when it does come," answered madame. " I have them both here, of a certainty ; and they are both here for their merits ; that is enough."

She rolled up her knitting when she had said those words, and presently took the rose out of the handkerchief that was wound about her head. Either Saint Antoine had an instinctive sense that the objectionable decoration was gone, or Saint Antoine was on the watch for its disappearance ; howbeit, the Saint took courage to lounge in, very shortly afterwards, and the wine-shop recovered its habitual aspect.

In the evening, at which season, of all others, Saint Antoine turned himself inside out, and sat on door-steps and window-ledges, and came to the corners of vile streets and courts, for a breath of air, Madame Defarge, with her work in her hand, was accustomed to pass from place to place and from group to group : a Missionary — there were many like her — such as the world will do well never to breed again. All the women knitted. They knitted worthless things ; but the mechanical work was a mechanical substitute for eating and drinking ; the hands moved for the jaws and the digestive apparatus ; if the bony fingers had been still, the stomachs would have been more famine-pinched.

But as the fingers went, the eyes went, and the thoughts.

And as Madame Defarge moved on from group to group, all three went quicker and fiercer among every little knot of women that she had spoken with, and left behind.

Her husband smoked at his door, looking after her with admiration. "A great woman," said he, "a strong woman, a grand woman, a frightfully grand woman."

Darkness closed around, and then came the ringing of church bells and the distant beating of the military drums in the Palace Courtyard, as the women sat knitting, knitting. Darkness encompassed them. Another darkness was closing in as surely, when the church bells, then ringing pleasantly in many an airy steeple over France, should be melted into thundering cannon; when the military drums should be beating to drown a wretched voice, that night all potent as the voice of Power and Plenty, Freedom and Life. So much was closing in about the women who sat knitting, knitting, that they their very selves were closing in around a structure yet unbuilt, where they were to sit knitting, knitting, counting dropping heads.

CHAPTER XVII

ONE NIGHT

NEVER did the sun go down with a brighter glory on the quiet corner in Soho, than one memorable evening when the doctor and his daughter sat under the plane-tree together. Never did the moon rise with a milder radiance over great London, than on that night when it found them still seated under the tree, and shone upon their faces through its leaves.

Lucie was to be married to-morrow. She had reserved this last evening for her father, and they sat alone under the plane-tree.

" You are happy, my dear father ? "

" Quite, my child."

They had said little, though they had been there a long time. When it was yet light enough to work and read, she had neither engaged herself in her usual work, nor had she read to him. She had employed herself in both ways, at his side under the tree, many and many a time; but this time was not quite like any other, and nothing could make it so.

" And I am very happy to-night, dear father. I am deeply happy in the love that Heaven has so blessed my love for Charles, and Charles's love for me. But if my life were not to be still consecrated to you, or if my marriage were so arranged as that it would part us, even by the length of a few of these streets, I should be more unhappy and self-reproachful now, than I can tell you. Even as it is — "

Even as it was, she could not command her voice.

In the sad moonlight, she clasped him by the neck, and laid her face upon his breast. In the moonlight, which is always sad, as the light of the sun itself is — as the light called human life is — at its coming and its going.

" Dearest dear ! Can you tell me, this last time, that you feel quite, quite sure, no new affections of mine, and no new duties of mine, will ever interpose between us ? *I* know it well, but do you know it? In your own heart, do you feel quite certain?"

Her father answered, with a cheerful firmness of conviction he could scarcely have assumed, "Quite sure, my darling! More than that," he added, as he tenderly kissed her; "my future is far brighter, Lucie, seen through your marriage, than it could have been — nay, than it ever was — without it."

"If I could hope *that*, my father! — "

"Believe it, love! Indeed it is so. Consider how natural and how plain it is, my dear, that it should be so. You, devoted and young, cannot fully appreciate the anxiety I have felt that your life should not be wasted — "

She moved her hand towards his lips, but he took it in his, and repeated the word.

" — wasted, my child — should not be wasted, struck aside from the natural order of things — for my sake. Your unselfishness cannot entirely comprehend how much my mind has gone on this; but only ask yourself, how could my happiness be perfect, while yours was incomplete?"

"If I had never seen Charles, my father, I should have been quite happy with you."

He smiled at her unconscious admission that she would have been unhappy without Charles, having seen him, and replied: —

"My child, you did see him, and it is Charles. If it had not been Charles, it would have been another. Or, if it had been no other, I should have been the cause, and then the dark part of my life would have cast its shadow beyond myself, and would have fallen on you."

It was the first time, except at the trial, of her ever hearing him refer to the period of his suffering. It gave her a strange and new sensation while his words were in her ears; and she remembered it long afterwards.

"See!" said the Doctor of Beauvais, raising his hand towards the moon. "I have looked at her from my prison window, when I could not bear her light. I have looked at her when it has been such torture to me to think of her shining upon what I had lost, that I have beaten my head against my prison walls. I have looked at her in a state so dulled and lethargic, that I have thought of nothing but the number of horizontal lines I could draw across her at the full, and the number of perpendicular lines with which I could intersect them." He added, in his inward and pondering manner, as he looked at the moon, " It was twenty either way, I remember, and the twentieth was difficult to squeeze in."

The strange thrill with which she heard him go back to that time deepened as he dwelt upon it; but there was nothing to shock her in the manner of his reference. He only seemed to contrast his present cheerfulness and felicity with the dire endurance that was over.

"I have looked at her, speculating thousands of times upon the unborn child from whom I had been rent. Whether it was alive. Whether it had been born alive, or the poor mother's shock had killed it. Whether it was a son who would some day avenge his father. (There was a time in my imprisonment when my desire for vengeance was unbearable.) Whether it was a son who would never know his father's story; who might even live to weigh the possibility of his father's having disappeared of his own will and act. Whether it was a daughter, who would grow to be a woman."

She drew closer to him, and kissed his cheek and his hand.

"I have pictured my daughter, to myself, as perfectly forgetful of me — rather, altogether ignorant of me, and unconscious of me. I have cast up the years of her age, year after year. I have seen her married to a man who knew nothing of my fate. I have altogether perished from the remembrance of the living, and in the next generation my place was a blank."

"My father! Even to hear that you had such thoughts of a daughter who never existed strikes to my heart as if I had been that child."

"You, Lucie? It is out of the consolation and restoration you have brought to me, that these remembrances arise, and pass between us and the moon on this last night. — What did I say, just now?"

"She knew nothing of you. She cared nothing for you."

"So! But on other moonlight nights, when the sadness and the silence have touched me in a different way, — have affected me with something as like a sorrowful sense of peace as any emotion that had pain for its foundations could, — I have imagined her as coming to me in my cell, and leading me out into the freedom beyond the fortress. I have seen her image in the moonlight, often, as I now see you; except that I never held her in my arms; it stood between the little grated window and the door. But you understand that that was not the child I am speaking of ? "

" The figure was not ; the — the — image ; the fancy ? "

" No. That was another thing. It stood before my disturbed sense of sight, but it never moved. The phantom that my mind pursued was another and more real child. Of her outward appearance I know no more than that she was like her mother. The other had that likeness too, — as you have, — but was not the same. Can you follow me, Lucie ? Hardly, I think ? I doubt you must have been a solitary prisoner to understand these perplexed distinctions."

His collected and calm manner could not prevent her blood from running cold, as he thus tried to anatomise his old condition.

" In that more peaceful state, I have imagined her, in the moonlight, coming to me and taking me out to show me that the home of her married life was full of her loving remembrance of her lost father. My picture was in her room, and I was in her prayers. Her life was active, cheerful, useful ; but my poor history pervaded it all."

" I was that child, my father. I was not half so good, but in my love that was I."

" And she showed me her children," said the Doctor of Beauvais, " and they had heard of me, and had been taught to pity me. When they passed a prison of the State, they kept far from its frowning walls, and looked up at its bars, and spoke in whispers. She could never deliver me ; I imagined that she always brought me back after showing me such things. But then, blessed with the relief of tears, I fell upon my knees, and blessed her."

" I am that child, I hope, my father. Oh, my dear, my dear, will you bless me as fervently to-morrow ? "

" Lucie, I recall these old troubles in the reason that I have to-night for loving you better than words can tell, and thanking God for my great happiness. My thoughts, when they were wildest, never rose near the happiness that I have known with you, and that we have before us."

He embraced her, solemnly commended her to Heaven, and humbly thanked Heaven for having bestowed her on him. By and by, they went into the house.

There was no one bidden to the marriage but Mr. Lorry ;

there was even to be no bridesmaid but the gaunt Miss Pross. The marriage was to make no change in their place of residence; they had been able to extend it, by taking to themselves the upper rooms formerly belonging to the apocryphal invisible lodger, and they desired nothing more.

Doctor Manette was very cheerful at the little supper. They were only three at table, and Miss Pross made the third. He regretted that Charles was not there; was more than half disposed to object to the loving little plot that kept him away; and drank to him affectionately.

So the time came for him to bid Lucie good night, and they separated. But in the stillness of the third hour of the morning, Lucie came down stairs again, and stole into his room : not free from unshaped fears, beforehand.

All things, however, were in their places; all was quiet; and he lay asleep, his white hair picturesque on the untroubled pillow, and his hands lying quiet on the coverlet. She put her needless candle in the shadow at a distance, crept up to his bed, and put her lips to his; then, leaned over him and looked at him.

Into his handsome face, the bitter waters of captivity had worn; but he covered up their tracks with a determination so strong, that he held the mastery of them, even in his sleep. A more remarkable face in its quiet, resolute, and guarded struggle with an unseen assailant, was not to be beheld in all the wide dominions of sleep, that night.

She timidly laid her hand on his dear breast, and put up a prayer that she might ever be as true to him as her love aspired to be, and as his sorrows deserved. Then she withdrew her hand, and kissed his lips once more, and went away. So the sunrise came, and the shadows of the leaves of the plane-tree moved upon his face, as softly as her lips had moved in praying for him.

to the chariot which Mr. Lorry had hired in honour of the day. The rest followed in another carriage, and soon, in a neighbouring church where no strange eyes looked on, Charles Darnay and Lucie Manette were happily married.

Besides the glancing tears that shone among the smiles of the little group when it was done, some diamonds, very bright and sparkling, glanced on the bride's hand, which were newly released from the dark obscurity of one of Mr. Lorry's pockets. They returned home to breakfast, and all went well, and in due course the golden hair that had mingled with the poor shoemaker's white locks in the Paris garret, was mingled with them again in the morning sunlight, on the threshold of the door at parting.

It was a hard parting, though it was not for long. But her father cheered her, and said at last, gently disengaging himself from her enfolding arms, " Take her, Charles ! She is yours ! " And her agitated hand waved to them from a chaise window, and she was gone.

The corner being out of the way of the idle and curious, and the preparations having been very simple and few, the doctor, Mr. Lorry, and Miss Pross, were left quite alone. It was when they turned into the welcome shade of the cool old hall, that Mr. Lorry observed a great change to have come over the doctor ; as if the golden arm uplifted there had struck him a poisoned blow.

He had naturally repressed much, and some revulsion might have been expected in him when the occasion for repression was gone. But it was the old scared lost look that troubled Mr. Lorry ; and through his absent manner of clasping his head and drearily wandering away into his own room when they got up stairs, Mr. Lorry was reminded of Defarge, the wine-shop keeper, and the starlight ride.

" I think," he whispered to Miss Pross, after anxious consideration, " I think we had best not speak to him just now, or at all disturb him. I must look in at Tellson's ; so I will go there at once and come back presently. Then we will take him a ride into the country, and dine there, and all will be well."

It was easier for Mr. Lorry to look in at Tellson's, than to look out of Tellson's. He was detained two hours. When he came back, he ascended the old staircase alone, having asked no

But Mr. Lorry thought he saw, as he leaned forward on his bench in the dusk, with his elbows on his knees and his head in his hands, that he was in some misty way asking himself, "Why not?" The sagacity of the man of business perceived an advantage here, and determined to hold it.

Miss Pross and he divided the night into two watches, and observed him at intervals from the adjoining room. He paced up and down for a long time before he lay down; but when he did finally lay himself down, he fell asleep. In the morning, he was up betimes, and went straight to his bench and to work.

On this second day Mr. Lorry saluted him cheerfully by his name, and spoke to him on topics that had been of late familiar to them. He returned no reply, but it was evident that he heard what was said, and that he thought about it, however confusedly. This encouraged Mr. Lorry to have Miss Pross in with her work, several times during the day; at those times, they quietly spoke of Lucie, and of her father then present, precisely in their usual manner, and as if there were nothing amiss. This was done without any demonstrative accompaniment, not long enough, or often enough to harass him; and it lightened Mr. Lorry's friendly heart to believe that he looked up oftener, and that he appeared to be stirred by some perception of inconsistencies surrounding him.

When it fell dark again, Mr. Lorry asked him, as before: —

"Dear Doctor, will you go out?"

As before, he repeated, "Out?"

"Yes; for a walk with me. Why not?"

This time Mr. Lorry feigned to go out when he could extract no answer from him, and, after remaining absent for an hour, returned. In the mean while, the doctor had removed to the seat in the window, and had sat there looking down at the plane-tree; but on Mr. Lorry's return, he slipped away to his bench.

The time went very slowly on, and Mr. Lorry's hope darkened, and his heart grew heavier again, and grew yet heavier and heavier every day. The third day came and went, the fourth, the fifth. Five days, six days, seven days, eight days, nine days.

With a hope ever darkening, and with a heart always growing heavier and heavier, Mr. Lorry passed through this anxious time. The secret was well kept, and Lucie was unconscious and happy; but he could not fail to observe that the shoemaker, whose hand had been a little out at first, was growing dreadfully skilful, and that he had never been so intent on his work, and that his hands had never been so nimble and expert, as in the dusk of the ninth evening.